# alpha dog

a novel by

# Jennifer Ziegler

Delacorte Press

Published by Delacorte Press
an imprint of Random House Children's Books
a division of Random House, Inc.
New York

Delacorte Press and colophon are registered trademarks of
Random House, Inc.

www.randomhouse.com/teens

Educators and librarians, for a variety of teaching tools, visit us at
www.randomhouse.com/teachers.

Library of Congress CataloginginPublication Data
[CIP Information tk]

The text of this book is set in [tk].

Printed in [tk]

10 9 8 7 6 5 4 3 2 1

First Edition

For my dog, Cutter,
the most devoted friend
I've ever had

# Acknowledgments

The author is deeply beholden to the following people: Stephanie Lane and her wonder dog, Gabby; Lisa Holden; Carla Birnberg; Julie Carolan; Joe and Louise McDermott; the Wethington family; Lisa Shubin; my muse, Lucie; and the incredibly kind staff at Griffith's Small Animal Hospital in Austin, Texas.

Special thanks to my parents, Jim and Esther Ford, for allowing me to become "alpha," and to my husband, Carl, for his limitless patience and encouragement.

"I'm gonna buy me a dog,
'cause I need a friend now. . . ."

— *The Monkees*

(Written by Tommy Boyce and Bobby Hart)

# prologue

You want to know something tragic about me? I hate birthdays. Not everyone's, I mean. Just my own.

I guess I'm what you might call birthday challenged. While most people have elaborate, fantasy-filled ceremonies on their birthdays, mine play out more like Shakespearean tragedies.

It started when I turned six and only one girl showed up for my party. Everyone else I invited was either going out of town or sick with a stomach flu. Later, when we were having cake, Rosemary Eggleston, my one and only guest, started throwing up all over the dining room table. To this day I can't look at Rosemary without being reminded of partially digested strawberry ice cream.

From then on, every one of my birthdays has been marred by some sort of disaster. A hired pony with a gastric disorder. Four stitches in my scalp after a piñata mishap. A rental flick so scary all my slumber party guests went home early.

At times I wondered if some powerful sorceress put a spell on me, dooming me to emotionally scarring birthdays for the rest of my life. In fact, in my entire seventeen years, I'd only had one magical birthday moment. . . .

The summer I turned thirteen my dad decided the whole McAllister family should go to Ireland to see his "homeland." (Actually my dad was born and raised here in San Marcos, Texas, but he's really into the whole family ancestry thing.) The day of my birthday we were taking a walking tour of Dublin. We saw a lot of cool historic buildings and heard a lot of Irish history, but I just couldn't get into it. Basically I was feeling sorry for myself. I hated missing out on a real birthday party and not being able to go to dance camp. So I kept lagging farther and farther behind until I wasn't even part of the tour group at all. Eventually I missed a light at a street crossing and got stranded on the corner.

Right then it started to rain—I mean really pour down. I could see my mom open our king-sized umbrella and look around for me. As soon as the light changed, I took off running across the street. Unfortunately, the cobblestones were slick, and three years of dance lessons hadn't made me any less of a klutz, so I ended up slipping and falling flat on my back. My head banged against the stone pavers, making me achy and woozy. And the worst part was, through the swirling rain, I could see a car coming around the corner—heading straight for me. Strangely, my only thought was, "Great. I'm about to die wearing the frilly unicorn underpants Grandma Hattie sent me."

Then all of a sudden, *he* was there.

Tall and muscular, maybe eighteen or nineteen, with dark messy-floppy hair and the biggest brown eyes I'd ever seen. He waved his arms to stop the approaching car and then bent over me. "Let me help ye up," he said in a husky brogue. He grasped my hands and pulled me upright so swiftly and easily, he probably could have sent me soaring over his shoulder had he wanted to.

After walking me to the curb, he bent toward me, pushed wet strands of hair out of my face and asked, "All right?"

I nodded and said something like "Ungah."

And then he smiled. A gorgeous, dimple-popping, eye-twinkling smile. I can't be totally sure, but it seemed that the clouds parted slightly and a ray of sunlight beamed down on him.

At that point a voice called out, "Katherine Anne! Where have you been?" Cringing, I glanced to the left and saw Mom trotting down the sidewalk toward me,

Dad lagging behind her, not wanting to miss a single second of the tour.

"No need to worry," the guy said as she approached. "She took a bit of a spill runnin' across the street, but I'm sure she'll be all right."

Mom's eyes widened. "You were running in the *rain*? I've warned you a thousand times not to do that. What is wrong with you, Katie? Why can't you be more careful?" She shook her head and let out a long, pained sigh.

"Sorry," I mumbled, hanging my head in embarrassment.

The guy took a step away from me and turned toward my mother. " 'Twas only an accident. I've slipped on these cobblestones a time or two meself. Seems the best thing to do would be to have a laugh and make her feel better instead of worse."

Mom's cheeks turned the color of raw salmon. "I was only . . ."

For the first time in my life, my mother was at a loss for words. It was astonishing and wonderful and amazing and all those words people use after witnessing a miracle.

A few seconds later, my dad finally caught up with us. "What's going on?" he asked, craning his head to keep his eye on the tour guide behind him.

"I fell in the street and he"—I gestured to my hero—"he helped me up."

Dad's eyebrows flew up. "Is that so?" He stepped

forward and held out his hand toward the guy. "Well, then. Thank you for your help, Mr. . . ."

"Seamus," the guy said, giving Dad's hand a shake. "Just Seamus." He gave me one last grin and a pat on the shoulder, then turned and walked away.

I never saw Seamus again, at least not in person. But for the next few years he had the starring role in all my romantic dreams—asleep or awake. All I had to do was close my eyes and I would see him, as if his image had been tattooed onto the backs of my eyelids. I could even smell the rain and the musty odor of wet wool on his clothes. For a long time I thought I was in love with him. Until finally I grew up and got real. A *real* boyfriend, that is.

Which brings me back to birthdays and the worst one ever.

On the morning of my seventeenth birthday, two days after my junior year ended, I was sitting in Taco Loco, my favorite restaurant in all of San Marcos, talking to my mom on the cell phone.

"I'm doing a huge favor letting you borrow my car. I expect you to follow all the rules of the road."

"I will."

"Don't speed and don't get on the interstate. You know that's where all the drunk drivers are."

"Mom, it's the middle of the day. It'll be fine."

"That's just the sort of lazy attitude that gets people

into wrecks. When I was your age, I knew the importance of driving defensively. Maybe that's why I never had an accident."

*When I was your age . . .* It was her favorite song—her mantra. My mom and dad are on record as the most perfect teenagers ever to exist in Hays County.

Just so you know, my dad is Shane McAllister. He's a lawyer for a group of local banks and is on the board of directors of many important civic groups, with names like Sons of Irish Immigrants, the Irish Heritage Club and Young Irish Professionals. And my mother is Laura McAllister (formerly Laura Keller), Junior League president, PTA vice president, and former beauty queen. In her day she was Cotton Princess and a first runner-up Miss San Marcos. But you'll have to check the *Daily Record*'s archives to figure out what year, because she won't say.

". . . and be sure to come back in an hour," she rambled on. "We have a ton of shopping to do and I have to speak at the city council meeting later tonight."

"Okay," I said irritably. *God, another meeting? What's she protesting now?* You'd think she'd be tired of telling me what to do 24/7. But no. Mom apparently feels the need to tell the greater population of San Marcos how to behave.

From there on, my end of the conversation went something like this: "Okay, Mom. Right. I know. Yes. All right. I promise. *Bye,* Mom!" By the time I hung up and tossed the cell into my purse, my ears were ringing with the staccato cadence of her voice.

"Can I get jou anything, *señorita*?" Chuy, the restaurant's grandfatherly owner, stood beside me, a wide smile lifting his gray-streaked, meticulous mustache.

"Two Macho Nacho platters," I said, tapping my finger against the laminated menu. "And two Cokes with lemon, please."

"*Ay yi yi*. So much food for such a little lady," Chuy teased as he set down the complimentary bowl of salsa and basket of tortilla chips.

"It's my birthday," I explained happily. "And it's not all for me. I'm meeting my boyfriend."

I glanced at the glass front door, searching for Chuck's tall silhouette. He was late, but that was typical. In the two years we'd been going out, he'd only been on time for a date twice. I'd learned to deal.

"*¡Feliz cumpleaños!*" exclaimed Chuy, clapping me on the back. "Happy birthday!"

"Thanks."

"How old are jou now? Sixteen?"

I could feel my face flush. People were always thinking I was younger, on account of my five foot-five frame, freckles, and round green eyes. "*Seven*teen," I corrected, a slight edge to my voice.

Chuy didn't seem to notice. "*Es muy especial*. I'll bring a free piece of flan."

I was about to tell him not to bother (I really can't eat flan; its gummy, gluey texture always makes me gag), but he'd already trotted off to the kitchen. *What-*

*ever,* I thought. *Maybe Chuck will eat it.*

Right then, I saw Chuck through the window. It was his stride I noticed first—the guy just couldn't *not* swagger. It was as if his body were a complicated system of gears and pulleys. His shoulders dipped and swayed, making his arms swing backward and powering the slightest, cutest circular motion in his rear end.

I smiled proudly as he pushed through the squeaky, grease-streaked door. Chuck Rhodes was one of San Marcos High School's major hotties, and he was all mine. Of course, I'd nabbed him two years ago when he was only a minor hottie. But as the older guys graduated and went away, Chuck had become known more and more as a superstud. Lately lots of girls had been telling me how lucky I was.

They were right. I took note of his many attributes as he strutted toward me: his tall, lean swimmer's build; his spiky, platinum-blond hair (with an occasional greenish tinge from the chlorine); his perpetual tan; and, since getting the braces off a year ago, his gleaming, movie-star smile.

I quickly pushed my hair over my shoulders and adjusted my new blouse. A pale green scrunched V-neck. I liked it because it made me look older. The color showed off my eyes, and the neckline created a slight optical illusion—making my B cups look more like Cs.

"Hi there." I greeted Chuck as he walked up to the table.

"Hey," he said, sliding into the chair opposite. I'd

been hoping he'd kiss me hello, but Chuck never could get mushy in public. Something else I'd learned to accept.

"You're late," I teased. It was protocol—our own little joke.

"Aw, come on. I had to get my hair just right." He ran a hand over his lime-gold bristles and flashed me a lopsided grin. He was so cute.

A big bubble of anticipation swelled inside my chest, helping me fill out my new top. "Well?" I asked, unable to contain it any longer. "What is it?"

"What?"

"You know," I whined, bouncing slightly in my seat. "Whatever it was you needed to tell me!"

"Yeah, that." Chuck swallowed and looked down at the tabletop.

*He's nervous.* A prickly flush spread over me. We'd been going out for almost two years now and Chuck had been starting to hint around about us getting more . . . serious. You know . . . physically. A lot of our friends had done it. And it was an unwritten school rule that anyone entering their senior year still a virgin was a certified loser. I wondered if Chuck wanted to celebrate my seventeenth birthday in a major way.

He drummed his hands against the table and looked up at me. "Uh . . . let's order first. Then I'll tell you."

"I already ordered."

"Really?" He looked surprised and slightly annoyed. "For both of us?"

"Well, yeah," I replied with a shrug. "I mean, we always get the same thing. Besides, I don't have much time. I'm sorry. Did you want something different?"

"No, it's okay," he said, still sounding a little put out. "It's too late anyway. Here comes Chuy now."

"Here jou go, *novios*." Chuy walked up behind me, holding a large tray aloft. He set down a plate of nachos and a Coke for each of us and placed a small bowl of lemons in the middle. Then he waved a gigantic piece of flan in front of my face. It jiggled and glistened like a square of compressed yellow snot. "For jour birthday," he said, plunking it next to my nachos.

"Thanks," I said.

Chuy looked extremely pleased. He opened his arms and said, "Enjoy!" then strode off to a nearby table.

I shoved the flan to the edge of the table and dug into the nachos.

"I've got to hurry. Mom's taking me shopping later. There's a bunch of stuff I need before I leave tomorrow."

He shook his head. "Man, I can't believe you actually signed up to go to *school* this summer." Chuck had been acting annoyed ever since I'd told him I'd been accepted to the University of Texas Core Curriculum Program—a summer session especially for high school students wanting to get credit for required subjects.

"I know. I don't want to go either, but my parents are making me." I rested my hand on his arm. "But hey, at least I get my own place. You can come visit." My mom had taken so long to decide whether I should attend or not, I missed the student housing deadline. So instead, I was going to stay in an off-campus condo. The bad part was, I would still get a roommate, and the old lady who owned the place would be right next door watching over us. But still, I'd basically be on my own.

"So, come on. Tell me." I clapped the dusting of chip fragments off my hands and sat back on the bench. "What's this big news of yours?"

"It can wait."

"No! I have to go meet my mom soon. Tell me now, *please*?" I leaned forward and pretended to pout.

"Okay." Chuck took a big breath and stared down at a spot on the table. "We've been going out a long time, right?"

"Yes." My breath quickened. It felt like warm syrup was slowly seeping over me.

"And I was thinking that . . . that . . ."

"Yes?" I prompted.

"I think we should see other people."

"What?" The warm, syrupy snugness slid away. "Ha, ha. Very funny."

"Katie, I, uh . . . I'm not joking."

Something in his voice made me freeze. An intense prickly feeling swept through me, as if I'd sprouted thorns. I looked up and met his gaze. There was no twinkle of mischief in his eyes, no barely restrained smile on his face. He was totally serious.

"You're . . . breaking up with me?" I asked almost noiselessly. A big chunk of something seemed to be jamming my throat—probably a section of my heart, which had just exploded.

Chuck stared back at me, all cramped and guilty looking.

"Is it because of the summer program? It's only two months long. But if you really don't want me to go I'll find a way out, I promise. I'll pretend I'm sick or make up a rumor about—"

"It's not about the stupid summer thing," he blurted.

"Then . . . what?" I asked squeakily.

"I've sort of started seeing someone else."

The thorns were morphing into butcher knives. "Wh-who?"

"Trina." He swallowed and looked away guiltily.

"You and . . ." I couldn't finish. A sick, gurgly feeling spread through my gut. All that cheese and grease seemed to be squirming their way back up my esophagus—as if my lunch were rejecting me too.

*Trina Manbeck?* She was my friend. She, Ariel, Tracy, Bethany, and I had been hanging out together since eighth grade. Of course, Trina was also one of those girls constantly telling me how *lucky* I was to have Chuck. Guess she decided to get *lucky* herself.

"So," I said shakily. "You really *did* want something different, huh?"

"Katie." Chuck reached toward my arm resting in front of me, but I jerked it away. My elbow hit the plate of flan, knocking it over the edge of the table. It crashed to the floor loudly. Judging from the silence that followed, all eyes were now upon us.

"Come on. Don't cause a scene," Chuck said in a whisper.

I couldn't stand it any longer. I leaped to my feet and strode toward the exit.

Unfortunately, I barely made it two steps before my foot hit the remains of the flan. The next thing I knew, I was flat on my back, my head slamming against the plank floorboards. The strands of chili pepper lights above me wavered in and out of focus. Then everything went blurry.

A figure bent over me. "Let me help ye up," came an echoey voice with a lilting Irish accent.

"Seamus?" I blinked and refocused. Chuck was kneeling over me. Behind him Chuy and a few nameless faces stood staring at me pityingly.

"Can I help you up?" This time it was Chuck's voice, all Texas-twangy and a little worried. He held out his hand.

"Go away!" I snapped. I shoved his arm and scrabbled about in the muck for a few seconds before making it to a standing position. My entire backside throbbed and my insides seemed to be doing a weird circus routine. Still, I somehow managed to stride out the door with my head held high.

As soon as I reached the front sidewalk, though, an intense rushing sensation doubled me over. It was as if my whole body had been transformed into a cannon. There I was, just like Rosemary Eggleston on my sixth birthday, spewing my stomach contents into the nearby nandina bushes.

The birthday curse had struck again.

# 1

I vaguely remember coming home from the restaurant. Mom didn't have to worry about my driving. I was in such a state of shock that I puttered down the streets like a stoned septuagenarian.

The rest of the day I spent sitting on the floor of my bedroom with the door locked and the CD mix Chuck made for me playing on my stereo, cranked up just enough to cover the sounds of my crying but not enough to bring Mom pounding on my door.

Everything Chuck had ever given me was spread around me in a semicircle. The first note he'd ever passed me ("Pick you up at 8. Dress hot."); ticket stubs from the first film we ever saw together (a Halloween rerelease of *The Blair Witch Project*); a couple of dried-up flowers; bells and ribbons from his homecoming mums; a few Shiner Beer bottle caps from the night we shared our first major kiss; and a picture of us taken at Leigh Ann Shaw's New Year's Eve party.

I ran my finger over the glossy photograph, staring at it intently. Chuck's arms were hanging over both of my shoulders, his eyes were half closed, and there was this big openmouthed smile on his face. The purple San Marcos Rattlers sweatshirt he was wearing in the shot was draped over me now, a keepsake from one of the best nights of my life.

I remember that was one of the very few times my mom had let me stay out past midnight, and it was a good thing, too. Chuck had drunk so much trash-can punch he ended up hurling all over Leigh Ann's rose-bushes. I sat beside him the whole time and he kept saying, "I love you, Katie. I really love you," over and over.

I threw the photo down and used a sleeve of the sweatshirt to wipe my eyes. The seam in the left armpit was ripped open, and there was a big greasy mark across the front, but I didn't care. It was still one of the most favorite things I owned. Chuck had worn it the night he said he loved me. It was the only time he'd said it, but I'd felt sure he really meant it—as if all that alcohol had crumbled his macho image for a few hours and his true feelings had been exposed. And now this?

I picked up the phone and called Ariel's cell number. After the third ring Ariel's breathy voice came over the line. "Hello?"

"Ariel, it's Katie," I croaked shakily. "You aren't going to believe this. But Chuck broke up with me. He's going out with Trina!"

"Um . . . yeah. We heard."

*We?* "Is everyone over there?"

"Yeah. Stacy and Bethany are here."

"Are you guys having a party?"

There was a pause. "Um, yeah. At my lake house. We kind of figured you wouldn't want to go, since Chuck's going to be here and everything."

"But it's my last night before I leave. Don't you guys want to hang out?"

"That's probably not a good idea. You need some time to get over this and all."

A cold realization tingled over me, from scalp to toenails. They were squeezing me out. They knew I was down, so they were distancing themselves.

I knew the drill. I was damaged goods. As long as I was the topic du jour, people had to avoid me or risk mucking up their own reputations. They probably knew about Chuck and Trina before I did, and no one wanted to tell me. They just automatically aligned themselves with Trina, who was more popular and powerful, leaving me to rot by myself.

"But . . . it's my birthday," I mumbled morosely.

Another pause. "Yeah . . . sorry. Um, maybe we can come by tomorrow morning and see you before you leave?"

A familiar laugh sounded in the background—a high-pitched cackle, like an incredibly chipper tree monkey. "Is that Trina?" I asked, choking on the name.

Another, longer silence. I could almost feel the guilt oozing through the phone line. For a few seconds, I considered screaming at Ariel to put the bitch on the phone and then hurling obscenities at Trina until I passed out from exhaustion. But I didn't. I couldn't.

I knew from experience that it was better to roll belly-up and play dead than to stand up to the social forces of San Marcos. Besides, it just wasn't in me to square off against Trina and her loud cheerleader mouth.

If only I was more like Mom. She was always taking a stand—always starting petitions against rezoning or convincing the school board not to allow off-campus lunches (yep, that really made me popular). Even Dad was known to write an occasional letter to the editor. But not this McAllister. Arguing with people and practically asking them to hate you seemed like one of those nightmares that could turn your hair white. I mean, why not wear a Please Pelt Me with Spit Wads sign on your back? Or break into song at every given chance? You'd get the same attention.

I couldn't change things. And going into meltdown mode would only make things worse. I just had to accept it.

"Yeah," Ariel finally answered, her voice low and

resigned. "Trina's here."

"Right. Well . . . you guys have fun," I said. My tongue felt thick with self-pity. It flopped about inside my mouth like a dying fish, slurring my words.

"Okay," she said. Again I could hear Trina's smug little screeches in the background.

"I'll see you guys tomorrow morning, right?"

"We'll really try. Bye, Katie."

I heard a click, followed by the mournful drone of the dial tone. My hands shook as I replaced my cordless phone on its base.

*That's it,* I thought as fresh tears dripped down my cheeks. *I'm done. I'm over. I've been totally abandoned.*

I shouldn't have been all that surprised. After all, I'd gone along with similar avoidance campaigns in the past. Besides, I'd been putting Chuck before them for the past two years. We weren't exactly a sisterhood.

And yet it still hurt like hell. *I've been dumped on my birthday and no one cares!* I'd barely made it to seventeen and my social life was ruined forever.

At least I had the college thing in Austin. I wouldn't have to stick around this summer and see Chuck and Trina making out at the mall or the river parties.

Now if I could just figure out a way to never come back.

"You're wearing too much makeup," Mom said, pulling the Volvo onto Interstate 35.

I didn't say anything. I just stared out the window at the passing scenery—mainly gas stations and strip malls repeating themselves endlessly, like the background in an old cartoon's chase scene.

We were headed to Austin, to the University of Texas campus. Classes didn't start until the next week, but Mom wanted me to have time to settle in, buy my books and supplies, and, as she put it, "meet some nice people." Only, for some reason, I was finding it difficult to feel excited.

"Really, Katie," Mom went on. "You are such a beautiful girl. Why do you insist on making yourself look like a prostitute?"

"God, Mom! Why do you have to say it like that?" I shrieked from my slouched position. "I'm not wearing any more makeup than other girls. And besides, I'm tired of everyone thinking I'm younger than I really am."

"When you're older, you'll be thankful." Mom waggled her finger at me. "Just think of Grandma Hattie and how young she looks."

"Great. I'll be the queen of the old folks' home," I mumbled, looking back out the window.

I could make out a vague reflection of myself in the glass. Personally I thought I could have added another layer of blush and eyeshadow. My face still had that puffy, marshmallowy look to it, the result of twenty hours of crying and moping, broken only by four hours of fitful sleep.

For about two seconds that morning, I'd forgotten everything. I'd woken up to beautiful Texas sunshine and mockingbirds singing in the distance. Then my butt throbbed where it had hit the floor of Taco Loco and I remembered: My boyfriend really did dump me on my seventeenth birthday. He really had fooled around with one of my co-best friends (*former* co-best friend). I truly did fall on my rear in front of a crowd of people and then barf all over the sidewalk outside. And yes, I was currently being shunned by all the popular kids within a twenty-mile radius of my home.

Just as I'd expected, Ariel, Bethany, and Tracy didn't show up to see me off—too gutless to go against Trina. Nor did they call or e-mail. I was a social leper. Relationship road kill. From now on I'd have to hang out with the chronic nose-pickers and hall monitors. High school life as I knew it was over.

I couldn't get out of town fast enough.

"Don't squint like that," Mom said, giving me another quick glance. "You'll get wrinkles, and then you really *will* look old."

"I can't help it. The sun's too bright right now," I whined.

"Then put on your sunglasses."

"I lost them." Actually, I'd left them on the table at Taco Loco, but no way was I going to tell her that. They were expensive, so she'd probably make me go back and get them. And I wasn't planning on entering that place for another millennium.

Mom let out one of her famous loud, lengthy sighs to let me know how much suffering I was causing her—a literal waste of breath, since she always followed up by saying it in words.

"This is why you should have come shopping with me yesterday. We could have bought you a new pair. I don't know why I bother trying to help you when you won't help yourself."

"It's okay, Mom. I can get sunglasses by myself. I can handle that one on my own."

"Don't get smart-mouthed with me!" Mom pouted. "I spent my entire afternoon yesterday shopping for *your* supplies and this is the thanks I get?"

"Mom! I wasn't talking back. I appreciate it. Really. You did a great job."

She'd done an okay job. Actually, there hadn't been that much to buy. The condo where I'd be staying with another girl was already stocked with furniture and pots and pans. We just had to bring our own towels and bedding. Mom bought me an assortment of pastel sheet sets, a white chenille coverlet and sham, six purple bath towels and washcloths and . . . a Scooby Doo alarm clock.

Normally I would have loved it, but this was college. I wanted to distance myself from everything that might look babyish. But when I tried to explain that nicely to Mom, she looked at me with a put-upon expression and said, "Well, you aren't planning on bringing lots of people into your bedroom, are you?"

Maybe she'd gotten the idea from her mom. Grandma Hattie had sent me another birthday care package, with more underwear in it (flowered this time, with an eyelet ruffle). Plus she must have gotten a little confused when I said I was going to a college a half hour north of home, because she also included some black mittens and a red-and-black-striped scarf.

"Next time you can do your own shopping," Mom went on, still miffed. "That's the last time I do a favor for you while you lie in bed feeling sorry for yourself."

"I was sick!" I exclaimed, gripping the seat in frustration. "Would you prefer that I went with you and left a trail of vomit through the mall?"

For a moment, no one said anything. Our angry sound waves richocheted around the interior of the Volvo like gunfire.

I glanced at Mom's frowning profile. She just didn't understand. The woman probably never got rejected in her life. Not only was she absurdly young-looking for her age, she was also glamorous. People were always saying she looked just like Sharon Stone, only with brown hair and without the nude scenes.

Mom took a deep breath. "Listen, I'm sorry you're upset that things didn't work out with Chuck. But I have to say, I always had a feeling something like this would happen. I warned you several times."

I slumped against the door and pressed my forehead against the window. I was beginning to wish I hadn't told her about Chuck and me breaking up. I'd had to give her some explanation for my crying jag the day before—and at least I'd withheld the particulars. But I should have known it would be like handing over a gold-framed license to nag. Now I was trapped in a plush, luxury-edition prison, unable to flee from her barrage of I-told-you-so's.

"I never did trust that boy," she went on, spitting out the last word as if "boy" were some sort of profanity. "You deserve someone who's decent and responsible. Someone like Bitsy's boy, Aaron. You know, he's living in Austin right now, finishing up his degree in design. You two should meet for lunch or something. I know you always liked him. Bitsy and I swear you two were made for each other!"

I stifled a groan. Aunt Bitsy isn't really my aunt, but a former sorority sister of my mother's. Her son Aaron really is decent and responsible and sweet and incredibly good-looking. I had the biggest crush on him until two years ago when I ran into him at the outlet mall and he introduced me to his boyfriend Chad.

"Mom, I don't think so. I probably won't have time to date. I'll be studying a lot."

"Who said anything about dating?" she asked in an oh-so-innocent voice. "I don't think your landlady will even allow dating. I'm talking about meeting up with an old friend, someone who can help get your mind off this Chuck person. . . ."

"Oh God," I moaned, twisting around in my seat and leaning against the door. I closed my eyes and tried to shut down the auditory section of my brain. The movement of the car was vibrating my still-aching skull and making my ear canals tickle. *Maybe my eardrums will rupture,* I thought hopefully. I really, really, *really* didn't want to hear her thoughts on how I should deal with the breakup—especially since that's all I'd been thinking about.

Over the past twenty hours, feelings had gone through all the stages described in *Cosmopolitan.* First anger, then total despair, then a denial that it really happened and the lame hope it was only a prank. Then anger again—only this time at myself.

If only I had gotten back at Chuck in some way. Kicked him in the crotch or shoved flan in his face, or told the whole restaurant that he drools slightly when we make out (something I never quite learned to deal with)—anything except the wimp-ass way I took it.

". . . You shouldn't be wallowing like this. You should see this as an opportunity. A chance to focus on your studies and meet some nice, upstanding people. . . ."

My fingers caressed the door handle. I imagined myself opening the car door and tumbling onto the road, free at last. Of course, since it was a fantasy, instead of ending up a mangled mess with premature eye wrinkles, I'd simply land on my feet and take off running. I'd hop the barbed-wire fence and race over the ridge until I was certain Mom had lost my trail. Then I'd find a nice farm or ranch family to take me in. I'd convince them I was being hunted by the mob and that they couldn't tell anyone I was there. Then I'd earn my keep by milking goats or something until I'd saved up some money. Then I'd fly to Ireland and find Seamus. . . .

"Katie? . . . Katherine Anne McAllister! Are you listening to me? . . . Stop squinting!"

My mood lifted as we pulled into Austin. First the traffic got thicker, and then the glass crown of the Frost Bank building appeared on the horizon. Soon other downtown buildings and the pink granite capitol dome came into view. And to the north loomed the infamous University of Texas Tower, its south-facing clock beckoning to me like a large smiley face.

*College,* I thought as a fluttery, pressurized sensation filled my chest. This was going to be perfect. No mom to fuss at me. No dad to tell embarrassing stories about me. No one constantly comparing me to my mother's perfect girlhood. And best of all, no one who knew I'd just been dumped like moldy leftovers.

Mom hadn't even finished easing the Volvo into the Pearl Street Condominiums parking lot before I was out on the curb unloading my bags. A couple of swoonworthy guys—frat boys, judging by the Greek letters on their baseball caps—were walking along the sidewalk. One of them smiled at me.

Suddenly it occurred to me that a real college summer session would be going on at the same time as the Core Curriculum Program. I could meet real college students—college *guys*. Maybe Seamus would be there, having just transferred for a specialized graduate degree. I could just see him sauntering through campus, his beefy chest snug inside a Texas Longhorns shirt instead of a crewneck sweater. . . .

"Katie!" Mom called, yanking me back into my present surroundings. I was still standing on the curb, gaping at the two hotties as they passed. She gave a disapproving glare and nodded toward my pile of luggage. "Let's hurry and get inside. I'm sure you need to relieve yourself after all that coffee you drank this morning. It's not healthy to hold it in, you know." She picked up one of my bags and headed for the entrance.

My face seemed to erupt into flames. I avoided looking at the two frat guys as I hoisted my last two bags and followed her into the building.

"That reminds me," she went on as we trudged up a Berber-carpeted staircase to the third floor. "All I see around here are burger and pizza joints. That kind of food is so bad for your complexion. If there's time before I leave, we should stock up at a grocery store. Just because you won't have me around to cook doesn't mean you can eat junk. I didn't get a scholarship by scarfing down sugar and fat all day, you know."

Every day Mom found a way to point out how blatantly inferior I was to herself at a young age. Even the words she used were repetitive: "When I was your age,

I didn't get to [insert feat of superhuman proportions] by [insert one of my regular, inferior habits]."

Eventually we reached the third floor and stood in front of unit 302. On the door hung a wooden cutout of a cat with a ruffled gingham heart glued to the chest and the name Krantz stenciled underneath.

Mom rapped on the door next to the wooden cat's faceless head. "Be on your best behavior," she whispered. "I'm sure you'll have a strict curfew, and she's probably going to check up on you all at least once a day, so you better keep things in order. No leaving your clothes and wet towels all over the place like you do at home."

"*Mo-om!* I know this already. You don't need to keep reminding me."

"Honey, I'm only telling you these things because I want you to succeed here. If you were more reliable I wouldn't have to—"

Just then, the door opened and an older woman stood before us, smiling. She was petite with a dyed black, Betty Boop–style hairdo and huge, clear-framed eyeglasses. Her long denim skirt and crisp white blouse looked freshly pressed, but both were covered with multicolored hairs. Probably from the smug-looking calico cat she held to her chest.

"Are these our new summer guests, Mrs. B?" she asked in a singsongy voice.

Mom and I exchanged brief, startled looks. Who the heck was she talking to?

"Yes, I do believe they are," she went on. "Just look at all the suitcases."

That's when it hit me. She was talking to the cat.

"Hi, I'm Agnes Krantz," she crooned, thrusting her hand toward my mother.

"Laura McAllister," Mom said, grasping her palm and shaking it. When they let go, Mom studied her hand. It was covered in cat fur.

"Oh, sorry about that. This awful heat's been making Mrs. B shed like crazy, hasn't it Missy-tootle?" She lifted her arms and nuzzled her face against the cat's head.

"Quite all right," Mom said with a nervous laugh. "May I introduce my daughter, Katie?"

"Hi," I greeted her with a wave, hoping to avoid the furry handshake.

It worked. Mrs. Krantz nodded and grinned at me. "Hello. I've heard so much about you. Would you like to see your place?"

"Sure."

Mrs. Krantz took a wad of keys out of her skirt pocket and walked next door to number 301. After unlocking the doorknob and two dead bolts, she opened the front door and gestured us inside.

As I stepped across the threshold, I could feel layer upon layer of stress slide off me. It was like the relief you feel when you finally fill your lungs with air after holding your breath a long time. I felt . . . home.

The place was small, much smaller than I'd imagined. But it didn't matter. I thought it was perfect in spite of the grizzled, dingy carpeting and odd chicken-soup smell. I could easily imagine myself eating Cocoa Puffs at the green laminated bar that separated the living room from the tiny galley-style kitchen. Or drinking a soda while flopped across the old but comfy-looking flowered sofa.

Mrs. Krantz set down the cat and puttered about, opening blinds and fluffing the cushions on the couch and two flanking armchairs. Rays of light streaming through the windows illuminated swirls of dust in the air.

"Don't worry. Everything is clean," Mrs. Krantz remarked, watching my mother run her finger along a built-in bookshelf. "It just needs to be lived in. Isn't that right, Mrs. B?"

I turned to look at the cat, half expecting her to answer. Mrs. B sauntered over to me, gave my shoes an indifferent sniff, and then jumped into the frayed yellow club chair.

"It's charming," Mom said, glancing around and giving an approving nod.

"Thank you." Mrs. Krantz beamed. "Let me show you my favorite part."

She pushed aside some vertical blinds to reveal a glass atrium door. Then she opened it up and led us onto a wide concrete balcony overlooking west campus.

"Wow," I breathed, leaning against the iron railing.

There, just a few miles east, stood the UT Tower. This time its western clock face was smiling at me. "What a view! Isn't it great, Mom?"

Mom walked up beside me and stared out at the sun-drenched panorama. For the first time that day, her expression softened and she actually smiled. "Yes, it's nice," she said. She turned and looked at me. "Remember not to squint."

"Right." I was way too happy to get annoyed. Shielding my eyes with my hand, I gazed out at the bustling streets, trying to picture myself scurrying along the sidewalk with my backpack slung over my shoulder.

"Yes, Mrs. B and I just love it out here," Mrs. Krantz said behind us. "That's our balcony right next door." I glanced to the right toward the other half of the concrete balcony, separated by another waist-high iron railing. It was crowded with plants and potted palms, and in the corner, two ceramic kittens appeared to chase a ceramic yarn ball.

"I'm glad you're so close by," Mom said, pivoting about and leaning back against the rail. "So, how often will you look in on Katie and her roommate?"

Mrs. Krantz tilted her head and pushed her glasses farther up her nose. "I beg your pardon?"

Mom stiffened slightly. I turned around to watch them, sensing trouble.

"I mean," Mom continued, "you will be chaperoning the girls, won't you? I assume you will have a set curfew and a strict no-boys-allowed policy?"

"Mrs. McAllister, I'm afraid there's been a misunderstanding." Mrs. Krantz's overly magnified eyes studied my mother cautiously. "I'm afraid my only roles here are that of landlady and neighbor, *not* chaperone."

Mom's mouth bunched up as if yanked by an invisible drawstring. "But in your letter you said you would be offering your guidance as well."

"I believe my exact words were that I could 'serve as a guide.' I've lived in Austin over thirty years and can give directions to places all over the city."

Mom appeared to be in shock. "Well, I just assumed . . . She's still in high school, after all. . . . She only just turned seventeen." She took a step toward Mrs. Krantz, clutching her purse in front of her. "Couldn't we make some sort of arrangement with you? Maybe for an extra fee?"

Mrs. Krantz seemed slightly offended. "I'm sorry, but that wouldn't be possible. As it is, Mrs. B and I are going out of town tomorrow to visit my sister. I won't even be here for the first several days."

"But . . . isn't there anyone else who could do it?" My mom's voice was rising steadily. "Shouldn't the college provide some sort of supervision?"

"The university has no responsibility over students off campus," Mrs. Krantz answered calmly. "Please don't worry. I understand how hard this must be, first time away from home and all, but I'm sure everything will be fine." She stepped toward me and patted my shoulder lightly. "Your daughter seems like a very smart, sweet girl. I'm sure she can look out for herself."

Mom regarded me closely, as if I were some piece of art she was thinking about buying. And just then, it was like I could read her mind. The breakup with Chuck, the lost sunglasses, the way I gawked at those two frat guys—everything I'd ever done that wasn't exactly to her specifications. I watched in horror as her head shook back and forth, slowly at first, then gaining speed.

"It'll be okay, Mom. You can trust me," I said, trying desperately *not* to sound desperate while shockwaves of panic shuddered through me.

There was no way I could go back home. Not now. I just couldn't face the fallout. Not with news of my humiliating breakup still making the rounds as the week's top story. I could just imagine the morbidly curious stares, the phony condolences, the fake excuses as people suddenly became too busy to hang out with me.

"No," Mom finally proclaimed. "I'm sorry, sweetie, but I don't like this. This is not what I agreed to at all. You are too young and irresponsible to be on your own."

"But—"

"My decision is final. There's no way you are staying here without constant adult supervision. Now let's get your things." She pivoted on her heel and stalked back through the patio door.

I looked at Mrs. Krantz in the faint hope that she

could somehow stop this, but her owl-like eyes only sagged with pity.

All the elation, all the tingly anticipation I'd been feeling now drained out of me. I slowly trudged after Mom, feeling a heavy sense of doom, knowing full well that I was marching toward my own social annihilation.

Back inside I glanced around at the small, sunny condo, the postcard view off the balcony, the distant UT Tower casting a long early-morning shadow our way as if stretching out to me. All this had been in my reach only to be snatched away at the last minute. I should have known it wouldn't work out. It was just too good. Too perfect.

"Excuse me. Is this number 301?"

We all turned in unison. A girl my age was standing in the front doorway, which Mrs. Krantz had left open. She was tall, with the most amazing upright, square-shouldered posture. Everything about her was thin and pointy. Squinty brown eyes, a small pinch of a nose, a chin so sharp it could probably puncture tin cans. Two skinny legs stuck out from the bottom of a denim skirt and continued for half a block until they reached long fingery toes poking out of leather flip-flops. Her sleeveless pink top was buttoned all the way to the collar, and two scrawny arms stuck out of either side, her shoulders so knobby they looked like bedposts. But what really got me was her straw sun hat with the matching pink band. The brim was so wide, I wasn't sure she could fit through the door.

"I'm Christine Hobbes," she said, stepping into the condo. The hat passed through the frame with just inches to spare.

"Hello, dear!" exclaimed Mrs. Krantz, returning to her previous, singsongy voice. She rushed forward and shook Christine's hands, leaving fur on her long, tapered fingers. "I'm Mrs. Krantz. And this is Mrs. B," she added, nodding down at the calico, who was weaving figure-eights around Christine's legs.

"What a beautiful cat!" Christine cooed, reaching down and scooping Mrs. B into her arms.

Mrs. Krantz beamed proudly. "Oh, and this is Mrs. McAllister and her daughter, Katie. Katie was to be your roommate, but her mother is having some . . . second thoughts."

"Yes, I understand completely," Christine said, nodding sympathetically at my mom. Her voice had a certain Zen-master quality to it, deep and oh-so-understanding, like Oprah Winfrey on happy pills. "My parents were also reluctant to let me come here. But they finally decided they didn't want me to miss out on this great educational opportunity. Besides, my dad will be dropping in all the time, whenever he doesn't have surgeries scheduled."

"Your father is a doctor?" Mom asked.

"Yes. A cardiologist. He's at University Hospital in San Antonio."

"And where is your mother, dear?" Mrs. Krantz asked. "Is she with you?"

"Unfortunately, no. She's out of the country doing some missionary work this summer. Which reminds me"—she looked down at a watch hanging loosely on her wrist—"I'm supposed to meet a prayer group later at University Christian. My mother is good friends with the pastor. In fact, he'll be stopping by a lot, too." She turned toward me and grinned a happy-pill grin. "It's too bad you're not staying, Katie. We could go together and meet some new people."

"Yeah, too bad," I said, trying to look glum. Inwardly I sensed a slight uptick in my mood. Maybe there would be one very minor bright side to going home. This girl seemed so goody-goody, living with her would probably be just like living with my mom.

Judging by the smile on Mom's face, she was thinking the same thing.

"So, you say your parents arranged lots of supervision for you?" Mom asked.

"Oh, yes, ma'am," Christine replied in her honey-coated voice. "Mainly because they worry about me, not because they don't trust me. I'm afraid I'm a hopeless creature of habit. Early to bed, early to rise. I'm probably the dullest person here." She laughed a birdlike, twittering laugh.

Mrs. Krantz laughed too.

"What about boys?" my mom's voice cut in. "Have your parents set any limits on having boys over?"

"Boys?" Christine looked surprised by the question. "Well . . . I mean, I'm hoping to host the prayer group here once or twice, and there are probably boy members. But a boy here, alone, with no grown-ups? No. No, no, no. That would not be appropriate."

My jaw practically came unhinged. I couldn't believe there existed a girl my age who felt that way about guys. I half expected her to say they were "icky" and "have cooties."

"Now, see there, Mrs. McAllister?" Mrs. Krantz trilled. "These girls are young, but they're sensible."

Mom just stood there, sizing me up again. Only this time I couldn't read her mind.

*Please, please, please,* I urged inwardly. *I'll make friends with Christine and go to her dumb prayer group. I'll eat nothing but brussels sprouts. I'll wear a stupid pith helmet to protect myself from the sun. Just please let me stay!*

"Okay," Mom finally replied.

I blinked, unable to process it fully. "Really?"

"Wonderful!" Mrs. Krantz gushed.

"But let me make the rules clear," Mom went on. "No late nights. No piles of junk food. And above all, no strange boys up here. Do you understand?"

"Yes," I said, my entire body nodding.

"And here's the thing," Mom added, her voice deepening. *Oh great,* I thought. I knew there'd be a catch. "I will be calling regularly, and I'll want to talk to Christine as well. As long as she reports that you are following the rules I've laid down, you can continue to stay."

"What?" I gasped. I couldn't believe it. Mom had

more confidence in a total stranger than she did in me? It was so unfair. I'd never done anything really wrong—other than gab a little too long on the cell phone or date someone she felt wasn't good enough for me. "You . . . you don't trust me?" I asked, my voice meek and whispery.

Mom didn't reply. "Christine, would that be all right with you?"

"Of course," she replied. "I'll be glad to help. Although I'm sure Katie will do everything you say."

"Fine." Mom looked at her watch. "Well then, if you all will excuse me, I have to get back to San Marcos for an important meeting. Bye, honey." She kissed my temple, shouldered her purse and headed toward the stairwell.

"I'll walk you out," said Mrs. Krantz, trotting behind her, cradling Mrs. B with one arm. In the doorway she swiveled about, whispered, "I'm so glad she changed her mind," and then shut the door behind her.

I heaved a sigh of relief. Okay, so it wasn't exactly the arrangement I wanted. But at least I didn't have to go back.

I glanced over at Christine. She was staring at the door with her head cocked slightly. As soon as the sounds of footsteps died away, she turned and met my gaze.

"Good, they're gone," she said. She quickly took off her hat and unbuttoned her top. Jagged jet-black hair tumbled down her back, and peeking out from beneath her white cami was an elaborate Celtic-looking tattoo. "Now help me unpack all the booze."

# 2

"This is a good place," Christine said, sticking her head into the cupboard beneath the sink. I peered past her shoulder. It was dark and dusty and one dead roach lay on its back in a far corner.

She sat on the floor and began pulling bottles of liquor out of a cardboard box marked Computer Stuff and standing them inside the cabinet.

"What if Mrs. Krantz finds this?" I asked, biting my left thumbnail.

Christine looked at me as if I'd suddenly broken into a hula dance. "Why would she ever look in here?"

"I don't know. . . . What if the sink needs plumbing?"

"No big deal," she said. She pushed the hair from her face and went back to lining up the liquor. "It's not like *she's* going to work on the pipes. She'd hire some guy. I'd be more afraid some jerk showing off his butt crack might swipe a bottle."

"Yeah, I guess so," I said, nodding. It did make sense. Obviously I had a lot to learn.

I was still trying to find a way to file Christine into my brain. The girl had such a sweet, wholesome face— the type you'd see on a box of biscuit mix. For a while there I'd been afraid I was rooming with Shirley Temple at seventeen. But the minute Mom and Mrs. Krantz left, her demeanor had completely transformed. Her calm, saintly gaze gave way to a keen-eyed stare and wry smile. And her sugary voice was gone, replaced by the perpetually bored monotone of the ultracool set.

"You going to help?" she asked.

I sat down beside her and pulled a bottle of rum out of the box. "So, where'd you get all this?" I asked.

"From my dad's liquor cabinet."

"Really? Won't he see that it's missing?" I knew I sounded like a total thumb sucker, but I didn't care. I just had to know. In my house I couldn't roll my eyes without Mom finding out and nagging me about it.

Christine made a little snorting sound. "Yeah, right. Like he'd care. As long as no one touches the scotch. That's all he drinks. Luckily I hate that crap."

I nodded as if I totally understood. "I bet you're glad he had that surgery today, huh?" I said, trying to regain cool points. "You didn't have to worry he might notice all this stuff."

She looked at me with both sympathy and amusement. "He didn't have surgery today. I just made that up."

"Oh."

"Besides, he knows I can take care of myself," she said, frowning. She grabbed another two bottles and noisily plunked them beside the others. "*And* he had a golf game he didn't want to miss."

I wasn't sure what to say. It was clear she had parent issues, but then so did I. Plus, I was afraid I was making a pathetic first impression. For some reason talking with Christine made me feel about five years younger and short fifty IQ points.

"What about *your* dad?" she asked. "Where is he today?"

"At work," I said.

"And I take it your mom doesn't work and instead runs her kids' lives?"

"Well . . . yeah." I guessed that was one way of putting it. "Is it the same with yours?"

She gave me an ironic and slightly scary smile. "Oh no. Not my mumsie. She's in Costa Rica with her new husband."

Again I wasn't sure what to say. *I'm sorry* seemed too presumptuous. And the standard social courtesies, like *I see* or *Is that so?* didn't really seem to fit here. In fact, I was pretty sure I should never resort to polite society banter with her.

Luckily we finished unpacking the booze at that point and Christine announced it was time for a break. She mixed up a couple of drinks, some sort of juice with a little bit of rum, and we sat down in the living room—me on the big flowered sofa and Christine in the harvest gold armchair.

"Okay, questions," she said, setting her drink on the coffee table. "Where do you go to school? Who do you hang out with? And what do you do for fun?"

I swished my drink and watched the ice cubes whirl around the glass. I was used to these sorts of inquiries—these half-cloaked attempts to figure out my worth as a human being. In my circle, they were more along the lines of "Who's your boyfriend and what does he drive?" I could answer the question of my school, but not the others. Mainly because I didn't know anymore.

I must have taken too long to answer because Christine made a little exasperated noise. "Man, I should have made coffee instead. Are you stoned or something?"

"Sorry."

"Oh no. Don't tell me. You miss your boyfriend, right?"

I stared at her in alarm. "What makes you say that? Why do you think I have a boyfriend?"

"Please. Pretty trendies like you always have boyfriends. It's like those Barbie sets where you get two for the price of one. You date all through high school and college. Then you get married. You quit teaching to raise the kids, and you all live happily ever after in a big plastic dream home with your painted smiles, perfect hair, and expensive tans."

My eyes narrowed in a stern glare. What a judgmental bitch! How could she would make so many cynical assumptions about me after knowing me only half an hour? But I was also a little spooked. She'd just described my dad and mom to the last detail—except for the tanning part. Mom was too terrified of wrinkles and cancer. "Well, you're wrong! Not that it's any of your business, but I don't have a boyfriend," I said. I was so eager to shoot down her theory, I sounded almost boastful. "I used to, but he dumped me. Just yesterday, in fact . . . On my birthday . . ." My voice died away. Once again my insides felt swollen and bruised.

"Man, I'm sorry." Christine's smug expression dropped from her face. "What a loser."

"Yeah," I said tentatively. I wasn't sure if she meant Chuck or me.

For the first time since she arrived, Christine seemed speechless. I decided to take the focus off me and ask her a few questions.

"What about you? Do you have a boyfriend?"

"Yeah," she replied. "We've been going out for about a year now. He's older. Just graduated."

She softened as she talked about him, like any other girl who's crushing majorly over someone—just like I probably used to. She tried to hide it, but it was there. In the glow of her eyes and the unconscious way she smoothed her hair. I felt a stab of envy.

"Where'd you meet him?" I asked, interested in spite of myself.

"At a club in San Antonio. He's in a band."

*Figures,* I thought, taking a long swig of my drink. She seemed like the clubbing type.

"Do you play an instrument too?" I asked, wanting to keep the conversation going.

She shook her head. "I love music, but I'm not good at it. I'm in theater."

"You're *definitely* good at that," I said. "You had my mom and Mrs. Krantz totally fooled. Me too. I thought you'd be making me say grace anytime I grabbed a potato chip."

She started laughing. "It really helps when dealing with adults."

"I imagine."

Christine sat back in the chair and pushed a few strands of hair out of her face. "Hey, um . . . I know I was kind of bitchy before, but I didn't mean it. I tend to do that sometimes. I don't really know why."

I shrugged. "It's okay."

"You know what?" she said, lifting her glass toward me. "I think it's going to work out, you and I living together. Here's to blowing our parents off and having fun."

"To fun," I echoed.

We clinked our glasses together and Christine downed the rest of her drink in one gulp.

"All right," she said, slamming her glass down on the coffee table. "I call dibs on the biggest closet."

I followed her down to her car (a restored candy-apple red Karmann Ghia) and helped her carry the rest of her bags and boxes into the creaky service elevator, onto the landing, and then down the hall to her room. Christine took the north bedroom, since it had the bigger closet and was farther away from the noise of the living room. I didn't really care. My east-facing bedroom had the better view. If I stood in the far left corner of my window and got on the tips of my toes, I could see the top of the UT Tower peeking up over the giant live oak tree across the street.

Christine asked me to keep her company while she unpacked. Maybe it was the rum, or maybe I was tipsy just being away from Mom, but for some reason, I really liked Christine a lot—even though she'd been kind of mean to me before. Christine was someone who probably never got dumped, and never would. She was far too savvy to ever get blindsided the way I had been. I found myself really wanting her to like me. If nothing else, I figured I could study her over the summer and pick up pointers on how to win Chuck back. Or, more realistically, how to win back my reputation.

"So what's with your mom?" Christine asked as she

tossed a pair of what could only be described as army boots into the floor of her closet. "Why is she on your ass so much? Do you have a history of holding up liquor stores or something?"

"You'd think," I mumbled, staring down at my ragged nails—another one of Mom's favorite nagging topics. "It's just that she's a big go-getter and my dad is super successful and I'm not all that special."

Christine looked at me in disbelief. "Come on. You're a total yuppie princess."

"No, I'm not. I'm no good at that super achievement stuff. Dad says I'm too much of a thinker and Mom thinks I'm just lazy—either that or purposefully rebelling just to make her mad."

"You mean you aren't?" Christine raised her eyebrows. "Hell, I do that all the time to my dad. I figure it's our basic right."

"Yeah," I said. I didn't want to tell her that it wasn't pure teenage rebellion that made me go against my mom's plans for me. Truth was, I knew I'd fail at them. I was too klutzy and cynical for the beauty pageants, too shy for the speeches and protests. And I had no leadership qualities whatsoever. In our entire family, probably only Grandma Hattie, who had a tendency to go places in her slippers and still thought Nixon was President, was a bigger embarrassment to Mom.

I watched Christine hang up an itty-bitty dress that seemed to be made out of black rubber. The girl even had her own unique style. Obviously, she'd only worn

47

the church mouse ensemble in order to make a strong first impression on Mrs. Krantz. The real Christine, I could see, was more retro punk meets shabby chic meets urban cool.

"Okay. I'm done," she announced as she set a three-tiered chrome makeup case on the wooden dresser. "Let's unpack your stuff."

After watching her unload her vintage dresses, hard-core rock tees, and loads of black leather you-name-its, my own clothes seemed horribly boring and safe (especially the ruffly underwear from Grandma, which I tossed into a dark corner of the closet floor when Christine wasn't looking). I was kind of embarrassed and kept shoving things into drawers and onto hangers at a frenzied pace, so I wasn't really paying attention when I pulled out the Scooby Doo alarm clock from the bottom of the box.

"Is that a clock?" she asked from her cross-legged position on my mattress.

I looked down, surprised to see Scooby's goofy face in my grasp. "Uh . . . yeah."

Christine rose up onto her knees and held out her hands. "Can I see?"

"Sure." As I gave it to her, my mind raced to come up with some sort of excuse as to why I had a cartoon character alarm clock. Let's see. . . . She already knew I didn't have any younger siblings. She'd never believe it was a family heirloom. . . .

"This is cool," she said, turning it around. "Makes

sense you would have it. You look just like Daphne," she added, handing it back to me. "I absolutely love dogs. You want to see my collection?"

"Sure!" I exclaimed, happy to throw the focus off me.

She hopped off the bed and headed back to her room, returning with one of the cardboard boxes. I watched as she pulled back the flaps and began lifting out wiener dogs, one by one. There were several small stuffed ones, a couple of dachshund-shaped pillows, a pair of dachshund oven mitts, a few framed photos of dachshunds wearing costumes, a dachshund finger puppet, and a giant beach towel with a big blown-up photo of a dachshund's face and the words *Lord of the Wiens* written in bold across the bottom.

"I even have some wiener dog earrings," Christine added. "And look at this." She lifted her skirt to reveal a tattoo of a dachshund on her upper thigh.

"Wow!" I exclaimed. "You really like wiener dogs."

"Always have. In fact, I'm going to adopt a real one while I'm here. Mrs. Krantz already wrote a letter saying it was okay."

"Really?"

"Yep." She smiled sappily. "After all, she thinks I'm super-responsible."

"And your dad doesn't mind?"

"Sure he does. But I've got it all planned," she said smugly. "I'll just tell him I got a dog and I won't come home unless I can bring it with me." She sat down on the mattress, glanced at the Scooby clock, and then sprang back up again. "Oh, crap. Is that clock right?"

I stared down at my wristwatch. "Yeah. It's almost twelve."

"Aw, hell. I'm supposed to meet my boyfriend for lunch."

I watched as she tossed her wiener dogs back into the box and hoisted it onto her hip. I recognized that focused excitement. She was a girl with a purpose—a girl with a boyfriend—and nothing else mattered at the moment. I used to be just like that.

"So, hey. Um. You want to grab some dinner later or something?" I asked as she turned toward the door.

"Maybe," she said. "I don't know how long I'll be gone. But maybe we can hang out some more when I get back. Okay?"

"Sounds cool," I said.

But she was already out the door.

*I'm sitting on the grass overlooking a windswept shoreline. Seamus is there beside me. He pulls me up against him, his broad shoulder making the perfect cradle for my head. As I nestle against his sweater, he strokes his fingers through my hair. I feel so safe, so happy. After a while I lift my face toward his and stare into his copper-brown eyes. My hands reach up and begin tracing the familiar terrain of his face—his perfectly carved cheekbones, wide jaw, pencil-point cleft in his chin. Seamus*

*clasps each of my hands in his and kisses them softly. Then he leans forward and presses his mouth to mine. The earth spins faster. Animated cherubs frolic and sing! Eventually, we pull apart. Seamus smiles down at me, his black curls framing his features like a fuzzy dark halo. Leaning forward, he opens his mouth and says . . .*

"Jellyfishing!"

"Huh?" I jerked awake and found myself stretched out on the couch with a Hot Pockets sandwich wrapper on my chest. The condo was completely dark except for the TV, which was blaring an old *SpongeBob Square-Pants* episode. It took me a moment to realize where I was and what was happening

I hit the Lower Volume button on the remote control and sat up, rubbing my eyes until the image of Seamus fragmented and dissolved. Strange that I was dreaming about him again. Was it because Chuck dumped me? Was my poor, mangled ego trying to repair itself by focusing on a better guy? A guy cobbled together from bits of memory?

Then again, who else did I have? All day long as I'd unpacked and shopped for groceries, it hit me at intervals just how alone I was. No boyfriend, no friends, no group to hang out with. I'd managed to keep busy and shrug it off, assuring myself that I could put it all behind me, that Christine and I would hang out later, and that would help me forget. Only, here it was almost ten-thirty and Christine still hadn't returned—probably still in the arms of what's-his-name.

Now, in the stillness of the condo, the pathetic-ness that was my life hit me like never before. I lay back down and hugged a ruffly throw pillow to my chest, surrendering myself to self-pity. I missed Chuck. I missed having his arm around me, the spicy scent of his deodorant, and the sound of his rumbly voice over the phone. More than anything I missed that relationship feeling—the sense of being part of something beyond just me.

Now I was just me. And frankly, I wasn't enjoying my company all that much.

The sound of knocking startled me. Someone was at the door. Christine? Chuck? Seamus? My imagination was still in overdrive. I heaved myself off the sofa, trudged to the front door and opened it. Mrs. Krantz was standing in the hallway holding Mrs. B to her chest.

"Katie, dear!" she said. "How are you girls doing? Are you finding everything you need?"

"Yes. Thanks," I said, hoping my disappointment wasn't too obvious.

She leaned sideways and peered past me into the apartment. "It sure is dark. Where is Christine?"

"She's out."

Mrs. Krantz's eyes widened in alarm and she stared down at her watch. "She's gone out? At this hour?"

I suddenly realized I was about to destroy Christine's carefully constructed alter ego. "Uh, no," I said quickly. "What I meant was, she's out like a light. She's already asleep."

Mrs. B narrowed her amber eyes at me in an accusing sort of way. *Can she tell I'm lying? Am I that obvious?*

Mrs. Krantz gave a birdlike titter into her left hand. "I see. Well then, we won't keep you. Mrs. B and I just wanted to check on you and say goodbye. We'll be leaving first thing tomorrow morning and won't be back until Sunday evening."

"Thanks, but don't worry about us," I said. "We'll be fine."

"I know you will." She reached out and patted my wrist where I held fast to the doorknob. "I'm so glad we were able to work things out with your mother."

"Me too." Again, maybe it was just my guilty conscience, but Mrs. B seemed to flash me another death stare.

"You girls have a good time together!" Mrs. Krantz sang out. "See you when I get back." She gave a little wave and tottered back toward her condo.

"Have a good trip!" I shut the door and leaned against it, rubbing the sleep out of my eyes. Have a good time together? Yeah, right. Christine obviously wasn't too interested in hanging out with me.

I switched off the TV set, headed into my room and fired up my laptop to check e-mail. Most of it was boring stuff—the booster club newsletter and a message from Mom reminding me to program Austin emergency numbers into my cell phone. Of course, there was absolutely nothing from Chuck or my friends. No one cared.

For a long moment I just at there, fighting the urge to scream or cry or toss the laptop into the street. And then . . . I looked around and smiled.

At least I was here. Thousands of people who had no idea who the heck Chuck was or that he shoved my ego through a shredder. No fake friends clucking false sympathy to my face and then laughing behind my back. No mom around to tell me what to do every minute of the day. And no one who thought of me as Laura McAllister's far-less-brilliant daughter.

It almost seemed too dreamlike. I wouldn't have even blinked if some megaphone-wielding director stepped out of the wings yelling, "*Cut!* That's a wrap! You! Go back to your lame reality!"

The fact was, I was getting a fresh start. And I was going to make the most of it.

# 3

Scooby woke me up at nine the next morning. The fricking thing sounded like it was having an electronic panic attack. *"(Click.) BLLLLEEP! Beep! Beep! Beep! Beep! Beepbeepbeepbeepbeep!"* It blared at close to 147 decibels. I was on the floor practically convulsing in disoriented terror, swiping aimlessly at the clock and hoping to get it to stop. But the big-nosed Scooby face just stared back as if mocking me. Finally I managed to knock the thing into the waste bin where it took on an eerie, tinny echo. I shoved my pillow on top of it to muffle the sound, stuck in my hand and fished around until I eventually hit a switch that shut it off.

At that point I felt as if I'd just drunk nine cups of

coffee, so I decided to go ahead and start my day.

I headed out into the living room. Rays of sunlight were squeezing around the cheesy fabric blinds that covered the patio doors. Everything was still and quiet. And then I remembered: I really was here—on my own. Away from all things high school and all things Chuck. My heartbeat slowed and a giddy, excited feeling spread through my limbs. The condo suddenly seemed to me the most beautiful spot on earth. I was in love with its grizzled gray carpet and chipped, pea soup green counters. The tacky 1980s furniture looked like priceless heirlooms. Even the clouds of dust swirling in the sunbeams added a magical, sparkly quality—like a live-action fairy movie.

I took a deep breath of musty air and walked over to open the blinds, hoping to spend some time quietly admiring the view before Christine woke up. I yanked down on the plastic chain and the blinds zipped apart, stirring up tiny eddies of grime.

"Oh, be a love and shut those bloody things will you?" came a voice from behind me.

I let out a little yelp and whirled around, the skirt of my nightgown catching up with me a second later.

A figure was lying on the sofa surrounded by stuffed wiener dogs—a guy wearing dark clothes. I couldn't see his face, though, since he was shielding it with his hands.

*There is a strange guy on our couch!* a voice shouted inside my head.

"Seriously, love, it's a bloomin' supernova out there!" he said, sitting up.

*A strange* British *guy is on our couch,* my mind went on, *and you're just standing there like a dumb ass in your Hello Kitty nightie!*

What to do? Should I scream? Run away? Grab a weapon? Offer him hot tea?

"Wh-what are you doing here?" I demanded, my vocal chords reactivating. "Who the hell are you?"

"I'm Robot," he muttered from behind his hands.

"You're a robot?"

"No-o. The name's Robot. Robert actually, but me mates call me Robot. I'm Christine's chap."

"You're . . . Christine's boyfriend?" I stumbled, my brain slowly sputtering back to life.

"Yes," he said irritably. "Charmed, I'm sure. Now could you *please shut the bloody blinds*?"

I yanked on the opposite cord and the blinds swished shut.

"Thank you," he said with a sigh. "You must be Christine's flatmate." He lowered his hands, revealing a long, pale face—unusually pale for Texas in June. His features appeared to have been sculpted from marshmallow: deep-set brown eyes like two finger pokes, a thin tweak of a nose, and a pinch of a chin that was trying manfully to sport a soul-patch goatee, but instead came across as a smudge of potting soil. His white skin was offset dramatically by spiky black hair and sideburns, as well as his rumpled dark T-shirt and jeans.

But he was cute, in a skinny, sloppy, creature-of-the-night sort of way.

"What are you doing here?" I asked.

"Christine said I was snoring," he said, sitting up and scratching his scalp with both hands, making his hair defy gravity even more. "She made me come out here."

I shook my head. "Uh . . . not what I meant. I mean, why are you in Austin? Don't you live in San Antonio?"

"Yeah, I crash there most nights. But when Christine told me about this new flat, I thought I'd come check out the scene awhile. You know, try to score some gigs for the band." He smiled at me as he said this—not taunting, but rather smugly, as if he thought I'd be squealing and wetting my undies with delight over this news. "My band's New Bile. You heard of us?"

He rattled off the question offhandedly but watched my reaction closely. I could tell he was waiting hungrily for my starstruck reaction—as if that were the blood his vampire body thrived on.

"Yeah," I said, somewhat squeaky with delight in spite of myself. All last year the cool kids at school were talking about these retro-punk guys called New Bile who were packing the clubs. Unfortunately, my mom would never let me go to one of their shows. "My boyfriend is a major fan," I added. His smile stretched further. My reply was acceptable.

*My boyfriend?* I wondered. Why didn't I tell the

truth? Why not say *ex*-boyfriend? Was it a slip of the tongue? Or was I trying to make myself seem more sought-after and attractive? As attractive as a girl with morning eye gunk and a cartoon cat on her chest can be.

Robot stretched his arms and propped his feet, covered in dingy moldy-looking socks, on the rickety coffee table. I had just opened my mouth to tell him to be careful of the furniture, that we could lose our deposits if we break anything, when I saw him lunge toward a leather jacket draped on one of the armchairs and pull out a pack of American Spirit cigarettes from one of the pockets. He saw me watching him and pointed the box toward me. "Fancy one?"

"Uh . . . no thanks. Um . . . we're not supposed to smoke in here."

He raised his eyebrows. "Says who?"

"Says our landlady."

He let out a snort. "Don't see the old bag around here," he mumbled, the words slightly garbled from the cigarette perched between his lips. He fished a metal Zippo lighter out of his pants pocket and lit the end. Then he leaned back and rested his arms along the back of the sofa. I eyed the cigarette smoldering between the first two fingers of his right hand, envisioning tiny burn holes in the upholstery.

"Feel free to have a seat, love," he said, gesturing to the striped chair. He let out a cackle that turned into a hacking cough.

A hot jet of anger burbled up inside me. Who the hell was this ponce to tell me when to sit in my living room? This place was supposed to belong to me—the *new* me. It was supposed to be about late-night talks with my new roomie while we painted our toenails burnt orange, or eating takeout Chinese while I read from a ten-pound college textbook. It was supposed to be about leftover pizza for breakfast, having *American Pie* DVD marathons, and rating the frat boys passing beneath the balcony. It was *not* supposed to include some MTV reject digging into our couch like a hermit crab.

I sucked in my breath, ready to tell Robot to take his *bloody* boots off our *bloody* furniture and put out his *bloody* stinkarette.

Yet . . . Christine had obviously invited him here. And I couldn't piss off Christine. If I did she could sabotage things with my mom whenever she called. Then I'd be packed off to San Marcos and my lame excuse of a life faster than you could say "Cheerio, old chap!"

My anger subsided until I could only stand there chewing my nails, hyperaware of the stubble on my legs and the layer of grease on my face.

At that moment the phone rang. I quickly snatched it up, grateful for the distraction, only to hear my mom's voice on the other end say, "Katie, do you realize you forgot your skin ointment?"

I shut my eyes and made a tiny whimpering noise in my throat. "Hi, Mom."

"I can't believe you left this behind! What if you start getting that rash again?"

Man alive. I get one minor outbreak of eczema on my elbow and now she thinks I'm ointment-dependent. "It'll be okay, Mom."

"You know, you might want to look into a highly recommended doctor someplace near you. That way if anything goes wrong, you'll know where to go. In fact," her voice went up an octave, "you could call Aaron and see if he knows anyone. He had a really good friend for a while who was studying to be a doctor. They were very close. I'm sure he would know . . ."

My hearing failed. My brain went AWOL. I just couldn't take her without caffeine. As I forced myself to remain upright I noticed Christine emerge from her room. She was wearing black boxer shorts and a white tank with the word *Goal!* in purple block letters across the chest, and her hair stuck out in all directions. She stumbled crookedly down the hallway and crawled on top of Robot, who was once again stretched along the couch. I felt a squeezing sensation behind my ribs as I watched them snuggle up together.

". . . And you might want to get a standing prescription in case you get bad menstrual cramps again. . . ."

Robot whispered something to Christine and she let out a shriek of laughter.

"What was that?" Mom asked suddenly. "Was that Christine?"

"Um, yeah," I said, cupping the receiver in case she accidentally overheard Robot's voice. "She must be watching TV or something."

"Let me talk to her."

"What?"

"You heard me, sweetheart. Let me speak to your roommate. I want to hear what you've been up to."

My chest grew tighter. So she was really going to go through with this? My word wasn't enough for her? I briefly considered complaining, and then realized it was a lost cause. Once Mom decided something, no amount of begging, battling or skillful debate would make her change her mind.

"Fine," I grouched. I took a step toward the sofa. "My mom wants to talk to you," I said, focusing on the dark-haired scalp I assumed was Christine's.

She struggled to a sitting position, followed by Robot. Both looked annoyed and slightly bewildered.

"Really," I said, holding up the phone.

Christine looked momentarily put out. Then she turned and pressed a finger to Robot's lips. "Stifle," I heard her mutter. Pushing her long, raven hair over her shoulders, she reached out and snatched the phone from my hand. "Yes, Mrs. McAllister?" she said, morphing into her goody-goody persona. Her face went placid and her voice turned sticky sweet, as if she'd just gargled with molasses. "Yes, ma'am. . . . Of course. . . . No, ma'am. No problems at all. . . . Oh, no. We would never do that. . . . Yes, ma'am . . . Right. . . . I understand. . . . You too. . . . Goodbye!"

She handed the receiver to me and rolled her eyes.

"Thanks," I said, flashing her an apologetic look.

As she snuggled back up to Robot, I lifted the phone to my ear. "Mom?"

"Well, it's good to hear you are behaving yourself so far. Your father sends his love. You take care, sweetie. I'll call back soon."

*I don't doubt it.* "Bye."

"What the hell was that all about?" Robot asked as soon as I hung up.

"Her mom is making me spy on her," Christine explained. "She calls me to make sure Katie has been a good girl."

"She calls *you*?" Robot let out a roar of laughter. "That's a good one!"

"Hey!" Christine thumped him playfully on the arm, but she was laughing too.

Feeling thoroughly stupid, I had no choice but to laugh along with them. I supposed it was a bizarre situation—but it wasn't *that* funny. I mean, Mom was only doing this because she cared about me. What was wrong with that?

"I mean, God! How can you stand it?" Christine went on. "Do you have to check in with her, like, twelve times a day?" She pantomimed holding a phone to her ear and said in a meek little voice, "Mother, should I turn left or right? Do I want strawberry or chocolate? Should I breathe in or out?" She cackled at her own joke, Robot guffawing along with her.

My eyes teared up a little. She had no right to make fun of me that way. It wasn't my fault my mom was doing this. I didn't ask for it.

*But it's not like you ever ask Mom to stop either,* came a voice from inside me.

I stood there in a daze, feeling simultaneously mad, hurt and ashamed. I'd always known my mom was a little much. But until that moment I'd never really thought I might have some part in it—by going along with it all the time.

"I guess I should be glad my mom and dad never call," Christine went on. "Which reminds me, I need to check my messages." She leaped off the couch and fished a sleek BlackBerry out of her leather messenger bag.

Her movement seemed to dislodge my emotional clog and snap me out of my trance. "I'm going to take a shower," I announced, to no one in particular.

"Alright, love," Robot said, flopping back against the cushions and shutting his eyes. "But don't use all the hot water. I'm next."

I wrinkled up my nose and headed for the bathroom. Just as I was turning the corner, Christine let out a little scream. "Oh my God!" she said, pointing to her cell. "He's here! She's here! They've got one for me!"

"One what?" I asked, interested in spite of myself.

"My wiener dog!" she exclaimed. "I just got an e-mail from the rescue league! And the dog's a red one—just like I wanted!" She grabbed Robot's shoulder and started shaking him. "Get up! You've got to come to the pound with me!"

"Christine! It's the sodding crack of dawn!" he whined.

"It's almost nine-thirty!"

"But I'm totally knackered, love. You know we had a late gig."

"Don't be such a wanker! I was up late too, you know!"

"But you weren't on stage."

She let out an exasperated sigh. "Fine! I'll get someone else."

I knew what would happen even before she swiveled around to face me, her eyes as big and round as beer coasters.

"Katie," she began in her syrupy sweet voice.

"But I really need to take a shower," I said, gesturing to my matted hair and stubbly legs.

"You can do that when we get back. *Please?* If I take too long, someone else will beat me to him!"

*Do I look as if I care?* I grumbled inwardly, still mad at her for laughing at me. But even as I thought this, I could feel my posture wilting in defeat. Christine noticed too. A triumphant grin began wriggling across her face. "Oh, okay," I heard myself say. But Christine had already grabbed my arm and was pulling me toward my bedroom.

"Hurry and get dressed," she ordered. "I'll meet

you at the door in five minutes."

So there I was on my first morning of freedom. In-stead of sipping coffee on the balcony after a record-long hot shower, I was caffeine-free and yanking on old sweats so I could accompany Christine to an animal shelter.

The last thing I saw before heading out of the apartment with Christine was steam snaking around the bathroom door. Robot's voice, singing a classic Green Day tune, echoed from within.

"Crap! You are freaking kidding me! How can he be gone already?"

Christine had transformed again. Two minutes before, she had been all schoolgirl charm and impeccable manners. Now an angry, messy-haired banshee stood in her place, yelling at a bespectacled woman at the reception counter.

"I'm sorry. The dog left just half an hour ago with someone else. They called yesterday evening right after we posted the e-mail."

"But that's not fair! I just got the message this morning! I can't help it if I had plans last night. I have a life!"

The woman smiled without curling up the sides of her mouth, making it look as if she were baring her teeth at Christine. "If you like, I can do a search of other nearby shelters to see if any dachshunds have been brought in recently. Sometimes they don't get on the rescue league's network."

"Yes. Do that."

"It might take a while," she said. I could tell she was hoping Christine might worry it would take up too much of her "life."

"Fine. Whatever," Christine said. She looked over at me. "That's not a problem, is it, Katie?"

*Yes. I'm hungry and in dire need of shampoo and a cup of coffee.* "No. No problem. I'll just have a look around."

The irritated woman led Christine into a glass-walled office and shut the door. I felt like a dweeb on display just standing there with nothing to do, so I wandered down the corridor where the dogs were displayed. With each step the soundscape of barks, grunts and whimpers grew louder, and the combined smell of kibble and animal dander became nearly over-whelming.

A middle-aged man holding a clipboard stood near the far end of the corridor. He nodded at me. "If you see one that interests you, let me know."

"Thanks but . . ." I paused, unsure how to say that I really wasn't interested in adopting a homeless pet, that I was just killing time while my roommate had me trapped there. After all, the guy probably put years of his life into saving these animals and probably wouldn't take kindly to window-shoppers like me. "I'm sort of in a temporary living situation right now.

So I'm looking around to just, you know, get a feel of what sort of dog I want to adopt when I head home this fall."

He gave a perfunctory nod and turned back toward his clipboard, clearly sorry he'd even spoken to me.

*No need to tell him your life story, you spaz!*

I slowly ambled down the corridor, peering into the Plexiglas stalls at all the different animals. For some reason I'd expected the kennels to resemble a bleak dungeon—like the scene in *The Lady in the Tramp*. But this place wasn't that bad at all. The dogs all looked healthy and well-cared for. They had mats and blankets and big bowls of food and water. And yet, it still made me sad. There were so many of them. Row after row, stall after stall, dogs of all shapes, sizes and colors. My eyes blurred trying to look at them all.

Just as the depression was starting to set in, I caught sight of a little face out of the corner of my eye. I turned and saw a dog sitting quietly at the front of his stall, studying me as if I were the one on display.

He was medium-sized with longish black, white and brown fur. His ears were raised, the left one flopping forward at the tip as if it were too heavy. His fur parted down the length of his snout and hung down like a giant mustache beneath his round, black-button nose. But what struck me the most were his eyes. Big and round and dark, with two streaks of light brown fur hanging over each one like eyebrows. He cocked his head and stared at me intently, looking sad or worried.

*Worried about me?*

I'd never seen a dog like him before. And yet, there was something jarringly familiar about him—something that made my mind wheel backwards. . . . Big brown eyes . . . messy, floppy hair . . . a kindly look of concern . . .

"Seamus," I said softly.

Suddenly the dog rose up on his haunches and placed his front paws against the glass, his tail a wagging blur. It seemed to me that his mouth curled into a smile.

"Seamus?" I said again. I knew it wasn't Seamus—not my Seamus. But for whatever reason, this dog responded to the name. I stared into his dark, soulful eyes, and he kept on gazing back as if terribly concerned for me.

A warm, snuggly feeling swept through me. I wanted so badly to hold him, to take him home and feed him and take care of him forever and ever. But I knew I couldn't. Mom would flip out if I got a dog. A decision this big required her input at every step. Hell, she'd probably want to pick it out herself. She'd insist I forget about this guy and instead talk me in to some perfect, fluffy poser dog. Or something more practical like a gi-normous watchdog that would attack any guy who came near me—except Aaron, of course. Not that it mattered. She'd never allow me to have a dog to begin with.

As I turned to walk away, the dog started whining.

I spun back around and looked at him.

Then again . . . there was no reason why we couldn't have a dog. No one in my family was allergic, and we had a big backyard. And why shouldn't I be able to pick out the one I wanted? I'd be the one taking care of him. It wasn't like I would be bringing home a camel, or a great white shark or a guy like Robot. It was just a little dog. What was the big deal anyway?

I was tired of consulting Mom on every little thing. Robot and Christine were right. I was practically an adult and I was still letting my mom run my life!

No more. I was going to make this decision myself. And if Mom didn't like it, tough! It would serve her right for not trusting me.

"I'd like to reserve this one," I heard myself call out to the man, who was still flipping pages and taking down notes.

He glanced over, somewhat taken aback after having written me off as a browser. Sticking the clipboard under his arm, he walked over and studied the tag on Seamus's kennel.

"Sorry," he said. "You'd have to take him now. This guy won't be available in a couple of months."

"Why?" Oh no. Just my luck. Someone else already asked for him! But he was *mine*! They had to understand.

The man looked into my eyes, his expression a little sad. "This one is scheduled to be euthanized in two days if he isn't adopted."

"Euthanized? You mean . . ." It felt as if I'd been poured over ice. *". . . killed?"*

"I'm sorry," the man said again, and he truly did look very sorry. "We get so many dogs here, and we have to accept them all. We simply don't have the space or resources to keep them indefinitely."

I stared back into the little dog's eyes. His head was tilting from side to side as if he were pondering me as well. A fluttery feeling filled my chest. Somehow I just knew, beyond any doubt or hesitation: This little guy was meant to be with me. No way could I let him die.

I could do this. In fact, this way might even be better. After all, Mom couldn't argue that I wasn't responsible enough for a dog if I'd been taking care of one all summer. Right?

"Then I'll take him now," I said firmly. "Today."

Two minutes later we were in a different glass-walled office and I was looking over the information on "Tex," as they called Seamus. According to their records, he was approximately ten months old and had been found abandoned in a strip center parking lot. He weighed eighteen pounds and was twenty-one inches long. In the box marked Breed, they had written, "Mixed," but the man said he would guess Black Russian terrier mixed with something else. Schnauzer maybe, or Lhasa. "Something more hyper," as he put it.

"Do you have anything with your current address?" he asked as he filled out a form with lots of tiny print on it.

"Yes. My student ID card," I said, pulling the orange-bordered card from my wallet. "I'm starting classes there Monday," I added, hoping it made me sound older. *Yup, that's me. A responsible, mature UT student. A worthy caregiver for a homeless dog.*

He stopped writing and glanced up at me. "You rent?"

"Yes." I nodded. "A nice, big condo. Plenty of space."

"Do you have a note from the owner clearing you to have an animal there?"

"Uh . . . not really," I replied, my voice puny with sudden panic.

The man sighed and set down his pen, his features sagging with disappointment.

A heavy, tingly feeling trilled through my limbs. They wouldn't let him die just because of a piece of paper, would they?

"But my roommate has a note!" I added hastily. "Christine Hobbes. H-o-b-b-e-s. We live in the exact same condo. She has a letter from our landlady allowing her to have a pet."

"I'm sorry, but I'll need one made out for you."

"But my landlady is out of town until next week! You said yourself, by then it will be too late." For some reason, I was really losing it—lips quivering, eyes tearing up, voice like a cartoon mouse.

The man shifted in his vinyl office chair and muttered a series of single-syllable nothing words. "Uh . . . well . . . um . . . hmmm." He eyed the door behind me longingly.

I leaned forward and wiped my eyes with the back of my hand. "Please," I croaked. "Just let me take him. Let me save his life."

"Well *that* was a major waste of time," Christine said as she stalked out of the patient lady's office. "Come on, Katie. Let's get out of here and go find a Starbucks."

"Um . . . maybe we should go home first?"

She looked down at Seamus, who was dancing around my feet, and came to a halt. "What's that?"

"A dog."

"I know that," she snapped. "Why is it *with* you?"

"I sort of . . . adopted him."

"*What?* Are you on dope? Why would you do that?"

"Why not? I thought you loved dogs."

"Well, yeah. Of course I do." Her voice grew defensive. "But that one seems like a real spaz."

By now Seamus was whirling around my legs, requiring me to step over his leash every few seconds to avoid being tripped. "No," I protested. "He's just excited. He'll be fine. Seamus, this is Christine," I called down toward my feet.

"Shame, huh?" she asked.

"Seamus. It's Irish."

"Yeah, great." She shook her head mournfully. "I can't believe you actually adopted a dog!"

I shrugged lamely and jumped over the leash again. "I know. Me either. But I had to. They were going to put him down."

She made a huffy noise and cocked one elbow while placing her weight on one of her scrawny, splayed legs, making her look like a giant letter R.

"I don't think it's fair that you didn't even consult me about this."

My heart started thrashing as I suddenly realized how much this depended on Christine. What if she told the shelter people I wasn't allowed? Or complained to Mrs. Krantz? Or—even worse—to Mom?

"You didn't tell me you were getting a dog until yesterday," I pointed out, my voice wobbly from all the cardiac activity. "You never asked me either."

Christine's eyes met mine. I couldn't tell if she was furious or just shocked.

"Think about it," I added quickly. "This could be good for your dog too. He'd have a friend to hang out with when we're in class."

She stared back down at Seamus, who was now jumping up onto my legs, his toenails making tiny holes in my blue workout pants.

"Whatever," she muttered finally. "Let's just get out of here." Veering wide around me and Seamus, she shouldered her leather messenger and stalked out of the building.

I stood in a daze, listening to the sound of traffic grow suddenly loud and then diminish as she headed out the door. My senses reeled with both relief and disbelief. Somehow I'd done it. I'd gotten my way.

"Come on, boy," I said, giving Seamus's lead a gentle tug. He looked up at me and wagged his tail, smiling that doggie smile of his. A warm, gooshy feeling spread through me and I reveled in the sweetness of the moment. Then, with a sudden burst of speed, he turned and raced toward the exit, sending me sprawling sideways on the vinyl floor.

# 4

"What the hell is that?" Robot was splayed on the couch when we got back, surrounded by a colorful mosaic of food wrappers—snacks *I* had bought the day before at the corner Fresh Mart. He picked up the remote and turned down the volume on a Bugs Bunny marathon. "That doesn't look like a wiener dog."

"It's not mine. It's Katie's," Christine snapped. She threw her car keys onto the coffee table and flopped down beside Robot.

She hadn't spoken much on the drive home—except for the times when she shrieked at Seamus to quit scratching the dashboard or slobbering on the window. He was acting a little nuts, but I could tell he was just overjoyed to be out of that shelter. It made me feel more than ever that I'd done the right thing.

I shuffled behind her to the sofa, cradling Seamus with one arm and lugging a bag of pet supplies with the other. After we hit the Starbucks drive-through, Christine had been nice enough to stop at one of those giant pet department stores on the way home—although I thought she was going to leave us stranded when Seamus accidentally knocked over a display of elderly-dog diapers.

So far, owning a pet was turning out to be expensive. Along with the ninety-five dollars I spent to adopt him, I also had to cough up an additional one hundred and fourteen dollars for kibble, a dog dish, a collar and leash, a special flea comb, a brush, some breath-freshening snacks, vitamins, and a chew toy fashioned like a miniature beach ball. There were tons of other things there I'd considered buying, but I'd already dipped heavily into my summer savings. Besides, I figured I could always go back later.

I sat down in the striped chair, still cradling Seamus as best I could. By now my face was glistening with dog saliva and my arms had red crisscross marks from his toenails. Now that I had Seamus safely back in the condo, I wasn't exactly sure what to do. I felt like there should be some formality associated with his homecoming, but I had no idea what it should be.

"I didn't know you were getting a dog too," Robot remarked.

"Yeah, well . . . I've always loved dogs. I've been searching for one for a while," I lied. Actually, the only pet I'd ever had was a gerbil named Farley who escaped after three weeks and somehow got into the dishwasher. I was pretty traumatized when I discovered his boiled little corpse, and we never did get a replacement.

I stroked Seamus's back as he wriggled around on my lap.

"Why'd you choose that dog?" Christine asked. I could tell she didn't feel any kind of pull toward Seamus.

I shrugged feebly. "You know how it is. He just spoke to me."

Judging by their blank stares, they did *not* know how it was.

"What sort of breed is it?" Christine asked.

I pursed my lips. Why did she keep referring to him as "it"? "He's mixed," I explained. "Terrier and something else."

"Brillo pad?" Robot joked. Christine chuckled appreciatively. I bit the inside of my cheek.

I looked down into Seamus's dark, round, sea-otter eyes. He cocked his head at me and then licked my cheek, as if trying to say, "It's okay. Don't listen to them. You did the right thing."

Figuring he seemed calm enough, I bent over and carefully set him on the carpet. "Here you go. Welcome to your new—" But he was already racing away. Down the corridor and back again. Into the kitchen and back. Round and round the sofa.

"Speedy little nutter, isn't he?" Robot remarked. "You sure he's all right? He's got a look in his eye like he's mental."

"He's just excited," I said. It had become my slogan for the day. Seamus was just incredibly happy to be out of the shelter. He knew I'd saved his life and taken him away from that cramped, dingy little cage. Now he was simply showing me how much he appreciated what I'd done.

Right then Seamus came charging out of the bathroom with one of Christine's bras in his mouth. He was growling and shaking his head back and forth, as if fearlessly attacking a lacy black snake.

Christine screamed and Robot burst out laughing. I jumped up and ran after Seamus with my arms stretched out, trying to grab him. Seamus, however, assumed it was a game and accelerated, making sure he was always several steps ahead of me. Occasionally he would stop and hunker down, sticking his heinie way up high and wagging his tail furiously.

Eventually he started barking, causing the bra to fall to the floor. I picked it up and handed it, slightly damp but otherwise intact, to Christine.

"Sorry," I mumbled.

She snatched it from me with an angry grunt and stalked toward the bathroom.

Meanwhile Robot was still laughing. "You sure he's

not mental?" he asked, gesturing toward Seamus, who was still barking and whirling in a circle, begging me to chase him again.

"He's just excited," I repeated, somewhat lamely.

In addition to Christine's bra, here are all the things Seamus chewed within the first two hours of coming home:

- An empty Doritos bag
- The striped chair cushion
- The lamp cord
- My messenger bag
- The sleeve of Robot's motorcycle jacket
- My sock (while it was on my foot)
- Christine's car keys
- The May issue of *Vogue*

This is what he did not chew: the chew toy.

Every time I'd toss it toward him, Seamus would stop to watch it plop to the ground with a lackluster squeak, and then he'd continue on his merry way.

He also tried several times to chew one of the stuffed wiener dogs, only to be reprimanded with a high-pitched shriek from Christine.

In addition to all the gnawing, Seamus knocked over the soda can Robot was using as an ashtray, completely twisted up the vertical blinds, and took a bite out of my Pop-Tart when I was watching Bugs Bunny take on the giant red monster in tennis shoes.

"Are you sure you didn't adopt a psycho dog?" Christine snapped when she caught him tugging on her leopard-spotted shoelaces.

I could tell her stress was building and was afraid she'd pressure me to take him back to the shelter. I swore up and down that I would never let him roam the condo unless I was there supervising him closely. Luckily, that seemed to make her feel better.

After a while I noticed Seamus's gait had slowed to a trot. He wandered about the living room, sniffing all the furniture. *Good,* I thought. *He's calming down.* He took a few sniffs of the big potted palm in the corner, turned around and lifted his left leg.

"No!" I cried, causing Robot to choke on his Red Bull. I jumped to my feet and ran toward Seamus, who took off in the other direction, dancing and barking in another game of chase.

"What's he doing now?" Christine groaned.

"Nothing," I said, thankful she'd missed his near-watering of the potted palm. "I'm going to take him for a walk."

"Thank God," I heard her mumble as we walked out the door with the leash.

It was an absolutely beautiful day—not too warm yet, and with an intermittent light breeze. It looked as if someone had swept a few dust-bunny-looking clouds off toward the western horizon and then colored everything with a turquoise crayon. *Ah yes. This is much better,* I thought. *The ideal way for both of us to chill out.* I took a deep breath, gave the leash a tug, and together we headed down the sidewalk.

And there I was: a girl walking her dog. It felt so right, as if Seamus completed me somehow. The perfect accessory for a perfect outfit.

Of course, if I wanted to be completely accurate, our scene was more "dog dragging girl." Seamus was surprisingly strong for his size. Basically I let him take me where he wanted to go, since I had no real plan myself. Occasionally he would stop abruptly, right in my path, forcing me to hurdle over him clumsily.

We lurched down Pearl Street, passing renovated turn-of-the-century bungalows, a redbrick apartment complex, and a large Greek-revival-style mansion that, judging by the tall, clean-cut, incredibly cute guys playing Frisbee on the front lawn, had been converted into a frat house.

Eventually we staggered around a corner, and there, just past a concrete tennis court, was a wide, tree-lined park. Seamus pulled me along the curving sidewalk toward a sea of pea gravel. There preschoolers kids clambered over a giant blue-and-yellow plastic playscape while their mothers sat on park benches, gabbing and nursing sling-swaddled babies. A few of the children stopped to gawk at us. One of the younger ones, a wild-haired tyke in a Thomas the Tank Engine shirt, shouted, "Yook! Goggie! Goggie!"

A boy who looked about five years old ran up to us. "I like your dog," he said, trying to pet Seamus on the back. Seamus was hopping around on his leash, eager to continue his walk.

"Thanks," I said proudly.

Seamus, realizing the boy wanted to pet him, turned his attention toward the child. His panted happily and his tail began a high-speed wag. I felt the shifting of his weight and recognized the eager glint in his eyes. But before I could do anything, he had already flung himself forward and leaped on the small boy, knocking him to a sitting position.

"Seamus, no!" I yelled, snatching him up.

Luckily the boy just laughed and stood back up again. "What's his name?" he asked, patting Seamus's head.

"Seamus," I said, straining to keep hold of my dog.

"Same as?" The boy stared up at me quizzically. "Same as what?"

I laughed and shook my head. "No. Seamus. *Shame . . . us,*" I explained, breaking it down for him. "It's a boy's name. Just like yours."

The boy's blue eyes grew large and round. "His name is the same as mine? William?"

"Uh, no. What I meant was—"

By this time his two companions were walking toward us. The boy turned toward them, shouting,

"Hey, guys, guess what? The dog's name is William too!"

"Ohhh. Hi, Will-ee-am," sang a small, pigtailed girl as she stroked Seamus's ears.

"Will-yum! Will-yum!" chanted the small one who'd called him "goggie."

I struggled to keep hold of Seamus, but he managed to squirm out of my arms and leap on the smaller boy. The boy shrieked with delight as he fell against the grass, Seamus licking every inch of his face.

"William and Michael, come here right now!" A woman stood up from one of the benches and gestured toward us. "You know you're not supposed to pet strange dogs!"

"You too, Alicia," called out a second woman.

"Sorry," I called out, scooping up Seamus again and holding him with all my might. The women just ignored me.

"Bye, goggie," said the smaller boy as he scrambled to his feet again. He waved at Seamus before toddling off toward his mother.

"Bye-bye, William," Alicia said sadly. Then she, too, skipped off toward the benches.

The older boy, William, lingered behind and continued to pet Seamus. His features were set in grim determination.

"William!" his mom repeated in a warning tone. "Right now! It's almost time for your swim lesson!"

At this the boy brightened slightly. "I can almost

swim," he announced proudly. "I can hold my breath a long time. Look." He inhaled deeply and puffed out his cheeks. For a long time he stood motionless—but I could still see his chest moving up and down.

"Very good!" I exclaimed. His cheeks deflated with a small pop.

"*William!*" the mom shrieked.

"Well . . . bye." The boy turned and charged back toward the benches. Seamus strained harder than ever to follow him, but I held on tight and didn't let go until I felt him relax.

"Come on, Seamus," I said, tugging him in the direction of the sidewalk. "Let's go, Seamus." After the "William" episode, I was a little worried he might get confused about his name.

It required a lot of pulling and coaxing, but eventually I was able to restart our walk along the sidewalk. Just beyond the playground lay a grassy field, completely empty except for a chain-link backstop—and lots and lots of squirrels.

As soon as one of the bushy-tailed critters came within two feet of us, Seamus lunged with a force more powerful than I'd assumed he'd be capable of. I heard him start yapping loudly, felt the leash slip from my grasp, and saw a dark blur zooming off into the distance.

"Seamus! No!" I cried, running after him.

It was like one of those cheesy chase scenes in a vintage comedy. The only thing missing was the rollicking music. Even though the squirrel (and every squirrel within a hundred yards) had climbed to safety two seconds after my dog took off after it, Seamus still kept racing around the park, wired on freedom and the infinite space around him.

"Come here, Seamus!" I called out over and over, but he kept ignoring me.

Soon I realized he thought it was a game. He would stop long enough for me to get within range; then, as soon as I reached for him, he'd get this possessed gleam in his eyes and take off again.

After a while I stopped and rested my hands on my knees, trying to catch my breath. I was beginning to panic. What if I *never* caught him?

A lady pushing a stroller stopped along the sidewalk behind me. "Excuse me, but dogs are not supposed to be off their leash at this park," she said in a snippy tone.

"He's not off his leash," I pointed out. I knew it was rude, but I was beyond caring. I was mad and embarrassed and tired as hell. Besides, the woman looked a lot like my mom.

She narrowed her eyes at me. "You know what I mean. They aren't supposed to run free!"

"Lady, if you want to try chasing him down for me, be my guest," I snapped. "Right now I'm taking a breather."

She glared at me for a few seconds and then resumed her walk, her stride now longer and faster. I watched as she headed into the crowd of mothers. Soon all of their heads were ducked together for a collective whisper. *What's the big deal exactly?* I thought, my cheeks stinging with anger and humiliation. *It's not as if Seamus is hurting anyone.*

Eventually my breathing steadied. I turned back around just in time to see Seamus running past the neighborhood pool. Thankfully, the fence surrounding it was still shut tight. A girl in a bright red maillot with the word *Lifeguard* across the chest was hosing down the area, pushing away bits of branches with the spray. All the runoff was coursing down the rough patio and pooling just beyond the chain-link fence.

Somehow I knew what would happen before it actually did.

"Seamus! No!" I watched helplessly as Seamus ran gleefully toward the puddle, his ears flapping in the breeze, tail wagging like an outboard motor. As soon as his paws hit the water, he began springing about gleefully, sending up small sprays of muddy rain. By the time I reached him he was on his back, rolling in the muck and snorting in joyous doggie rapture. He saw me and paused in mid-roll, his tail splashing in delight, as if to say, "Look how fun this is! Come on and give it a try!"

*At least I can grab him now,* I grumbled inwardly. Gathering my nerve, I squatted down and scooped Seamus up out of the puddle. I tried to hold him out at arms' length, away from my yellow tee, but ended up having to squish him up against me anyway since he wriggled so much. Meanwhile, giant clumps of brown sludge rained down off him onto the ground and all over my tennis shoes.

I tried not to look at the park bench crowd as we made our way back down the walkway, splattering bits of muck and leaving a dirty trail as Seamus's filthy leash dragged behind us. My jaw clenched from both intense frustration and a fierce need to defend my dog against criticism.

"Yook! Goggie messy!" I heard Michael say.

*"Eeeuw,"* said Alicia.

Still I refused to look. My cheeks were already on slow cook from just imagining those mothers' scolding glares.

They didn't understand. Seamus had only just gotten out of the shelter that morning. He was just a little high on freedom right then. Once he calmed down, he'd behave better.

As soon as we turned the corner and moved out of sight of the park, I stopped and stared down into Seamus's round brown eyes. "Bad boy," I said, carefully enunciating each word as if he were an infant. Seamus cocked his head at me, his ears pricking slightly. "That's right," I went on. "Rolling in mud is bad. Very, very bad."

He studied me for a moment, his expression droopy and sad. But just when I was starting to feel guilty, his nose was in my face and his pink tongue slurped against my mouth.

"No, no. *Bad* dog," I repeated, wiping dirt clods off my lips. "I'm *mad* at you."

It was no use. The more I scolded, the more he wiggled and panted excitedly.

"Oh, okay. I'll let you off easy this time," I said, scratching his neck. "Besides, you'll do better from now on, right? No more problems."

By the time we got back to the condo, the hot sun had begun to dry the layer of mud on Seamus so that it resembled a rich chocolate glaze, yet his underside was still soggy and dripping. I knew we would leave a messy trail leading all the way to our door if I took him up the stairs, so as soon as we entered the lobby, I swooped to the left toward the service elevator. It was already open.

I sucked in my breath to find myself face to face with a guy. A tall, lean guy with saggy gray-green eyes, pouty lips and a thatch of wavy hair that tumbled across his brow like a forelock. A *gorgeous* guy.

"H-hi," I said, pausing in the doorway. I prayed that the loud panting sounds were coming from Seamus and not me.

"Hi," the guy said back, rebalancing the television set in his arms. "Come on in. There's room." The tiny lift was crammed full of boxes, so the only place I could stand was right beside him.

"What floor?" he asked.

"Three."

"Same as me. Button's already pushed."

"Oh," was all I could think to say.

I took my place in the empty spot next to him. Unfortunately the configuration of the space required me to stand sideways. Assuming it would be both rude and weird to stand with my back to the guy, I sidled in facing him. Together we waited in silence, smiling and nodding at each other. Finally the metal doors creaked shut.

I couldn't help staring at him, mainly because I had nowhere else to look. If I wanted to watch the floor display numbers, I had to crane my neck up and sideways—a movement both excruciating and extremely obvious. And staring down was not an option because it meant making eye contact with Seamus, who took it as an invitation to slobber on me.

So I stared at the way the guy's hair waved around his ears and up over the back strap of his baseball cap. I stared at the smooth hollow just below his cheekbone. I stared at his arm muscles, which rippled as he shifted around the TV set. Eventually my gaze ventured up to his eyes . . . and found them staring at me.

Almost instantly my cheeks felt prickly, as if they were giving off showers of sparks. I was just about to break off my gaze when he smiled. It was an adorable, lopsided smile—simultaneously shy and mischievous. My mouth boinged upward automatically. *Wow!* I kept thinking. I hadn't felt this woozy and gelatinous over a guy since Chuck first asked me out.

Seamus must have caught a whiff of my newly charged hormones because he suddenly squirmed around in my grasp, stretching out his snout to sniff the guy.

"Stop, Seamus," I said. I pulled him back, but not before he'd licked the guy's arm and left a grubby paw mark on his elbow.

"Sorry about that," I said. I glanced back up at the guy, grinning apologetically, but he gave no notice of me. Instead he was staring intensely at Seamus. His mouth was pursed in a grim line and his brows had bunched together, lowering over his eyes like a canopy.

*Oh no,* I thought. *He doesn't like Seamus!* It felt as if the cable had snapped, and the elevator was plummeting toward the earth. This changed everything. If the guy didn't like dogs, I had no chance—if I even had one to begin with.

For the rest of the ride there was total silence. Nothing but the squeaks and rattles of the old lift's pulley system and the occasional plops of dirty water dripping off Seamus onto the rubber floor. I didn't even try to meet the guy's sleepy-eyed gaze again, focusing instead on Seamus's mud-caked fur. And the guy didn't say another word.

Cute or not, I had to ignore him. It was for the best.

Giving Seamus a bath ended up taking the rest of the afternoon. Seamus absolutely loved it. For the first time since I brought him home, he stayed calm, standing stock-still while I washed him. His fur was thick and tangled and somewhat resistant to water. Every couple of minutes or so, he would shake his entire body, spraying the whole bathroom (including me) with dirty droplets. But I didn't mind too much. And he looked so cute while wet, like a skinny baby harp seal.

"You're a good boy, aren't you?" I crooned as I poured warm water over his haunches with a giant plastic tumbler. "Dat's right. Such a goo' boy!" Normally I hated when people talked like that, and I was surprised to hear it coming out of my own mouth. But Seamus seemed to love it. He smiled back at me, standing tall and proud in the suds.

I wondered if maybe this was a turning point. Maybe Seamus had gotten all that restlessness out of his system and would finally calm down. I really hoped so. I was turning into a nervous wreck chasing after him all the time. Besides, classes were starting on Monday, just four days from now. If he didn't settle down by then, I didn't know what I would do.

Once Seamus was clean and I'd wiped up all the dirty splatters, I picked him up and swaddled him in one of my towels. "Goo' boy," I whispered again. He stared up at me, his chocolate brown eyes droopy and serious-looking, and I felt that same yanking sensation in my chest that I'd felt at the shelter—as if my heart had been lassoed and hog-tied. I was such a sucker.

I carried him into the living room and sank into the yellow armchair.

"*Phew*. He smells like wet dog," Christine said from the couch, waving her hand in the air. Beside her, Robot wrinkled up his nose.

They were right. Even though he was clean, Seamus gave off a definite odor—sort of musty and mildewy, with only the barest hint of Pantene.

I stood back up. "Don't worry. I'll take him outside," I said, somewhat morosely. It seemed like everywhere I went, I was an instant reject.

As soon as we stepped onto the balcony, Seamus started thrashing in the towel, eager to be set down. I untangled him and stooped to let him loose. Almost immediately Seamus shot out of my arms and began dashing around the perimeter, stopping occasionally to shake off any residual bathwater.

As I sat down against the outer wall and watched him, a brand-new dread brewed up inside me. It was clear Seamus was no less of a spaz than he was before the bath. I could almost see that familiar maniacal gleam return to his eyes, and if anything, he seemed to have a little extra speed in his step.

In the back of my mind a dark thought was taking shape. Slowly, steadily it gathered weight and form until I couldn't ignore it any longer. *Was this why he was abandoned? Did his previous owner find him too much of a spaz?*

I pictured Seamus racing around an asphalt parking lot, hungry and afraid. In my mind I saw him as slightly younger and smaller, just two sorrowful black eyes and a gaunt, undernourished frame.

What kind of creep would leave him there like that? I could only conjure images of a withered, haglike woman or a twisted gnome of a man. A creature so evil its body had warped grotesquely.

*Why do people do that?* I wondered. *Why do they say they love you and then drop you at the first sign of a problem?*

I wondered how Seamus handled his rejection. Had he been glad to get away from those people, even if he was scared? Or had it broken his heart?

"Poor guy," I said aloud. "You can't help it, can you?"

Seamus stopped running and regarded me for a moment. He tilted his head sideways and studied me intently, looking as if he might pull out a tiny easel and render me in watercolors. Then he trotted forward, jumped on my lap and began sniffing my face, nudging me with his cold wet nose. "Stop," I said, giggling as his bristly fur tickled my cheeks. But Seamus kept on slurping away, stabbing me with his sharp little toenails.

After a while I grabbed his forelegs and held him an inch or so away from me. "I promise," I said, staring into his mournful eyes, "I will never ever abandon you."

A feeling of calm came over me as we held each other's gaze. It was one of those sweet, life-defining moments. The kind I would write about in a journal—if I kept a journal. The kind you see in movies accompanied by swelling violin music and the muffled sobs of tenderhearted audience members.

The kind of moment that gives your life meaning.

The rest of the day I spent chasing after Seamus, walking Seamus, or sitting on the balcony with Seamus. After a while, I was getting sort of lonely for human contact.

I had hoped to spend more time getting to know Christine, but all she wanted to do was hang out with Robot. For long hours they remained camped on the living room sofa with their limbs intertwined. They seemed really close—the sort of couple that finishes each other's sentences and had pet names for each other (in their case, he called her "Christini-bopper" and she called him "Beer-breath"). The sort of couple I'd hoped Chuck and I would become.

Just being in the living room made me feel like a pathetic third wheel. And Seamus was forever being banished for barking or chewing or running around like a rubber-room escapee. I tried hanging out in my bedroom with him, but it was too cramped and boring and he kept knocking stuff over and chewing up stuff. So while Christine and Robot lounged about, watching cable and eating junk food, I could only watch them from the patio like some sniveling peon gazing through the palace windows.

Even the balcony—the thing I'd loved best about the condo—was starting to lose its charm. My butt hurt from sitting on the concrete so much, and apparently the balcony stood downwind from the building's Dumpster—something I hadn't noticed the day before. Whenever the breeze picked up, an awful smell spiked the air, especially in the heat of the afternoon.

At dinnertime I left Seamus on the patio and ate my microwave meal at the bar, trying to ignore Christine and Robot's love chatter. In the middle of my low-cal penne with pesto, the phone started ringing. Christine and Robot made no move to get off the couch, so I slid from my stool and picked it up.

"Hello?" I said through a mouthful of pasta.

"Katie? It's Mom again."

"Oh, hi." I swallowed hard. That morning I had been determined to adopt Seamus no matter what Mom might say. But now as I listened to her voice, my confidence drained away and guilt automatically burbled to the surface.

What was I thinking? How was I ever going to tell her about Seamus?

I decided not to say anything—at least for a while. I just needed to buy some time and figure out what to do.

"You sound like you're eating," she said. "I hope it's

something good for you?"

"Some noodle dish with vegetables."

"Very good. I forgot to ask you earlier, have you called Aunt Bitsy to see about getting together with Aaron?"

"Not yet." I shut my eyes, bracing for impact.

"Well, why not?" she asked, her voice rising slightly.

"I've just been too busy."

"Busy? Doing what? Classes don't start for four more days."

"Just, you know, getting settled and stuff." I paced around in a small circle, biting my left thumbnail.

"Uh-huh." She sounded doubtful. "You're mumbling. Are you biting your nails?"

"No," I lied.

She heaved a great sigh. "I hope you're not planning to throw yourself at the wrong sorts of boys just because I'm not there."

"Of course not!" Why did she assume that just because she wasn't around to boss me, I would automatically end up in a *Girls Gone Wild* video?

"I just don't understand you. All I'm asking is that you spend a little time with a very nice, very handsome boy, and you aren't the least bit interested. Are you just trying to be difficult?"

"Mom, I just . . ." I paused. How could I tell her the real reason? If she didn't know he was gay, that meant his mother didn't know. And I certainly wasn't going to be the one to out him. "I just don't think I'm his type."

"Why, of course you are!" she said in a reassuring voice. "You're very pretty and sweet. You may not be as outgoing or self-assured or artistically talented as he is, but I'm sure that doesn't matter. Who knows, maybe he could be a positive influence on you."

By now instead of just biting my nail, I was chomping the first knuckle of my index finger.

"You need to meet some nice, hardworking young people who can teach you some responsibility," she continued. "People like Aaron. And Christine."

I bit down harder, resisting the urge to tell her that Christine was currently drinking a beer and painting her rocker boyfriend's fingernails black.

"That reminds me, why don't I speak with Christine."

"What? But you talked to her this morning," I protested.

"I only want to ask her a couple of questions. Why must you oppose me on everything?"

"Fine," I grumbled. I took a step toward the sofa. "My mom wants to talk to you, Christine."

"Again?" she mouthed, making a face. Robot chuckled softly.

I shrugged helplessly and pressed the receiver tightly to my chest. "Please don't tell her about Seamus," I said in an urgent whisper.

"Okay, whatever," she grunted, snatching up the phone. "Hello again, Mrs. McAllister," she crooned.

"How are you? . . . Today? Let's see. . . . We organized the condo, and then Katie helped me bag groceries at the local food pantry. It was very rewarding. . . . Why yes, I suppose it will look good on her college application. . . . Boys? No, Mrs. McAllister. . . . No, I haven't seen her flirting. . . . Yes. . . . All right. . . . Goodbye."

She covered the receiver and handed it back to me. "I didn't say a word," she muttered, her tough-broad attitude back in place.

"Thanks." I flashed her a grateful smile and pressed the phone to my ear. "Feel better?"

"No need to get snide, Katie. You know I'm only trying to take care of you," she said in an injured voice.

"Is Dad there?"

"Yes. Hang on, let me see if he has anything to tell you."

In the background I heard my dad's voice call out, "Tell her she missed the world's greatest brisket the other night."

I smiled. Dad and his barbecuing. In the summertime he was always grilling something. He'd stand outside and pour beer on the meat, then pour some down his throat, then a little more on the meat, then a lot more down his throat. By the time we ate he'd be hiccupping and pronouncing it the best goddamn thing he'd ever cooked. I never had the heart to say it was usually too tough.

I could hear my mom scolding him. "Is that all you're going to say to her?" She sighed loudly and got back on the line. "He misses you, sweetie. We both do."

"Me too," I mumbled, surprised to feel a flicker of homesickness in the midst of my exasperation. "Bye, Mom."

"Bye, honey. Don't do anything a McAllister wouldn't do."

I hung up and stood there for a moment, staring through the glass at Seamus scampering on the patio.

*Too late for that, Mom.*

That night I made a little doggie bed out of some of the towels Mom bought for me. I arranged them into a circular pattern like a bright purple nest and plopped Seamus right in the middle.

He immediately got up and sprang onto my bed, trying to lick my face.

"No!" I said, laughing. "This is my bed. This"—I stood and deposited him back on the towels—"is *your* bed."

I tried to position his body so that he would be lying curled among the folds of the towels, but the best I could do with his stocky little frame was set him stiffly on his side. Each time I let go, however, he would immediately leap to his feet, panting excitedly.

"Come on," I begged, pushing down on his rear end. "I'm not playing."

Seamus licked my ear.

I forced him into a lying-down position again. This

time, I decided to keep him there until he relaxed. "It's okay. Calm down and rest," I said, stroking his thick wavy fur with one hand while holding him down with the other. Gradually I could feel him grow less rigid. His muscles softened and his body flattened until, finally, he settled back and laid his head on the towels.

"Good boy," I whispered, tiptoeing backward to my bed. I smiled as I slipped beneath the covers, congratulating myself on my little triumph.

Just as I was reaching for the lamp switch, Seamus leaped to his feet. He ran over to the side of the bed, crouched down and barked.

"No," I pleaded. "Go back to—" Too late. Seamus had already jumped onto the covers and was dancing around my legs, panting and wagging his tail merrily.

I lay back with a frustrated grunt and put my pillow over my head. The events of the day had left me feeling incredibly tired. My limbs felt heavy and floppy and my yawns were so big, each one seemed to widen my mouth about a half inch. Plus there was a weird dull throbbing behind my eyes, as if some small creature were trying to claw itself out of my sinus cavity. How could I make Seamus understand that I had to get to sleep?

I pulled off the pillow and rose up onto my elbows. Seamus was sitting to my left, watching me.

"What am I going to do with you?" I asked. His tail began to drum against the mattress, causing the whole bed to shimmy. He scooted up closer and snuffled around my face, making a rattling whiny noise in his throat.

"Okay. Okay!" I said, gently pushing away his snout. "You can sleep up here. But you've got to go to sleep. No more playing."

I knew I was totally giving up, but I couldn't help it. I was zonked. Besides, I figured it probably wouldn't hurt anything. After all, it would only be for one night.

# 5

Seamus snored all night. The first time that it woke me, I was in a groggy rage at the idiot operating electric power tools nearby. I couldn't believe so much noise could come out of such a small dog. I shook his back, and he immediately flipped onto his feet. "Please be quiet," I rasped. For the next few minutes I could feel him wriggle and snuffle beside me until he finally fell still. After a while, I relaxed and began fluttering back off to sleep, only to hear Seamus's snores start up all over again.

And so on and so on until Scooby began his high-pitched bleeping. At the first beep, Seamus jumped upright. A crooked line of fur rose up along his back and he reversed down the mattress, growling and barking at the alarm clock until he fell off the bed.

*Great,* I thought, fumbling with the clock until I finally switched it off. *Now I have two dogs that won't let me sleep.*

"Come on," I said to Seamus, who was still whining and barking. I scooped him up and padded out into the living room. Pushing aside the dusty blinds, I opened the patio door and set him onto the concrete. "There you go." I shut the door and watched as he trotted over to the railing, staring out at the birds that were busily twittering and flying about the treetops.

"Hi there."

*Waaagh!* I spun around at the nasal sound. Just like the morning before, there was a guy lying on the couch. Only this guy wasn't Robot. This guy was shorter and his head was completely shaved. "Who . . . What . . . ?" I stammered. *Just how many boyfriends did Christine have?*

"Man, sorry if I scared you. I'm Lyle."

He said his name as if it would explain everything. *Oh yes, Lyle. By all means, make yourself at home. Care for some Froot Loops?*

I stated the obvious. "I have no idea who you are."

"I'm the drummer." He rummaged around the coffee table, picked up a small, pocket-sized paper bag of french fries and began to eat them. "Want one?" he asked, holding out a limp fry.

"No thanks," I said, shuddering.

Just then I heard the toilet flush and the door to the bathroom banged open. Out walked another strange guy. Tall and pimply, with a shock of super curly brown hair that extended the circumference of his head by two inches in every direction.

He trudged into the room, scratching his scalp with one hand and hiking up his drawstring pants with the other. As soon as he saw me, he stopped in his tracks. "Whoa," he said, with a slow, dippy-sounding chuckle. "A girl."

"And that's Kinky," Lyle said to me, gesturing with his thumb. "Bass player."

Kinky restarted his slow stride, heading for the yellow armchair as he continued to look me over. "Is this the roomie Robot talked about?" he asked. "He's right. She's cute."

I blinked back at him, my systems jammed by competing emotions. On the one hand I was pissed off that our condo was fast becoming a halfway house for wayward wannabe rock stars. But I was also mindful of the fact that I couldn't make a big stink about it. Plus I had to admit, even though my attraction to Kinky was in the negative range, it still felt good to hear someone call me cute.

Lyle groped around on the coffee table until he found a pair of yellow-tinted, round-framed John Lennon glasses. He put them on and stared at me.

I began to feel incredibly self-conscious. My sleep apparel for the previous night had consisted of nothing but an oversized Dallas Cowboys shirt that used to belong to Chuck and a pair of mismatched athletic socks. I yanked down on the hem of the shirt and sidled along the wall, afraid the strong morning sunlight might have infiltrated the thin material, revealing everything underneath as clearly as an X-ray.

Again, I decided to ask the obvious. "Why are you guys here?"

"We played a gig last night," Lyle replied.

"Yeah. It ended real late," Kinky added. "So Robot said we might as well sleep over."

"Ohhh. *Robot* invited you to stay," I muttered. "How nice of him."

"Oh, yeah," Kinky said, nodding. "Robot's great."

"Excuse me." I scurried off to my room, sat down on the bed and took deep breaths until I didn't feel like screaming anymore. Then I threw on a pair of shorts and halter, and pulled my hair into a sloppy ponytail. When I returned, Kinky and Lyle were standing side by side at the French doors, peering out onto the patio.

"What is that?" I heard Kinky ask.

"I think it's a dog," said Lyle.

"It is," I said. "He's my dog."

Kinky chuckled—a series of short exhales through his beak nose. "He's funny-looking. Kind of reminds me of my science teacher's toupee, only messier."

"You should talk, frizz-head," Lyle quipped.

By now Seamus had seen them and was barking and twirling about.

"What's wrong with him?" Lyle asked.

"Nothing," I said, my voice whiny and defensive. "He just needs to go for a walk."

"Right." Kinky nodded, his frizzy mane bouncing up and down. "Probably has to go to the bathroom. Do you use a scooper? Or do you just leave it there?"

"Man! I hate it when people just leave it," Lyle whined. "I always step in it."

"No," I said hastily. "I pick it up." But a nagging thought was screeching through my mind. It suddenly occurred to me that I actually hadn't picked up anything since I got Seamus. *Because Seamus hadn't made anything for me to pick up!*

I was, without a doubt, the lamest of all dog owners. No wonder he'd been acting a little batty. The poor little guy was about to bust!

Twenty minutes later we were wandering around the park. I'd expected Seamus to really let loose once we got there, but other than watering a couple of trees, he didn't do anything.

"Come on," I urged. I was all set with several plastic grocery bags. I'd seen our neighbor back home, Mr. Floyd, use them while walking his Pomeranian. He'd slip a couple of them over his hand like gloves, pick up his dog's droppings, and pull his hand out backward, sealing the mess inside. Then he'd tie up the ends and toss the whole thing into the nearest garbage can.

Only Seamus wasn't giving me anything to scoop up. Instead he yanked me this way and that as he barked at squirrels, sniffed out various odors and then rolled in the grass, making a variety of throaty grunts and whines.

"Quit playing, Seamus," I begged. "I'm starving."

I should have been paying better attention, but I hadn't had my coffee yet and I was daffy from lack of sleep. Apparently the pool opened early on Saturdays, and as we staggered down the sidewalk, Seamus's ears pricked at the sounds of splashing and the giddy squeals of little kids. The next thing I knew, the leash had slipped out of my grasp again.

*"Seamus!"*

I gasped in terror as he raced toward the pool like a furry cannonball. Seamus shot past the open gate and then launched himself into the air. He sailed magnificently over the water for a split second before descending with a loud splash.

At that point the entire scene picked up volume and tempo. Children shrieked with delight. The lifeguard began blowing his whistle and shouting. Several onlookers burst out laughing. Meanwhile Seamus swam about happily and oblivious, his little paws briskly treading the surface as if he were an oversized windup toy.

"Seamus!" I ran through the gate and over to the side of the pool. "Seamus, come here!"

"Is that your dog?" growled an incredibly buff, mean-looking lifeguard.

"Yes," I replied with a sigh. "Sorry."

"Get him out of there!"

"Okay, but—" I glanced down at my clothes. Did he expect me to dive in there myself?

"Now!" the lifeguard added. "He's scaring the kids."

From what I could see, the kids were moving *toward* him, crowding about so they could pat his head or wave pool toys in his face in the hopes that he might play fetch.

Something wet poked my foot. I glanced down and saw the boy I'd met in the park the day before. He grinned at me and pointed toward Seamus. "Can I play with William?" he asked.

"Actually his name is—" *Oh, what the hell.* "Sure," I said. "Only William isn't allowed in the pool. Could you help bring him over here so I can pull him out?"

"Yeah!" he said, hopping up and down. "I'm a good swimmer."

"Well, don't go where it's too deep," I cautioned. "Just try to make him swim this way."

He dog-paddled a few feet over to Seamus and called to him. "Come on, William," he said. "Come this way."

It worked. Slowly and steadily, Seamus followed the boy toward the side of the pool. As soon as he got close enough, I reached in with both arms and pulled him up. He was all wet and thrashing, and it hurt my lower back to lift him out of the water, but eventually I was staggering upright, pressing his wriggling frame to my chest.

"Thanks," I said to the boy. "You really are a good swimmer."

His little chest puffed proudly. "Can we do that again?"

I didn't want to take a chance on Seamus slipping away again, so I carried him all the way back to the condo. As we stepped into the building, I could hear the familiar rattle and squeak of the service elevator. I turned the corner in time to see the door sliding shut.

"Wait! Hold the door, please!" I called out.

A hand poked through the opening and the doors reversed themselves.

"Thanks," I said, stepping inside.

My face flushed as I saw the owner of the hand. The same guy from the day before stood leaning against another stack of boxes.

"Hey," he said with a nod. His eyes passed over Seamus in all his soggy, reeking glory before swiveling up to the number display.

He didn't glance at us again for the rest of the ride—which seemed to take a few archaeological eras. Seamus kept writhing about in my arms trying to sniff the guy, but I held him tight in my arms. By the time the elevator squealed to a stop, I was lightheaded from wet doggie aroma.

The doors parted and I stepped out onto the landing, taking a deep breath of cleaner air. The guy began hurriedly moving his boxes out of the lift.

"You want me to hold the door for you?" I asked.

"No thanks, I got it," he said, without looking at me.

*Fine. Be that way,* I thought as I marched toward my door. What was that guy's problem, anyway? I could tell he wasn't crazy about Seamus (and considering Seamus's present state, I couldn't exactly blame him), but he didn't have to be rude.

I was hoping to give Seamus an immediate bath, but Christine was holed up in the bathroom with a radio going. Lyle, Kinky and Robot were sitting around the living room watching MTV and eating cold Pop-Tarts.

"Hey!" Lyle called, waving a half-eaten chocolate tart at me. "Want one?"

*They're mine, you hairless, bug-eyed cretin.* "No thanks," I mumbled, struggling to keep a grip on Seamus, who was twisting his lower body like a champion hula hoop artist.

I knocked on the bathroom door. "Um, Christine? Are you going to be a while?"

There was no answer. All I could hear was the rushing of shower water and Christine trying to warble along with Franz Ferdinand.

I walked Seamus into my room and shrouded him in one of the towels I'd set down for his bed. Clutching him against me once again, I went into the kitchen and got the coffee pot going one-handed. By the time I'd finished my arms were sore and aching, so I returned to the living room and settled on the opposite end of the couch from Robot.

"What happened to him?" Robot asked, nodding toward Seamus, his upper lip curling in disgust.

"He fell into a pool," I grumbled as I rubbed the water out of his fur. I really didn't want to tell them the whole story, and thankfully they didn't ask.

"Were you at our gig last night?" Kinky asked. He sat sprawled in the yellow chair, his long legs stretched way out in front of him.

I shook my head. "No."

"Why not?"

*Because I wasn't invited.* "I was busy."

"Man, you should have come," Lyle said. "We were pretty awesome."

Just then the phone rang. I saw Robot turn to grab the receiver and screeched, "Don't!" Seamus jumped slightly in my arms and all the guys froze, staring at me in alarm. "It could be my mom," I explained. "She'd freak if a guy answered."

Robot lifted his hands as if in surrender. "Whatever, love. You answer the bloody thing."

I set Seamus down on the floor and wagged my finger in his face. "Stay put," I said. Then I snatched the cordless off its base. "Hello?" I said, trying to sound calm and collected.

"Hello?" came a deep, male voice. "May I please speak with Ms. Katherine McAllister?"

"Speaking," I replied hesitantly.

"Ms. McAllister, this is Alan Wethington from the shelter. I was just calling to see how your dog was doing."

I looked at Seamus. He was sitting on the floor with his snout poking out from beneath the towel, looking like an incredibly small, bearded monk. "Um . . . okay, I guess. I do have sort of a problem, though."

"Really? What's that?"

I couldn't tell if the guys were listening to me or to the talk show on TV. Just in case, I went into my room and shut the door halfway.

"Seamus doesn't seem to be, you know, going," I explained. "It's been two days, but he hasn't had a bowel movement."

"I see. Is he eating?"

"Yes."

"Is he lethargic?"

"Not at all."

"Well, if he doesn't seem sick, I wouldn't worry about it too much. He'll go. You might try taking him on a long walk to get things moving."

*Duh. Been there.* "Okay."

Just then, there came a huge crashing sound from the main living area. An uneasy feeling came over me.

"Uh . . . gotta go now," I said quickly. "Thanks for calling!"

I turned off the phone and sprinted out of my room. I checked the spot where I'd left Seamus, but he wasn't there. The towel was lying about a foot away.

"Where's Seamus?" I asked.

"Beats me," Robot said.

Lyle and Kinky just shrugged.

A tinkling noise emanated from the kitchen nook. I raced around the bar and skidded to a stop. The tall yellow plastic trash can had been knocked forward, its lid halfway open, disgorging coffee grounds, used tissues, and ketchup-frosted wrappings all over the kitchen floor. In the middle of the mess stood Seamus, his wet fur grainy with Folgers and other unidentifiable fragments. He was chewing on something brown and drippy.

The guys ran up behind me.

"*Eew!* What's that?" Lyle asked.

"It's my burrito from last night," Robot replied.

"*Eew!*"

"Drop it, Seamus!" I lunged for him, but he quickly cut sideways. His eyes drooped guiltily and his tail curved between his hind legs, but I could tell he had no intention of letting go his loot. "Please, Seamus! Put it down!" I stepped over the upturned can and made another grab for him. Seamus jogged in place for a split second, his paws slipping on the gooey debris, then finally got up enough traction to race from the room. "No! Stop!"

But there was nothing I could do. Seamus was tearing around the living room, leaving behind a mucky path and the fragrance of wet, slimy dog.

It took me over half an hour to clean the kitchen and vacuum up the trail of coffee grounds. The others sat on the couch eating Pop-Tarts and watching TV. Every now and then Lyle would flash me a look of pity, and Kinky even offered to help, but I refused. As it was, tears of frustration were already collecting in my eyes, and their sympathy only made me feel more pathetic. When I finally did spring a leak and start crying, I didn't want it to be in front of them.

Meanwhile Seamus sat whining on the patio, watching me through the cracks in the blinds. Pity and anger took turns squeezing my heart. As embarrassed and aggravated as I was, I also knew he didn't really know what he was doing. He was just being a dog: a sloppy, curious, clueless dog.

*Finally* Christine emerged from the steamy bathroom and I was able to get Seamus cleaned up—his second bath in as many days.

Just as I was heading into the hallway with Seamus bundled in a towel, Christine came out of her room. She was wearing a black minidress, ripped tights and clunky black leather shoes. Her hair had been scrunched into thick dreds, and her eyes were outlined in dark, Cleopatra-like streaks.

"You ready to go to orientation?" she asked me, her

brows furrowed as she took in my sloppy outfit and droopy ponytail.

"Is it that late already?" I asked. I leaned sideways to check the clock above the oven. Sure enough, it was almost noon.

The university was officially kicking off its Core Curriculum Program with a big mandatory assembly. I had sort of been looking forward to meeting some other students and hanging out with Christine minus Robot. Only the day's crises had disrupted my schedule and I was caught completely off guard.

"You better get a move on," Christine said.

"Yeah. Um . . . right." I was walking around in a circle, trying to think everything through. "I guess I don't have time to shower or change. I should probably bring a pen. Oh, no! What about Seamus?"

She frowned at me. "What about him?"

"He's sort of had a bad day," I explained, staring down at him. His brown eyes nervously darted back and forth. "I'm not sure if I should leave him."

"But you have to. This thing is required." She walked into the living room and faced the guys. "You all will watch Katie's dog while we're at this orientation, right?"

"Right." "Sure." "No prob." They answered without taking their eyes off the NASCAR race on TV.

"There," she said, turning back to me. "See? It's all taken care of. Your precious dog is going to be fine."

The orientation lasted longer than I'd expected. Christine and I had piled into a giant lecture hall along with a couple hundred other students and listened to speech after speech. One officially welcomed us. One gave a shortened history of the university and its summer program. And one reminded us of campus rules.

I started to take notes and caught Christine giving me a look. The rest of the time I doodled on my notebook page while she slouched way down in the seat and shut her eyes.

"God, I hope college isn't like that all the time." She was still complaining as we walked through the door of the condo.

"About bloody time!" Robot said, sitting up on the couch.

"What's wrong with you?" Christine asked. "Where are the other guys?"

"They went off to find food," he explained. "That daft dog went postal after you left."

"What happened?" I asked, setting down my book bag.

"Beats the hell out of me. We were just hanging around, programming tracks on Lyle's drum machine, when he started charging around, barking like a lunatic."

"Did you guys hurt him? I mean . . . accidentally?"

"No one laid a bloody finger on him." He stretched

out along the couch and folded his arms across his chest. "Dog's just a freaking mental case, that's all."

"No, he's not," I said, feeling really defensive. "He's just . . . just . . ." *immensely constipated,* I finished silently. Poor thing was probably in pain. "Where is he?" I asked, grabbing his leash.

"On the balcony. Took us forever to catch the nutter."

I rushed to the patio door. "He's not out there."

"Yes, he is."

I opened the door and glanced around the balcony. "No, he isn't!"

Robot's scowl disappeared. "What do you mean? That's where we put him. I swear!"

"Well, it's not like he could fly away. . . . Oh God!" Cold tingles were spreading down my scalp and over my body. "You don't think . . . ?"

I bolted back onto the patio and raced over to the railing. Bracing myself for the worst, I stared down over the side to the ground below.

But there was no crumpled little doggie. No blood-stains or tufts of fur or four-legged chalk outline. All I could see was grass.

Christine and Robot ran up beside me. "Thank God," Christine said as she looked over the railing. "But then . . . where *is* he?"

"Seamus!" I called out.

*Chiiinnng!* A clanging noise sounded nearby.

"Seamus?"

*Chiiinng! Chiiinng!*

The noise was coming from my right. Turning around, I spotted Seamus on Mrs. Krantz's side of the balcony. He was standing against the iron rail that divided the concrete ledge, his tail wagging happily.

"Seamus!" I cried in relief.

He bounced around in an excited circle and threw himself against the railing again, causing his tags to bang against the bars. *Chiinnng!*

"What the hell?" Robot scratched his left sideburn. "We didn't put him over there. I swear!"

Right as he said that, Seamus flopped onto his side and wriggled his head through the space beneath the railing. The rest of his body followed.

"Hey, you! What were you doing over there?" I exclaimed as he ran up to me. He stopped at my feet, wagging his tail and staring up at me with his pink tongue halfway out of his mouth, looking very proud of himself. I bent over and started fluffing his fur. After that brief scare, I was really glad to see him.

"I can't believe the little bloke fit through that space," Robot said, shaking his head in astonishment.

"And he was so fast," Christine added. "Like he'd been doing it forever."

My hand froze in midpet as I thought about what Christine said. It did seem like Seamus had done that before. Maybe several times. I straightened up and walked over to the railing, scanning Mrs. Krantz's side of the balcony.

"Oh, no! Crap, no!" I exclaimed.

Crap *yes*. Lots of it. Some fresh, and some a day or two old. All neatly scattered about the patio along with Mrs. Krantz's potted plants.

"Gross!" Christine said, plugging her nose.

Robot burst out laughing.

"You little doofus!" I shouted, rounding on Seamus. He skipped about on his feet and looked even more pleased. Judging by the mess, he *should* have felt light on his feet.

So the mystery was solved. The good news was my dog wasn't going to burst open from retaining too much poo. The bad news was I just might get evicted—after living there only a couple of days.

For the next forty-five minutes, I cleaned my dog's manure off Mrs. Krantz's ledge. It was by far the most disgusting thing I'd ever done in my life. But it also gave me real practice at scooping, something I'd been spared since adopting Seamus. For example, I learned quite a bit about consistency, how sometimes the droppings would come right up, and sometimes they . . . uh . . . didn't.

Seamus watched the entire time from our side of the balcony. Thankfully, he couldn't join me, because I'd blocked the opening beneath the rail with rocks "borrowed" from the landscaping around the building.

"Why do you do this?" I whined as I scraped and cleaned. "Why can't you just calm down already? If you don't stop this stuff, they're going to kick us both out!"

Seamus just looked back at me with his big expressive eyes, giving an occasional whimper.

At last I'd bagged up the entire mess and scrubbed away any telltale stains, including a particularly horrible one on one of her ceramic kittens. Judging by the smell, I was pretty sure Seamus had also watered a few of her plants, but I wasn't sure what I could do about that.

I heaved myself back over the railing, holding the bag of droppings and soiled cleaning rags. As soon as I entered the condo, Robot and Christine scrunched up their faces.

"Ugh! You're not bringing that in here, are you?" Christine said, waving her arms and shrinking into the couch cushions as if I were planning to toss the stuff at her.

"Of course not," I replied. "I'm just cutting through on the way to the Dumpster."

A sizzling sensation crept over my neck and cheeks as I stepped out onto the landing. I was really tired of dealing with one humiliation after another. Wasn't my move to Austin supposed to be about reinventing myself? If I'd wanted to live with constant embarrassment, I could have stayed home and faced the fallout from my breakup.

I was just about to head down the steps when I got a bright idea. Why not take the service elevator instead, to avoid as many people as possible?

*See? You can do this,* I thought as I pushed the elevator button. *You can think ahead and avoid these little disasters.* From now on I would keep everything under control. No more surprises. No more shame.

Just then the elevator dinged. I stepped forward, holding the bag out in front of me to distance myself from the smell. Slowly the doors slid open, and there stood that same guy from before, the cute one from unit 303, this time surrounded by several large paper grocery sacks.

"Uh . . . hi," I said lamely.

"Hi." He looked from me to the bag dangling at the end of my arm, his features creased in confusion.

I couldn't imagine how I must have looked, looming in front of him with a sack of poop. I watched his nose wriggle slightly as he caught his first whiff.

"Nevermind," I said quickly. "I'll take the stairs." I spun around on my heels and charged down the steps, refusing to look back at the elevator guy.

Okay, new strategy. Maybe I could embarrass myself so thoroughly in Austin that I actually ended up looking forward to returning to San Marcos and the mangled remains of my reputation there.

That evening when the guys went out to get us pizza, I tried to teach Seamus to sit—much to Christine's amusement.

"Sit," I would say, slapping my hand against the carpet. Only Seamus just kept watching my hand and sniffing the floor, positive I had some sort of treat for him. When he couldn't find anything, he'd leap on me as if trying to frisk me for it.

"Give it up already. He's too stupid for tricks," Christine said the fifth time Seamus jumped on me. She laughed as I stumbled and fell forward, doubling over Seamus like a human overpass.

"No, he's not," I said, pushing myself upright. "He's smart."

"Yeah, sure," she said, snorting.

Just then the phone started ringing. I didn't want to answer it. I could almost tell who it was by the ring—shrill and persistent. Seamus started barking and I quickly set him on the patio, grabbing the receiver right before the answering machine came on.

"Hello?"

"Katie? It's Mom." *Of course.* "Honey, I just heard on the local news that crime rates are going up in Austin. You girls are keeping the doors locked, right?"

"Yeah."

"Windows too?"

I frowned. "Uh . . . but we're on the third floor. How could someone break in through our windows?"

"Are you saying criminals have no idea how to use ladders?" she asked, her voice rising slightly.

"No, but—"

"Well, there you go. Promise me you'll keep your

windows locked from now on."

"Fine," I said wearily. "Maybe Mrs. Krantz can put bars on them."

"Oh, no! Not them. You could be trapped during a fire. Which reminds me . . . Do you girls have a working fire extinguisher?"

I slapped my forehead and concentrated on my breathing while Mom prattled on about escape routes and smoke detectors and the importance of natural-fiber clothing. Soon after, Christine took the phone and assured her that yes, I was eating whole grain foods. No, I wasn't leaving towels all over the place, and yes, we were remembering to turn off the coffeepot before leaving the condo.

By the time we hung up, I was feeble and dizzy from all my pent-up frustration.

"Man, when is she going to get a life and let you live yours?" Christine muttered, flopping back onto the couch.

"I don't know," I grumbled. "I guess when she thinks I can actually handle it." It was so aggravating. I still couldn't get a break from Mom—even when I lived thirty miles away.

The worst part was, I was beginning to think she was right to worry so much. Maybe I really couldn't handle stuff on my own. I was certainly making a mess of things so far. I hadn't made any friends except Christine (and I wasn't even sure she counted). I had already spent a good third of my savings. And my new dog was systematically destroying all my belongings, scratching up my limbs, and basically doing everything he wasn't supposed to—and I couldn't stop him.

I glanced toward the patio door, where Seamus was on his back legs, barking and trying to dig through the glass. "Okay, okay. I'm coming," I said, grabbing up the leash.

I couldn't help loving the guy. I just wished it were easier.

The next morning I woke to find Lyle and Kinky sitting on the couch watching *Sesame Street*. By now I'd given up on ever having an empty living room, so I automatically threw on a pair of cropped jeans and a white tank before leaving my room.

I stumbled toward the patio door and let Seamus out.

"Morning," Kinky said.

"Hey, Katie," said Lyle.

"Mornin', love," Robot greeted.

I tried to say "morning" back to them, but it came out sounding more like a moo than an actual word. I fumbled for the knob through the blinds, pushed open the door and set Seamus on the patio. Immediately he began running laps, his tongue hanging out, ears flapping in the breeze. It was so unfair. How could he keep me up all night and then have this much energy in the morning?

I staggered over to the yellow armchair, pushed aside a couple of stuffed wiener dogs, and collapsed into it, sinking down as far as the cushions would allow. Not only were my limbs stiff and heavy from lack of sleep, but it was difficult to follow a coherent train of thought. My brain felt cloudy and murky, with occasional lightning bolts of lucid thought, like "need coffee" and "must walk Seamus soon."

"Where's Christine?" I croaked, glancing around the room.

"Sleeping late," Robot replied.

*Glad someone can,* I thought glumly. "So . . . you guys crashed here again?" I asked rather stupidly.

"Yeah. Had a gig at Area 54 last night. Freaking brilliant!" Robot said proudly, his smile extending into his sideburns.

"That's great," I mumbled, getting a twisty feeling in my gut. That made three nights in a row that Christine had gone out and had fun. Without me.

"Hey, you want some breakfast?" Lyle asked, lifting a piece of bread and spraying on a layer of Cheez Whiz.

"No thanks," I replied, my throat closing up in defense. I turned away and tried to focus on the TV, where

Elmo was having an earnest conversation with . . . something. It looked like a shoe with Ping-Pong-ball eyes.

"What the hell is that thing?" Robot asked, gesturing toward the TV set with his orange-slathered bread slice.

Lyle frowned at the screen. "It's a loafer."

"How come he's talking to a shoe?" Kinky asked with his mouth full.

"Ah, you know." Lyle shrugged. "It's educational."

Robot shook his head. "Looks bloody freaky to me."

Kinky nodded briskly, his hair bouncing a half second behind his head. "Yeah, that's the thing about *Sesame Street*. Everything can talk. Shoes. Chairs. Broccoli. But I think you're right, dude. If there was such a place, I'd be way too spooked to live there."

"Aw, man, I know," Lyle agreed. "The Muppets used to really mess with me. I mean, how come Miss Piggy wants Kermit? Could they actually mate? It used to keep me up at night wondering what their offspring would look like. Piglets with flippers? Tadpoles with big snouts and curly tails?" He closed his eyes and shuddered.

I let out a moan and rubbed my aching temples. I really needed caffeine to handle this conversation.

"I don't think so," Kinky said, rubbing his stubbly chin as he pondered the ceiling. "I think it would be more like in *Lady and the Tramp* where Lady has, like, three puppies that look like her and one that looks like Tramp. So Miss Piggy would probably have a couple of frogs mixed in with her litter of piglets."

"That's insane!" I blurted out, scooting to the end of the chair and leaning toward them. "Miss Piggy is a mammal. She can't give birth to amphibians! Amphibians have to hatch in water and— " I paused and pressed my fingertips to my eyelids. "What the *hell* am I saying? It's a freaking kid's show! It won't happen."

"Man," Lyle drawled, giving me wary look. "You're, like, Katie-the-Grouch today."

"She's right, though," Kinky said, nodding. "It would never happen. Kermit just isn't all that into Piggy."

I groaned and sank back against the chair cushions again. I wanted to dissolve away and become nothing for a while. Just a free-floating mass of particles. A nebulous blob that didn't have to deal with hyper pets or nosy moms or weird roommates. Closing my eyes, I strained to concentrate on nothing. . . .

"You okay?" came Lyle's twangy voice.

I could hear Robot mumble something about "being mental," followed by Elmo's falsetto laugh.

"Sorry," I said, struggling upright. "I'm just really, really tired."

"Yeah, you do look pretty bad," Kinky said sympathetically.

"Thanks," I mumbled.

A loud bang made me jump. Then a scratchy, rapping noise that could only be my dog's toenails on glass. It sounded like Seamus was throwing himself against the patio door.

"Time for walkies," Lyle sang out.

"Great," I grumbled, forcing my tired muscles to move me up and out of the chair. My head throbbed from the change in altitude.

As soon as I opened the patio door, Seamus charged past me and headed straight for the front door.

"Okay, okay," I said, hurrying to clip the leash on him. Now that I'd discovered his secret potty place and barricaded the railing, I had no idea what he might do—or *when* he might do.

As I slipped on my sandals and headed out into the foyer, I overheard Kinky musing aloud, "So like, if Pepé Le Pew and that cat had babies, they'd probably be—"

"Dude," Lyle interrupted. "Don't go there."

I returned forty-five minutes later, red-faced and limping. The good news was that Seamus didn't come back in desperate need of a bath. However . . .

"Freaking dog," I grumbled, wincing with every step. Blood was trickling from a gash over my left kneecap. I'd tripped over the leash trying to grab Seamus, who had just stolen a cracker from a kid in a stroller.

Of course, Seamus was completely clueless to the fact that he'd done something wrong. He glanced up at me as I fumbled with the keys, his tail wagging so hard his whole back end was doing a shimmy.

"Quit being so damn happy. You got me in trouble. *Again,*" I snapped, remembering the toddler's yowls of protest and the mother's irate glare.

Seamus made a small, guttural bark and danced about the welcome mat, thrilled just to be talked to.

Finally I unlocked the door and Seamus rushed inside, pulling me with him. "Hang on," I said, freeing my keys from the knob. I turned to set them on the small console table—only the table wasn't there. My keys plummeted right to the carpet. "What the . . . ?"

I glanced around the living room in shock. All the furniture had been pushed up against the far wall and draped with sheets. Even Seamus looked taken aback, his tail lowered as he sniffed the air cautiously, backing up against my legs.

"Christine?" I called shakily. There was no answer.

I looked up at the number on the front door, just to make sure I was in the right place. I was.

"Okay. Don't panic," I mumbled, pulling the door shut.

"Don't close it!" came a voice from behind me. It was Lyle coming out of the service elevator, balancing two round black boxes in his arms. "Thanks," he said as he lurched past me and set the teetering stack on the floor.

"Uh . . . Lyle? What's going on?"

"Setting up my drum set," he replied, unclasping

the top case.

"Yeah, I see. But why?"

He gave me a puzzled look. "For the party," he said slowly, as if I hadn't quite mastered English yet.

"What are you talking about?"

At that moment, Robot and Kinky ambled through the open door, each one lugging a boxy black amp. Christine sashayed in behind them. She paused when she saw me and pointed at my leg. "Oh my God, Katie. Do you know you're bleeding?"

"We're having a party?" I asked, too stunned even to feel pain anymore.

She grinned gigantically. "Yeah! It was Robot's idea."

"Um . . . are you sure we should? I mean, we are, you know, renting."

"Who gives a crap?" she snapped. "It's the last weekend before school starts. We deserve some fun, don't we?"

"I guess," I said lamely.

"Come on! You've got to go with the flow," she said, nudging me with her elbow. "Besides, if you don't, I can always tell your mom you've been hosting orgies." She threw back her head and laughed.

I chuckled nervously, wondering if her threat was serious or not. Before I could figure it out, Christine had trotted off in the direction of her room, leaving me standing there in a daze.

I didn't know what to do. There were no chairs to

sit on or tables to set my things on. For the next couple of minutes I watched helplessly as the guys unloaded different bits of equipment and plugged in different colored cords. Seamus kept whining and weaving around my legs, binding me up with his leash.

Kinky plugged in a shiny white bass guitar and began plucking the strings. The deep, trembly notes reverberated throughout the condo, vibrating my sternum. A throaty growl emanated from Seamus, and he backed against my legs, his whole body shaking. I had to brace myself against the wall to keep from falling again.

Freeing myself from his leash by twirling around a few times, I carefully picked him up and took him over to the patio. As soon as I set him outside, he ran to the far railing and stood there, still growling and shuddering.

"Don't worry," I said. "I'm going to fix my knee and then I'll be right back."

"You say something, love?"

I shut the door and whirled about to find Robot standing behind me.

"Uh, no. I mean, yeah. I was talking to Seamus," I replied, ducking my head to hide my blazing cheeks. I was getting as bad as Mrs. Krantz.

Robot smiled crookedly. "Whatever you say, love."

I headed into the bathroom and shut the door, immediately comforted by the cramped, solitary space.

"What the hell is going on?" I mumbled as I carefully washed my wound with a damp washcloth. "Everything's out of control."

Ever since I'd arrived in Austin, I'd been dealing with one major surprise after another, and I knew my stress was building on some subterranean level. I could feel it inside me, twisting and expanding into various shapes, like some radioactive, hell-spawned amoeba. Any day now it would burst out of me in all its hideous glory in a scene to rival any sci-fi horror flick.

And now it had this to feed on.

A party? With a rock band and a condo full of Christine and Robot's friends? That seemed to me a bad idea on so many levels. My mind reeled with images of angry-looking police officers storming our living room. I wondered how Mom would react if I called her in the middle of the night from the slammer, or if my mug shot appeared in the society section of the *San Marcos Daily Record*. Most likely I'd be spending my senior year with Grandma Hattie, watching Lawrence Welk reruns and learning how to knit.

But then, there really wasn't anything I could do about it. If I complained, Christine was likely to wield her greatest power of all—squealing to Mom about Seamus and anything else she could dream up.

So which would I rather face . . . jail or Mom?

The rest of the day I didn't utter a single complaint about the impending party. I held my tongue when

Robot dug my spare sheets out of the linen closet and used them to drape the stacked-up furniture. And I said absolutely nothing when I saw Christine open my bags of pretzels and pour them into large plastic bowls for the guests to munch on. When Kinky and Lyle carried in a giant rubber trash can with the keg floating in it, I dutifully scooped up Seamus from the balcony and took him to my room.

At first Seamus ran around like a furry motorized toy, leaping on everything and play-fighting with anything not nailed down. Eventually he settled down a bit, and I tried to pass the time by aimlessly flipping through an issue of *Cosmopolitan*. A few minutes later the band started practicing in the living room.

*Wang! Wang! Wa-a-a-aaannngg!* went Robot's guitar.

*Blangity, blangity, bow, bow, bow!* went Kinky's bass.

*Tappity, boppity, crash, boom, thud!* went Lyle's drumming.

*Bark! Bark! Growl! Whimper!* went Seamus beside me.

I lay on my side with my pillow wrapped around my head, trying desperately to concentrate on the "Is He a Commitment-Phobe?" quiz, but it was no use. All I could do was stare at the graphic—a guy holding hands with one girl while putting the moves on a redhead behind her back—while Robot, Lyle and Kinky provided a weird, dissonant sound track.

All that suppressed frustration felt like a tumor inside me. It didn't help that the guy in the magazine photo looked amazingly like Chuck, only in hipster clothes and with longer hair. I answered the quiz questions as if it were two weeks ago and Chuck and I had never broken up. After tallying up the answers, I read the corresponding analysis, which—surprise, surprise!—diagnosed our relationship as "rocky" and "imbalanced." Their so-called expert advice was for me to stop surrendering so much control to my boyfriend. "Show him you have more in your life than just him. Join a cool club and hang out with friends now and then. Be more mysterious. Guys who think there's nothing more to learn about you will want to move on."

Sadly, it made some sense. Looking back, it was obvious I had let my social life revolve around Chuck. And now here I was with no social life whatsoever. With a roommate who had a constant good time, as if it was her birthright, her superpower. Christine had so much social life it followed her all the way to Austin. Unfortunately, it didn't extend to me.

*Wang, wang, waaaaanggg! Tappity, tappity!*

Except for tonight. Christine's fun-filled existence was going to be rubbed in my face all night long. I knew that I was invited, but I also knew it was a mere technicality—a default caused by my living arrangements. If I didn't live here, Christine would have never included me.

I rolled over, letting my arm dangle lazily over the side of the bed. My fingers brushed against something soft and wet. Sensing something was wrong, I raised up and peered over the edge. The floor was completely white, as if a freak blizzard had hit the confines of my room. Seamus had somehow gotten my new carton of Kleenex off the desk and had ripped the box and all five hundred white tissues into small, soggy bits. I must not have heard it with the band so loud in the next room.

"Seamus!" I yelled, glancing around for him. I finally spotted him in the corner, chewing on the remainder of the box. He saw me and abandoned it, trotting forward with a satisfied look on his face. I was all ready to scold him loudly when I thought, *What's the use?* It wasn't like he understood what I was saying. No one ever listened to me, so why should I expect him to?

I forced myself upright and cleaned up the mess, muttering the whole time. As soon as I'd finished and sprawled back across my mattress, someone knocked. I didn't actually hear it, but Seamus's ears pricked and he ran to the door, barking so hard his whole body scooted backward a few millimeters with every yap.

"Come in!" I hollered, too lazy with self-pity to get off the bed.

The door cracked open and Christine poked her head in. "You got any nail clippers I can borrow?" she asked.

"Sure. On top of the dresser," I said with a sloppy wave.

"Thanks." Pushing Seamus gently with her foot to keep him from escaping, she slipped around the door and shut it behind her. She was already dressed in a short black skirt, black-and-red Ramones T-shirt, red Pumas, and studded leather bands on each wrist, and her hair was perfectly messed up and slightly greased. She looked like a rock chick superhero.

Midway to my dresser she paused and frowned at me. "Why aren't you dressed?"

I shrugged lamely.

"Come on! People will start showing up soon." She did a quick about-face and headed for my closet. "Let's see what you've got."

Without even asking, she pushed open the louvered doors of my closet and with amazing speed began flipping through my clothes, the thick plastic hangers making a rhythmic thwacking sound as she pushed them aside. Seamus trotted up beside her and watched, utterly fascinated.

"You don't have to do this," I protested from my prone position.

Christine ignored me. "No, no, no . . . ," she mumbled as she pawed through the rack. She was already halfway down the row of garments and nothing had passed inspection yet. Obviously in her eyes I even dressed like a loser.

I felt like a sniffly serving wench—a clueless Cinderella being aided by a pushy, gum-smacking, whippet-thin fairy godmother.

Then suddenly she halted and lifted out one of my blouses—a green-and-black-striped wraparound cami. "This is awesome. It's, like, mod or something. Where'd you get it?"

"Ireland." I'd forgotten I'd packed it. It had been a thrift store find in Cork. I'd thought it looked cool, and it was the same Kelly green as all the souvenirs. Even though it was low-cut, Mom let me keep it as a novelty memento of our trip.

Christine dangled the top by the crook of the hanger and turned it around, admiring it from all angles. "Man, if I had boobs I would totally wear this." She turned and thrust it toward me. "Okay, you need to wear this tonight. Do you have a black skirt?"

I squinted at her, trying to figure out why she was helping me. Did she pity me? Was she afraid I'd embarrass her? Or did she actually think of me as a friend?

"I have a black pleated mini," I replied.

"Perfect." She tossed the blouse next to me. Seamus immediately jumped on the bed and began sniffing and walking all over it. "You should probably hurry. People will be here any minute."

As she resumed her trajectory toward the dresser for the clippers, I bit my lip, wondering how I should tell her I was planning on hiding out in the bedroom all night. "Umm . . . Christine?"

"Yeah?" she said, without looking around at me.

"I don't know about tonight. I was sort of thinking I should stay in here."

She turned and gaped at me. "Why the hell would you want to do that?"

I bit the inside of my cheek, unsure how to explain. She obviously wouldn't understand my fear—fear of not fitting in, fear of meeting new people, fear of getting thrown in the slammer. "What about Seamus?" I said, scooping him up off my blouse. "I can't just leave him in here by himself." That was another fear. One she could probably grasp.

"Why can't you?"

"Well . . . what if he gets out?"

"Can he turn doorknobs?"

"No."

"Then he can't get out. He'll probably just sleep through the whole thing." She folded her arms across her chest. "Quit making excuses. You need this party more than anyone. That was part of the reason I thought it was such a good idea."

"Really?" My mood lifted a bit. So she had been thinking of me.

"Yeah. You need to forget all about what's-his-name and meet some new guys. I'm tired of you moping around."

My eyes widened. "Have I been moping?" I asked as my face went all tingly. I really thought I'd been doing a good job of playing it cool.

Christine sat down on the end of my bed. "You haven't been whining and crying or anything—which, by the way, thank you for that—but yeah, you've been kind of out of it. You have this perpetual crack in the middle of your forehead." She leaned over and tapped me right above the eyebrows with my nail clippers. "Makes you look fragile, like if someone yells *boo!* loud enough, you would split right down the middle."

I didn't know what to say. I had no idea Christine had been paying that much attention to me.

"So that's that," she said, heading for the door. "Get dressed pronto and get your ass out there and have fun." She flashed me one last stern glance and marched out of the room.

I looked down at Seamus and ran my hand through his bristly fur. She was right. He probably would just crash all night. And it wasn't like I had to rock him to sleep or anything.

I smiled slightly as I fingered the smooth fabric of my striped top. So Christine really had been playing fairy godmother —in her own stone-ground, abrasive way. A little more "boo" and a little less "bibbity-bobbity."

Fine. I would give the party a chance. And who knew? Maybe a little fairy-tale magic would come my way.

An hour or so later I was studying my new party self in the dresser mirror. I was packed tight in the green-striped top, which I'd paired with my pleated mini and scuffed, clunky Mary Janes. My eyes and lips were freshly painted in the darkest makeup shades I owned. And after wrangling my hair into a dozen different twists and shoots, I'd finally given up and let it hang loose. Ironically, though, all that battling with it created an ideal mussed-up look.

Judging from the rumbling of voices on the other side of the door, the party was officially under way. I turned toward Seamus, who was rolling on my bed, growling and chewing up my headband.

"Be good," I said, backing toward the door. My voice came out low and wavery. Was I hesitant to leave him or hesitant to go out there? Probably both.

Seamus leaped off the bed and ran over.

"No, no. You're not coming," I said.

He cocked his head and looked at me quizzically. I opened the door behind me and slowly backed out.

"Stay," I said, blocking the way out with my foot. "Good boy. Go to sleep."

The last thing I saw before shutting the door was Seamus's baby-deer eyes gazing up at me sadly. As soon as the latch clicked, I turned around with my back to the door, facing our transformed condo.

It was like standing in the mouth of a cave. The place was cramped and dark, lit only by some strategically placed lamps Christine had draped with colored scarves, and a row of Christmas lights along the bar.

"Whoa, Katie." Lyle seemed to appear out of thin air. "You look . . ." He shook his head. "Whoa."

"Yeah," said Kinky, who was standing farther down the corridor, his bushy hair bobbing up and down.

"You do."

"Thanks." I didn't quite understand what they were saying, but I liked it. "How come you guys aren't playing?"

"We'll start up in an hour or so," Lyle explained. "Now's our chance to mingle."

"Plus we need to find an extension cord," Kinky added. "That one outlet keeps giving off sparks."

Great. Now I had to worry about a freak fire as well.

"Come on. Let's go check the van," Lyle said. The two of them loped off toward the front door.

*Here goes nothing.* I smoothed my skirt and ventured out into the living room. An odd, hyperaware feeling came over me—like the nightmares I've had of walking through school naked. I'd never gone to a party by myself before. I'd always been with Chuck. Before him, on the rare occasions Mom allowed me to go to a party, I at least had a couple of friends in tow. But not now.

Christine and Robot were nowhere to be seen. And except for Lyle and Kinky, who were heading out the door, I didn't know a single person. The others looked like irregular versions of Christine and Robot. All were dressed in dark, trashy-hip clothes, which disappeared in the dim light, making their pale faces look like floating, disembodied heads. Almost everyone wore heavy black eye makeup—the guys too—and had obviously dyed hair that was either ironed straight or stylishly messy. They even had matching expressions: apathy with a touch of cynicism.

The parties I'd gone to with Chuck were all jock keggers, but this one seemed to follow the same dynamic. People stood in small clusters, sipping beers or puffing on cigarettes, talking in low, bored tones. When someone else spoke, they'd nod along while scanning the rest of the room, taking careful mental notes of who had arrived and who was with whom. As I walked through the room, a few pairs of eyes passed over me. Some seemed momentarily interested, as if trying to figure out who I was. But no one spoke or otherwise made contact.

I wended my way through the crowd, trying to look as if I had a purpose, while secretly hoping a conversation or other opportunity to mix would present itself along the way. Eventually I reached the patio doors, which had been propped open with cinderblocks.

There were twice as many people on the balcony, all hovering around the keg as if it were a watering hole in the middle of the Serengeti. Robot was manning the pump, and Christine stood against the balcony railing—the queen surveying her royal ball.

She saw me and waved me over.

"Look at you," she said as I approached. "I bet the guys are leaving little slobber trails on the carpet."

"Just Seamus," I said. "And maybe Lyle and Kinky. But don't they always?"

"Right, huh," she said, laughing. Suddenly she

grabbed my elbow and pulled me closer. "See that guy next to Robot?" she muttered in my ear. "You should totally go after him. He just broke up with his girlfriend. Total hag—couldn't stand her. But don't you think he's cute?"

I squinted at him. He was . . . okay. Long bangs, Elvis sideburns. And he obviously thought painting a checkerboard design on a pair of boots was some sort of anti-fashion fashion statement. I tried to picture myself with him. Going to clubs, sharing eyeliner, sucking on the same Thai noodle à la *Lady and the Tramp*. Of course, we could only go out after dark due to the whole sun-aversion issue. And I'd probably end up chucking him on his butt when he painted bull's-eyes on my favorite wedges.

"I don't know," I mumbled back. "He's not really my type."

Christine flashed me number seven of her perturbed expression collection: eyes hooded, mouth open with a slightly curled upper lip. "Then what is your type?"

I stared over her head at the darkness beyond, trying to assemble my thoughts. My type? Chuck's face loomed in my mind. I always thought he was cute, but was he my archetypical dreamboat? I didn't think so. Or rather, it was impossible to tell, since any mental image of him made me feel punctured and shriveled inside.

I then thought of Seamus—the original Seamus.

Seamus the hunky Irish guy. His face still made me swoon. And I never felt gutted thinking about him. But there was no one at the party even remotely Seamus-like.

"I don't know," I confessed.

"I was just trying to help," she said rather irritably. "But if you think my friends aren't good enough for you, then fine."

I stared at her blankly for a moment, too stunned to speak. "No," I said finally. "That's not what I think at all. I just . . . need more time."

"Whatever," she said, turning back toward the assembled crowd as if dismissing me. "Just don't expect me to hang with you all night."

Two hours later I was in the exact same spot. Christine had blown me off in the first thirty minutes, and I was too terrified to actually wander up to anyone I didn't know. So I interjected myself into a conversation with Lyle, Kinky and a Kelly Osbourne look-alike named Genesee.

"No, man, the acoustics at the Hidey-Hole are much better," Lyle was saying.

I nodded like I knew what he was talking about.

"No way, dude," Kinky said. "The Danger Zone totally kicks its butt. Besides, they have cheese fries."

"I think both clubs have an excellent vibe, but"—Genesee paused to take a dramatic puff on her cigarette—

"the Hidey-Hole does have better feng shui. The energy flow is much stronger there."

"Hah! Told you," Lyle whooped.

Kinky shook his bushy head. "You guys are high. What do you think, Katie?" he said, turning to me. "Which club is better?"

They had obviously mistaken me for one of them, and I realized I was about to be revealed as a trendie in clubber's clothing. "Actually I like anyplace that has a clean rest room," I quipped.

The guys cracked up, but Genesee gave me a penetrating stare—looking very much like Mrs. B. I supposed in her mind, two-ply toilet paper had nothing to do with good energy flow.

"So, how about that new place on Red River?" she said, angling her body ever so slightly away from me. "I hear they do yoga workshops there during the day."

I leaned against the wall and blinked several times to keep my eyes from glazing over. This was easily the least fun I'd ever had at a party. For one thing, the creepy Euro-disco tunes and everyone's black clothing and listless expressions made it feel more like a wake. And as the night wore on, the consumption of alcohol only made the scene more surreal.

Some partygoers got louder the more they drank. Others got quieter and quieter until they were reduced to head-bobbing mutely along to the music with their eyes closed. Then there was the Romeo Christine had wanted to set me up with. After positioning himself at the keg and drinking an unfathomable amount of beer, the guy suddenly took off his T-shirt and started dancing spasmodically to the techno song on the stereo. At one point he even climbed onto the bar and tried to dance up there—the low ceiling requiring him to squat like a chicken. When Christine marched over and started yelling at him to get down, he hollered, "Stage dive!" and fell backward into the crowd. It was amazing to see everyone simultaneously step aside, protecting their beers. The guy hit the carpet and lay there looking a little cross-eyed until someone dragged him onto the balcony.

". . . because music is like water," Genesee was saying. "It's like, if you don't have it, you die inside . . ."

My ears shut down. I just couldn't fake it anymore. I scanned the crowd for another spot to retreat to, but couldn't find anything. By this time the small huddles of people had begun splitting into pairs. It was past midnight and couples were everywhere, talking in low tones with their heads bent together or fading into dark corners to make out. No matter how hard I tried not to think about him, my masochistic mind kept dredging up memories of me and Chuck. Me sitting on Chuck's lap at Debby Ellis's party. The two of us cuddling under a blanket at the lake. Chuck pulling me onto the school dance floor during a slow song . . .

"Katie? You all right?" Lyle asked. He peered at me worriedly, his eyes as round as his eyeglass frames.

"Yeah, I'm fine," I replied. My tongue felt thick and

my face got all twitchy. I knew I was close to crying. "Excuse me for a sec."

I weaved around several couples until I reached the bathroom. Luckily it was empty, save for the cigarette smoke. I locked the door and braced myself against the sink basin, filling my lungs with the noxious air and trying to get a grip. Eventually my breathing steadied and the glob in my throat dwindled. I lifted my head and glanced at my reflection in the square chrome-rimmed mirror. My hair was all frizzy and staticky-looking, and my eye makeup was starting to smear, making me look like a feral raccoon.

But that didn't bother me as much as the glint of fear in my face. Christine had been right. A deep furrow had been cleaved down the middle of my forehead, and my gaze constantly darted from one eye to the other, as if too freaked to stay in one place for long. What was wrong with me? I used to have a cool boyfriend and popular friends. I used to welcome the chance to hang out with people. Now I was hiding in a bathroom during my own party.

"Hey! Check out that dog!" someone yelled.

"What's he got?" shouted someone else.

*Dog? Oh no!* I charged out of the bathroom and ran into my room. "Seamus?" I called, flicking on the light. The room looked as if it had been ransacked. Stuff had been knocked off my dresser and desk, much of it soggy and chewed. But Seamus wasn't there. Instead a guy and girl were lying on my bed in the middle an extremely steamy make-out session.

"Hey!" the guy said, squinting at me as if the light hurt him. "Do you mind?"

"Do *I* mind? This is my room!" I shrieked. "That's *my* bed!"

"Sorry," the girl said in a snooty voice. They got to their feet and began straightening their clothes.

"There was a dog in here," I said. "Where did he go?"

"I don't know." The guy answered impatiently. "Out there somewhere."

*"Katie!"* Christine's voice cut through all other noise like a pneumatic drill.

I followed it into the living room, knowing full well what she was screaming about.

"Your dog is going bonkers again!" she shouted as soon as she saw me.

"But where is he?"

Right when I said that, I saw a dark shape streak through the living room. "Seamus!" I called, lunging after his blur. It was hard to follow him in the dim light and dense crowd. But even when I lost sight of him I could tell where he was by how the partygoers bobbed upward as if they were doing the wave.

Eventually I cornered him beside one of the big black amps set up for the band. "Come on," I muttered. "We're going for a walk." I carried him, babylike, back through the throng of onlookers.

"What's that in his mouth?" someone asked.

I glanced down. Sure enough, some frilly piece of clothing was between Seamus's jaws. Without thinking, I pulled it out and held it up. Immediately, the people around us started laughing.

It was one of the panties I'd thrown in the bottom of my closet. The big ruffly ones Grandma Hattie had sent.

"Come on, boy! Hold still!"

I was in the corridor outside our condo trying to wrestle the leash onto Seamus. Ten minutes had already passed and I still hadn't managed to get it on him. Each time I tried, he would hunker way down and lower his head.

*Wang! Wang! Waaaanggg! K'boom! Bow! Bow! Bow!*

The sounds of New Bile's instrument tuning penetrated the walls, making Seamus go even stiffer. *Why do they have to be so damn loud?* I grumbled inwardly. Someone was going to call the cops. That or our eardrums would shrivel up like rotting vegetables.

Suddenly the door to unit 303 opened and Hunky Elevator Guy stepped out onto the landing.

"Hi," he said without smiling. "You guys having a party?"

"Actually my roommate—" I paused, sighing wearily. "Yeah. I guess we are."

"Do you have to have a live band?" he went on. "I can't hear myself think!" He was obviously mad as hell.

His voice had a growling quality to it that amazed Seamus. For the first time since we stepped out there, he relaxed and lifted his head. I quickly snapped the leash on his collar.

"Please." The guy clapped his hands together in a prayer gesture and pressed them against his chest. "Could you please just make them stop? I've got to work tomorrow. I've got to get some sleep."

I tried to picture myself going back in there and hollering for the band to quit playing. I pictured them laughing at me or simply ignoring me altogether. On the slim chance they actually obeyed, Christine would still be majorly pissed. I then pictured her gabbing with my mom on the phone, sneering smugly as she listed various true and untrue crimes.

"No," I replied. "I can't. I'm sorry."

He glared at me. "You can't? Or you just won't?"

I heaved a weary sigh. "I'd like to help, but it's just not possible."

"Why? What's the big deal?"

"It's just . . . complicated."

"Complicated *how*?"

Something inside me, some loose cog of machinery, seemed to snap into place. Before I realized it, I was on my feet, yelling. "I just can't do it, okay? Believe me, I don't like it any more than you! People are making out in my room, throwing trash off the balcony, smoking everywhere, asking me about my vibes! Meanwhile my mom's trying to set me up with a gay guy, my roommate is miffed because I won't date the drunk stage diver, *and my dog is eating my underwear!*"

For a second, no one spoke or moved. Both the guy and Seamus wore matching looks of shock.

*Oh God. Delete! Delete!* If this were all a kind and just universe, it would smite me down with a freak lightning bolt and turn my red-faced, flashlight-waving body into a steaming lump of jelly.

Eventually the guy's mouth twisted into a wry smile. "Are you drunk?" he asked. "Or are you always like this?"

"Sorry," I mumbled, backing up a step, not wanting to look at him. Now that my pent-up rage had spewed out like the contents of a punctured aerosol can, I felt completely drained— and petrified with humiliation. *Dear Lord, did I actually scream about my underwear in front of him? What is wrong with me?*

"You okay?" he asked. All the anger had left his voice. Now he just sounded concerned. After all, loud rock bands pale in comparison to living next to a raging psycho.

"I'm just sorry," I repeated morosely as I fumbled with Seamus's leash. "Maybe you should just call the cops or something. We'll probably get kicked out, but maybe that's not such a bad thing. It's not like things are working out here anyway." I turned and trudged toward the stairwell.

"Whoa. Wait a minute. . . . Wait!"

I spun around, eyeing him suspiciously.

"Let me see your flashlight," he said, holding out his hand. "I have an idea."

I followed him outside, not saying a word. After screeching about my panties, I decided not to take any more chances with conversation. He led me along the front of the building, beneath the balconies. The noise of our party spilled into the night, shrill and discordant.

"Here it is," Elevator Guy announced, stopping just around the corner and pointing to a spot on the building's north wall. "Could you please take the flashlight and shine it on my hands?"

"Sure." I hooked the handle of Seamus's leash over my wrist and clumsily grabbed the flashlight. I had no idea what he was doing and wondered if I should be worried. After all, he clearly didn't like Seamus, and he couldn't be all that fond of me after I refused to help him and had that grand mal hissy fit. But for some strange reason, I trusted the guy. Even Seamus was more subdued around him. Too bad the guy didn't like dogs, because Seamus clearly liked him.

As he reached toward a dark rectangle on the brick exterior, I shakily aimed the flashlight beam over his shoulder. I then recognized the shape as the building's breaker box. *What the hell?* I wondered, feeling the first stirrings of doubt.

"A little higher please?" he asked.

I dutifully complied.

"Three, three, three," he mumbled. "Yes. Here it is. Three-oh-one." I heard a couple of clicks and then suddenly the screeches and throbbing rhythms of New Bile's music died away, leaving only the faint rat-a-tat of Lyle's drumming. I poked my head around the corner and looked up at our balcony. The condo was pitch dark. Only the red glowing tops of lighted cigarettes remained, like a large cluster of fireflies.

There came a few shrieks of surprise and someone exclaimed, "Aw, dude! I think you blew the electric!"

I retracted my head and leaned against the wall, laughing into my hand. "That was brilliant," I whispered. My grip loosened on the flashlight and the beam hit Elevator Guy square on the chest, illuminating the outer tips of his face as if he were sitting at a campfire. His mouth was open in a wide grin, teeth gleaming, and the tops of his cheeks pushed his droopy eyes upright. My heart tumbled inside me. Maybe it was wishful thinking, but it seemed like there was something between us—most likely just the camaraderie that stems from being partners in crime.

"Do you have anywhere you need to be tomorrow morning?" he asked.

My face felt suddenly hot. *Are all college guys this direct?* "Uh . . . n-no," I stammered truthfully.

"Good. 'Cause your alarm might not work with the power off. I promise I'll flip the switches back before I leave for work tomorrow."

"Oh. Thanks." Stupid. Stupid. He'd only been concerned about our lack of electricity. He had no idea my hellhound alarm clock had a backup battery.

"I guess we should head back," he said. "Let's go this way. We don't want anyone to see what we're up to." He placed his hand in the center of my back and started steering me down the building's north end.

I nodded in a slow rotating motion, ultra-conscious of his touch. "Yeah. . . . I mean, no. I should probably finish walking him first," I said, gesturing toward Seamus, who was busy gnawing on a stick.

"Okay. I'll go with you."

"What?" I looked at him, feeling another sproingy sensation behind my ribs. "It's okay. I mean . . . you don't have to. Don't you need to sleep?"

"Look, it's Saturday night. There are weirdos behind every rock. I'm going with you, and then I'll sleep." He said the last part firmly, implying there would be no arguing about it.

Not that I really wanted to.

"Okay," I said. "Thanks."

"So, what's your name?" he asked as we headed for the sidewalk. Seamus realized we were walking and abandoned his stick, eagerly pulling me forward.

"Katie."

"Nice to meet you, Katie." He reached down, grasped my hand in his and shook it gently. "I'm Matt."

We ended up at a picnic table in the park. Matt sat on the tabletop and I sat on the bench below, occasionally tugging on Seamus's leash as if I were fly-fishing. Meanwhile Seamus scampered about the four-foot radius allowed by the leash, exploring every inch of ground with his nose.

"So why wasn't the party any fun?" Matt asked.

I sat still for a moment, mulling over my answer. "It just wasn't my scene," I said finally.

"Why not?"

*Because I don't fit into the shadow world of Christine's hip friends. Because I have posttraumatic-getting-dumped-disorder. Because I don't know who I am now that I'm not Chuck's girlfriend.* "I just don't have much in common with those guys."

"You aren't musical?"

I let out a snort. "I do a mean Sheryl Crow karaoke. But that probably doesn't count."

To my surprise, he burst out laughing. "No, it probably doesn't. Not to those guys anyway."

We fell into another silence, but it was less awkward this time. Seamus charged under the bench to investigate some new odors, requiring me to turn around. Now I could see Matt's face, and he mine.

After a while the silence seemed to stretch on too long.

"Where are you from?" I asked suddenly.

"Niederwald."

"Oh, so *you're* the Niederwald teenager. I heard about you."

He laughed again. "Hey. We're not that small a town. Besides, I'm not a teenager anymore. I turned twenty two months ago."

I raised my eyebrows. "You aren't in the Core Curriculum Program?"

"Nope. I'm a sophomore."

"Oh."

Again we got quiet. I shifted uncomfortably on the bench. For some reason it depressed me a little to find out he was older. Obviously he would only see me as a young, immature, and slightly strange kid. Not that I had much chance with him anyway. But it would have been nice to have a new guy to daydream about— someone other than a creep ex-boyfriend or a perfect stranger who lived an ocean away.

"So what do you do for work?" I blurted out, more to kill the silence than anything else.

"Uh . . . well, it's kind of weird." He hunched his shoulders slightly. "I hold rats."

"You hold . . . what?" I asked.

"Rats. For the psych department. They do testing and watch their responses to stimuli and stuff. Anyway, they've found that if the rats aren't held regularly, they tend to die. They just waste away. Maybe it's from being caged up and all. Anyway, the researchers are too busy to pet them, so they hire idealistic psych majors to do it."

"And you're an idealistic psych major?"

He lifted his hand. "Guilty."

"So you just hold them?"

"Pretty much. I do other stuff too, though. A few of the rats have been coming down with some virus or something, so I'm supposed to go in early tomorrow and make sure none of the others are sick. Things like that can really throw off their data." He stopped talking and studied me. "You're a little freaked out, huh?"

"No. I think it's sort of . . ." I paused, searching for the right word. ". . . sweet."

"Even though it's rats?"

"Yeah. I mean, I don't have much experience with rats, but I did have a pet gerbil once. He—um . . . died."

"I'm sorry."

His comment was packed with so much sincere emotion that I had to turn and look at him. I thought maybe he was putting me on, but he seemed totally sincere. A warm feeling oozed over me as I pictured him standing in some musty, paper-strewn lab stroking the fur of a beady-eyed white rat.

*Lucky rat.*

Suddenly Matt cried, "Hey!" I looked over and saw that Seamus had stuck his head between the bench and tabletop. Matt was holding his left hand in his right.

"Oh my God! Did he bite you?" I asked, leaping to my feet.

Matt shook his head. "No. He just . . . licked me. It surprised me, that's all."

Sure enough, Seamus was pawing Matt's pant legs and slobbering all over him, begging for attention. He looked like an obsessed thirteen-year-old girl who'd run into Orlando Bloom on the street.

I would have been funny, except that Matt didn't do anything. He just sat there, holding his hand and staring strangely at Seamus. It was clear he was not enjoying it at all.

"Seamus, down!" I called out. "Leave him alone!"

But Seamus just glanced over at me as if to say, "Come on, girl. Help me out. You grab him from behind and together we'll get an autograph *and* a hair sample!"

Matt's face was a series of crisscrossed lines. Something seemed to be building inside him. Fearing he might lose it and begin kicking Seamus, I bent down and grabbed my whining, salivating dog. It wasn't easy, since his leash was wrapped around the bench, but eventually I pulled him off Matt and held him tight in my arms.

"Sorry," I said to Matt.

He blinked at me as if awakening from deep hypnosis. "It's okay. No problem." He unclasped his hands and rubbed them on his pants. "I guess we should get back," he said, stepping down from the table.

"Yeah."

We headed down the curved, dimly lit sidewalk. Matt stayed by my side as Seamus dragged me forward, but neither one of us spoke. Unlike before, it was an excruciating silence. I felt like I'd crash-landed.

*Oh, well. Love me, love Seamus,* I told myself. I was just going to have to get over this new crush. Matt obviously hated dogs, and that blew any chance of a friendship or fill-in-the-blank relationship between us.

Too bad I hadn't adopted a rat.

# 7

*Bam! Bam! Bam!*

*Scooby?*

*Bam! Bam! Bam! Bam! Bam!*

"Arf! Arf! Arf!"

"Shhh! Seamus, be quiet." I rolled over and looked at my Scooby clock. It was eight-fifteen in the morning, and someone was pounding a giant bass drum. I was going to strangle Lyle. I would shish-kebob him with his own drumsticks. I'd play "Wipeout" on his cranium. What did it take to get some quality sleep in this place?

*Bam! Bam! Bam!*

I sat up, suddenly realizing the pounding was

someone knocking on our front door. *What the hell?*

Thinking it might be Matt, I leaped out of bed and scurried about my room, throwing on a pair of shorts beneath my oversized T-shirt and running a brush through my wild tumbleweed, post-party hairdo.

"Stay here," I ordered Seamus, shutting the door in his face.

I headed through the living room, where Kinky lay asleep on the carpet, his arms thrown over a chair pillow like a shipwreck victim clutching a piece of flotsam. Robot was sprawled spread-eagle only a couple of feet away. His shirt was off and someone had written BUZZ BOY across his chest in something yellow— mustard, probably. And somewhere in the vicinity of the sheet-draped furniture, I could hear Lyle snoring.

More knocking rattled the door. Kinky writhed slightly and let out a small moan, but Robot made no reaction at all.

"Hello? Hello-o? Is anyone home?"

The warbly voice stopped me in my tracks. *Mrs. Krantz! She's back early!*

"Uh . . . just a second!" I called out.

With a superhuman surge of adrenaline that only sheer terror can produce, I raced over to Kinky, clamped my hand over his drool-glazed mouth *(eee!)*, and shook him till his eyes were wide and spooked-looking.

"My landlady is here," I whispered into his ear, my words crackling with extreme urgency. "You and Robot and Lyle need to stay out of sight and keep quiet. Okay?"

He nodded solemnly and I let go of his mouth, wiping my hand on my shorts. Kinky crawled over to Robot and performed a similar procedure on him. Robot mumbled, "Bloody hell!" and the two of them crawled off under the sheets. I could hear some loud, sizzling whispers and the snapping and creaking of furniture. Finally the sheets fell motionless and everything became silent.

*Bam! Bam!* "Hello? Katie?"

*Okay. You can do this,* I told myself as I kicked several plastic cups out of the way. *Just don't let her in. And if she asks about the furniture . . . say we're getting the carpet cleaned.*

Taking a deep breath, I unlocked the door and opened it just wide enough for my face.

"Mrs. Krantz!" I exclaimed, trying to sound surprised. "You're back."

"Yes, we are!" she sang out. She grinned and nuzzled Mrs. B with her chin. The cat stared at me with that same sharp expression. I gulped in spite of myself.

"Well, uh . . . welcome back," I said nervously, trying to avoid Mrs. B's laser-eyed gaze.

"Thank you." Mrs. Krantz grinned at me. "May we come in?" She started to move forward.

Instinctively, I shoved my shoulder into the opening, blocking her entrance. "Um . . . I don't think that's a good idea," I said, shutting the door as far as it would go and squeezing myself in the frame.

Mrs. Krantz gaped at me with her overly magnified eyes. "Why not?"

"Because . . ." My mind raced frantically. "Because Christine is really sick."

"She is?" Mrs. Krantz retracted slightly.

"Yep. Has been all weekend. And her doctor said she should stay clear of people and not invite anyone over. Airborne germs and all."

"Oh my. That sounds serious." She shook her head and made a sympathetic clucking noise. "Is there anything we can do to help?"

"No. Not a thing," I quickly replied. "She'll be okay. It's just a bad virus. The doc even thinks she'll be well enough tomorrow to go to classes, but we don't want to take any chances until then."

"I understand. Well, we won't keep you. Mrs. B and I just wanted to let you know that we were back."

"Thanks." I moved to shut the door.

"Oh, and one more thing," Mrs. Krantz added, holding up a finger. "Could you please move your trash can back inside?"

"Our . . . trash can?"

"Yes. On the balcony."

I peered over my free shoulder and saw the empty keg floating upside down in the black plastic garbage pail. "Oh, right," I said. "That trash can."

"Please bring it back in," she repeated. "It's making my balcony smell horrible."

*Er, yeah. That would be Seamus's fault,* I thought,

my guilt doubling. "Sorry. We'll bring it in right away."

"I appreciate it. Please tell Christine I hope she feels better very soon. So nice of you to take care of her." She pushed her glasses up her nose and peered at me closely. "I'm amazed you haven't come down with it."

"Yeah." I nodded in a circular motion. "It's a miracle."

"Knock wood!" Mrs. Krantz trilled, rapping on the door.

Behind me I could hear Kinky moan.

"Speaking of, I really should check on her," I said quickly. "See you soon!" As I shut the door, I caught one last sight of Mrs. B's accusatory glare, and an itchy sensation snaked down my spine. Witch cat. I had no idea how Mrs. Krantz found her so lovable.

"Okay, guys," I said, lifting up one of the sheets. "You better come out. We've got a lot of work to do."

Robot came creeping on all fours, the mustard smeared and his hair stuck to his pasty face. It was amazing how different he looked in the daylight. "Crap!" he griped. "Why did that old bag have to come back so soon?"

"Beats me," I replied, staring at him. Something was strange. All his "coolness" was gone. But that wasn't all.

His British accent was gone too.

Two hours after I had sounded the alarm and

woken Christine, we'd cleared the condo of most of the trash, the mood lighting, and a guy named Ken who had passed out in the bathroom.

Everyone except me was hungover. They whined and groaned and clutched their heads as they slowly moved things around. And when Lyle saw me dunking a fruit roll into my coffee, he turned the color of celery and ran for the toilet.

My lie about Christine hadn't been far from the truth. She certainly looked sick. Her fair skin had taken on a clammy, mayonnaise color, and her face seemed incapable of changing expression, leaving her with a perpetual zombie gaze.

"Damn old lady," she grumbled as she slowly and shakily helped me pull the sheets off our furniture. "Why the hell couldn't she give us another day? Just one lousy day."

"Daft old biddy," Robot joined in. Again I noticed the absence of his English lilt. But no one else seemed to pick up on it. Probably too hungover to care.

As Robot, Lyle and Kinky pushed and pulled the sofa back to its original spot—pausing several times to grip their foreheads and curse—one of the seat cushions slid to the floor. And there underneath lay three pairs of frilly underwear. My underwear from Grandma Hattie.

"Wo-ho! What have we here?" Lyle picked one up and studied it as if it were a rare and valuable artifact.

I let go of the sheet I was helping Christine fold and

grabbed it. "Give me that!" I cried.

The others burst into puny guffaws.

"Aw, man." Lyle pretended to be upset. "I was gonna add them to my collection."

I could feel my face turn the color of picante sauce. "Seamus did it," I whined.

That made them laugh even more.

"You should have called him Under-dog," Kinky chuckled.

"Very funny," I muttered. I scooped up the remaining pairs of panties and stomped off to my room.

The second I opened my bedroom door, Seamus shot out and ran right for the balcony door, barking and whining loudly.

The others yelled out protests and grabbed their skulls, as if fearing they might explode like giant popcorn kernels.

"Shut him up! *Please!*" Christine yelled.

"He needs to go to the bathroom," I tried to explain, as if they cared. I ran over to him and tried to pick him up, but he dove out of my arms and continued running around in circles, yapping insistently.

"You can't go out there," I tried to explain, as if *he* cared—or understood.

Just then, someone rapped on the front door. Everyone froze, including Seamus briefly. "Katie? Christine?" came Mrs. Krantz's muffled voice.

"Dammit!" Christine cried. "Your stupid dog!"

"Okay. It's okay. It'll all be okay," I babbled, holding out my hands. "You guys hide and I'll get rid of her."

"Don't let her see the band equipment," Christine said, gesturing to the pile of amps and cases.

"I won't."

As they ambled down the hall to Christine's room, I snatched up Seamus and tossed him, still barking, into my room. "Please just hold it for a few more minutes," I begged him.

Mrs. Krantz pounded again. "Hello, girls? Please open up."

I opened the door wide enough for my nose. "Hi again, Mrs. Krantz," I greeted.

"I heard some noises," Mrs. Krantz said, her expression full of worry. Again, Mrs. B sat in her arms, sneering at me.

"Noises? Like what?"

"Well, like. . . ." She paused, cocking her head, the chain on her eyeglasses falling sideways and draping her left jowl. "Like that. Do you hear barking?"

My chest felt tight as if I'd been holding my breath a long time. This was it. I had to confess sometime; it might as well be now. "Actually, Mrs. Krantz, I need to talk to you about that."

A half hour later I headed over to Mrs. Krantz's place with Seamus in my arms. I'd promised I'd come over to discuss the "situation," and figured it would also give the guys an opportunity to clear out their band stuff and the keg while I kept her distracted.

Taking a cue from Christine, I was wearing my most innocent, Sunday school teacher–type clothes—white sleeveless blouse, long khaki skirt and flower-patterned hair clip. And Seamus had been walked, watered, fed, and brushed until his fur looked poofy with static.

But I should have known it would turn out badly the moment I stopped outside her door. As soon as I knocked on the cutout cat, Seamus went rigid in my arms. A low growl welled up in his throat and continued unremittingly, as if his engine were idling.

Mrs. Krantz opened the door, took one look at Seamus, and heaved a great sigh. "Come in," she said, her voice lacking its usual singsongy pitch.

Seamus kept on growling, even revving it up slightly. "It's okay," I whispered as I headed into her dainty living room, my ballet flats clapping against the hardwood floor.

Like Seamus, Mrs. Krantz seemed extra stiff as she shut the door and waltzed to a loveseat. Her face was flat and her nose was more upturned than usual, as if she were constantly sniffing the air around her. But there was something else vastly changed about her— something I couldn't quite place.

"Have a seat," she said with the minimum amount of courtesy.

Just as my rear began descending into a fur-lined rocker, she cried, "No! Not that one. That's Mrs. B's chair."

It was then I realized what else was different about her. Her ubiquitous cat was nowhere to be seen. I'd gotten used to seeing her constantly held over Mrs. Krantz's abdomen, like a live, smug-looking muff.

As I sank into a stiff green parlor chair, I noticed the rocker didn't have a fur seat cushion after all. It was simply covered inch-deep in feline hair.

"Where is Mrs. B?" I asked.

"She's napping in the next room. We'll need to keep our voices down."

"Sure."

Mrs. Krantz pushed her glasses up her nose and then folded her hands primly in her lap. "So this is the one you told me about," she said, peering at Seamus. I could tell she was trying to be cordial, but she just couldn't. As she attempted a smile, the corners of her mouth wavered and twitched. She seemed almost disgusted—as if I were presenting her a shined-up turd in a red collar.

"Yes. This is Seamus," I said, lifting him up slightly. Seamus's rumbling had kicked into first gear and his body trembled in my grasp.

"Mmm." She nodded politely. "And what sort of breed is Seamus?"

"He's a . . . well . . . he's a mutt, I guess. A terrier mix. Normally he's very sweet."

Mrs. Krantz fiddled with her glasses as an excuse to look away. "You'll pardon me for saying this, but he doesn't seem all that sweet to me right now."

"He's just uncomfortable, that's all. He actually loves people. Or . . . most people. He's always licking me. And he loves Matt, one of our neighbors." I nodded in the direction of Matt's condo.

"Really?" she said, perking up slightly. "So you've met Matthew?"

"Yes. He, um, helped us out while you were gone."

She smiled her first real smile since we'd arrived. "Such a nice boy," she said, staring toward his place. Then she turned and pointed at Seamus. "Our Matthew's a sweetheart, isn't he?" she asked him playfully. "I'm not surprised that you like him."

*Yeah. Too bad it isn't mutual,* I thought glumly. Still, I felt better overall. Dropping Matt's name seemed to raise her opinion of Seamus a little.

Only I should never have gotten my hopes up. Because right at that moment, everything went berserk.

Something colorful streaked into the room, and Seamus leaped out of my arms and charged after it. It was Mrs. B, who looked nothing like her normal composed self. She was all hissing and yowling and porcupine-like. She ran for Mrs. Krantz, who shrieked and tried to grab her. Instead Mrs. B used her as a human launchpad, jumping from Mrs. Krantz's arms to her shoulders, up to her bouffant bob, and eventually to a high wall shelf crammed with several tiny porcelain kittens and, now, one live, freaked-out cat.

"No! No! Bad boy!" I yelled. I lunged for Seamus

and instead grabbed air as he ran under the glass-topped coffee table and pounced on Mrs. Krantz, trying to follow Mrs. B's path to the overhead shelf.

By the time I skirted the table and snatched him, Mrs. Krantz was in a doddering, slack-jawed state of shock. Tufts of her heavily sprayed hair stuck out at all angles, her glasses hung lopsided, and her blouse was bunched and half untucked. On her right arm, a long C-shaped scratch glistened with blood.

"Mrs. Krantz! I'm so sorry!" I cried, clamping down harder on Seamus as he struggled in my grasp. "Are you all right?"

"I—I—I'm okay, I think," she stammered. Her eyes blinked rapidly, growing gradually sharper. "Yes, I'm all right." Suddenly she spun around and lifted her hands up toward Mrs. B. "Oh, my poor little cupcake! It's okay, Missy-boo! Come to Mommy!"

Seamus let out a loud bark and Mrs. B skittered backward along the narrow ledge, knocking off a ceramic Siamese. It bounced off the top of Mrs. Krantz's head and crashed onto the wooden floor, where it broke into several pieces.

"I'm so sorry!" I cried again. By this point all I could do was shuffle slowly backward, shaking my head as if I could somehow erase the scene before me like a gigantic Etch A Sketch.

Mrs. Krantz regained her composure first. With surprising agility, she climbed onto the loveseat, pulled Mrs. B down from her perch, and carried her to the bedroom, cooing to her the entire time. Once the cat was safely stowed, she smoothed her blouse and strode over to me.

"You're hurt," I said, staring in horror as tiny drips of blood striped her arm.

She straightened her glasses and looked down at the wound. "It'll be all right," she said tersely. "But about your dog—"

"Please," I interrupted. I had to stop her from saying it. For some muddled reason, I felt I could stop the inevitable by simply preventing the words from leaving her mouth. "He's not a bad dog. Really."

Mrs. Krantz blew out her breath. "Be that as it may, I feel—"

"I'll keep him away from Mrs. B at all times. I promise. You'll never see him. Never."

She shook her head. "No. I'm afraid it's best if—"

"But they'll kill him!" I screeched, my voice breaking on the word *kill*. "If I take him back to the shelter, they'll put him to sleep! Please don't let that happen. He's not bad. He's just a dog. He doesn't know what he's doing." My lips were trembling something terrible. I pursed them together, holding my breath as I watched her reaction.

Mrs. Krantz let out a long sigh, her battle stance gradually crumpling. Her shoulders slumped, her chin lowered, and her large, golf-ball eyes sagged with pity. "I'll think about it," she said finally.

"Thank you! Thank you, Mrs. Krantz!" I exclaimed, my voice airy from holding my breath so long.

"You'll have my final answer tomorrow night. In the meantime, you have to promise me he won't come near Mrs. B."

"I promise. Not a problem. They'll never see each other." I gave Seamus a squeeze, nuzzling the top of his head with my chin. "You won't be sorry," I went on, heading for the door. "Everything will work out great."

Mrs. Krantz smiled feebly and cradled her bloody arm. "Yes, well . . . we'll see."

When I got back to the condo, the band had cleared out with their equipment, and the rest of the furniture had been returned to its usual layout. Christine was sprawled across the couch holding a can of Coke to her forehead.

"How're you feeling?" I asked, putting Seamus out on the balcony.

"Uhhhhhh," she replied.

I fixed a crooked cushion on the yellow armchair and plopped into it. "So Mrs. Krantz and I had a little . . . talk. I guess."

"Uhh?" Her head tilted toward me slightly.

"Yeah. Seamus is on probation. She wants to think about it and will let me know her verdict tomorrow night." I decided not to bring up the fight, the blood or the broken figurine.

Christine set the soda on the coffee table and struggled onto her elbows. "That's good. I guess," she said in a monotone. "By the way, your mom called. She wanted to know if you'd called some guy named Aaron?"

My stomach clenched. "God, I wish she'd leave me alone about that." I filled her in on how Mom wanted to fix me up with the gay son of her old college roommate. For some reason Christine thought that was really funny.

"Your mom is a piece of work," she said, chuckling weakly. "Oh yeah. And she also wanted to know if you'd bought your textbooks yet. Something about not waiting till the last minute. Yadda, yadda."

"What did you say?"

"I said you had." She popped back against the cushions, closed her eyes, and began massaging the triangular space between her eyebrows.

"Thanks."

"You mean you haven't got them yet?"

"No," I said, yawning. "Have you?"

"Uh-uh."

I toyed with a loose thread on my skirt. "I guess we should, huh? Classes start tomorrow." It was hard to think about school after everything that had happened. I knew it was the main reason I was there, but with all the other stuff I was dealing with, it suddenly seemed a real nuisance.

Christine grabbed her head and struggled to a sitting position. "Yeah, I guess you're right. Want to go together?"

"Now? Are you sure you're up for it?"

She shrugged lazily. "I have nothing left to puke."

Right then Seamus started barking loudly. Leaning sideways, I peered through the glass patio door and saw him lunging toward the railing that separated our balcony from Mrs. Krantz's.

"Oh no!"

I raced outside. Seamus had his forepaws perched on one of the big stones and his head was thrust between two rails, the studs on his collar clanging against the metal each time he barked.

Sure enough, Mrs. B stood in the middle of their balcony, eyeing Seamus warily.

"Stop!" I cried. "You're supposed to stay away from her!" I tied to pick him up, but only managed to slide his head a few inches up the balusters. Crouching down, I threw my arms around him and tugged again. But just like before, I could only move him up or down—not back. He was stuck!

Seamus was just figuring that out himself. His barking had stopped and he whined and fretted as he tried unsuccessfully to back out of there. He hunched his body, bracing himself as he yanked his head, but all he managed to do was clang his ID tag against the bars over and over.

Behind me Christine started laughing and clutching her head. "Ha, ha, ha, *ow*! Ha, ha, ha!"

"How the hell did you get in this mess?" I grumbled to Seamus while trying to flatten his ears.

Mrs. B craned her head, fascinated by Seamus's plight. She took a few steps toward us, stopped, and sniffed the air, as if pretending she was just out for a stroll among the potted plants. Again she glanced at him, her tail twitching, and ventured a little closer, then closer still, until she stood right in front of him, staying just out of reach of his jaws. There she sat herself down and stared at him with a smug little look on her face. I could almost hear a breathy femme fatale voice taunting, "Ha, ha, ha, ha, *ha*, ha!"

I grunted in frustration as I desperately tried to guide Seamus's head back between the balusters. Each time I pulled, he would let out a high-pitched yelp as if scared or in pain. "Sorry," I said again and again. After a while, I sat back on my rear and rubbed my aching fingers on my skirt.

Seamus let out another yowl.

"I didn't even touch you," I snapped.

And then I saw. It was Mrs. B. She had risen up on her haunches and was batting his face over and over like a punching bag. *Pow!* went her left paw across his snout. *Bam!* came her right hook. Poor Seamus could only stand there helplessly and take it.

Behind me Christine took turns screeching with laughter and groaning in agony.

I reached over the railing and swiped at Mrs. B. "Stop it, you little—!"

"My baby!" Mrs. Krantz came barreling into view wearing a bathrobe and towel turban. "What's he doing to my baby?"

I stood there frozen, my hand still raised over Mrs. B. *O-o-okay. This doesn't look good.* Mrs. B ran right to her master's feet, like some furry, namby-pamby little tattletale. She even had the nerve to look frightened.

Somehow, in the midst of all this, Seamus managed to wrench his head back forcefully enough to free himself from the bars. He wandered around our balcony, whimpering and shaking his head over and over.

"Are you all right, Missy-Bee?" Mrs. Krantz clucked as she snatched her up. "Did that doggie hurt you?"

"But she was attacking *him*. He was stuck and she was whacking him with her claws!" I explained, my voice high and shrill.

"I find that very hard to believe," Mrs. Krantz said huffily.

"It's true." Christine stepped onto the balcony. "I'm sure Mrs. B thought she was defending herself. And I have to say, she did an excellent job." She was speaking in that honey-coated voice again—the one that hypnotized anyone over the age of forty—and her features were reset into her placid, goody-goody mode (although still drawn and pale).

"Christine, dear. My, you do look sick, you poor thing. I hope this little to-do didn't wake you." Mrs. Krantz was speaking to her in the same gooey, cooing voice she used with Mrs. B.

"No, I was up," she replied, smiling beatifically. "Like I said, your cat really taught Seamus a lesson. I'm sure he won't be bothering her anymore. Right, Katie?" She glanced over to where I stood fussing over Seamus and raised her eyebrows pointedly.

I got the message. "Right," I muttered.

Mrs. Krantz relaxed visibly. "Well . . . I'm sure she didn't harm him. Her front paws are declawed."

"He's fine," I said. "Not hurt at all." Traumatized, maybe. Humiliated, definitely. But not hurt.

Mrs. Krantz nodded. "All right, then. If you'll excuse us, I'm going to finish my bath." As she walked back into her condo, I could hear her whispering to Mrs. B. "You showed that mean doggie, didn't you? Yes, you did."

"Thanks," I said to Christine as soon as they disappeared inside. "I thought Seamus would be kicked out of here for sure. I wouldn't have been surprised if she tossed him off the balcony herself."

"Don't mention it," Christine said, staring down at her nails, her voice back to normal again. "I hate that stupid cat."

"Me too."

"So let's get out of here and get those books while I still have enough energy to walk."

"But . . . what about *him*?" I looked at Seamus, who was hunkered down beside me, looking kind of hung-over and depressed.

"What about him?" she asked.

"I can't just leave him like this."

"Well, don't leave him out here, that's for sure. Just put him in your room. He'll be okay."

I bit my lip. "Are you sure?"

"He'll be fine. Trust me."

When we returned two and a half hours later, Mrs. Krantz met us on the landing.

Christine saw her first. After griping about the service elevator being out of order and how climbing the stairs made her head throb, she suddenly stopped in mid-complaint and broke into one of her blissed-out smiles. "Good afternoon, Mrs. Krantz," she said in her Disney princess voice.

"Afternoon, girls," Mrs. Krantz called. I could tell by her clipped tone that something was really wrong.

Christine didn't seem to pick up on it, though. "How's your arm?" she went on, as if trying for extra credit.

"It's fine, dear. Thank you." Mrs. Krantz turned toward me, her expression instantly grim. "Katie, may I speak with you a moment?"

My limbs turned to icicles. "Uh . . . sure."

"Here, give me your bag, Katie. I'll wait for you inside," Christine said, her pitch all hush-hush and her face so solemn it made me want to punch her. I was really getting tired of this whole good-renter, bad-renter routine she thought we were playing.

"Thanks," I muttered, enjoying her slight wince as I handed over my bulging Co-op Bookstore sack.

Mrs. Krantz smiled benignly and waited until Christine shut the door behind her. Then she pushed her glasses up her nose and cleared her throat. "I'm afraid we had a little . . . incident while you were gone."

"An incident?" I repeated. "What kind of an incident?" I could guess what kind. A Seamus-related one, I was sure. But I wanted to play this as innocent as possible.

"Soon after you girls left, your dog began howling nonstop. Such loud, anguished cries." She touched her hand to heart for some reason, as if to demonstrate the drama of it all. "It really upset poor Mrs. B."

*Dammit!* I knew I shouldn't have left him. He was still so freaked out and I abandoned him.

"I'm really sorry." I paused, listening. "But . . . how did you get him to stop?"

She fiddled with her eyeglass chain. "Well, I have to admit, after the little ruckus this morning, I was too afraid to go near him. But luckily Matthew showed up."

"Matthew? You mean Matt?"

She nodded, smiling. "Such a sweet young man. He offered to take your dog and keep him quiet until you came home. So we let ourselves in and got him. I hope you don't mind."

"You mean . . . Seamus is over at Matt's?"

She nodded again, her glasses slipping to the tip of her nose. "Yes. He's there now. I just wanted you to know."

"Thanks."

Mrs. Krantz headed into her condo. "Oh, and Katie?" she added, pausing on the threshold.

"Yes?"

"I haven't made up my mind yet. But you have to know, this cannot happen again."

"I understand. Thanks."

After she shut her door, I began pacing the landing. My mind was so stockpiled with stress, I didn't know what to think. Obviously things were not working. And I was beginning to wonder if even Seamus would be happier elsewhere. But if I took him back to the shelter, he'd be finished. Gone. Mrs. Krantz would let me keep him if he behaved. Only I couldn't put him on the balcony or he might chase her precious devil-spawn cat. I couldn't let him roam the apartment or he would chew and ingest various things. And thanks to this latest development, it seemed I couldn't leave him in my room either.

Basically, I was screwed. *Seamus* was screwed.

Now Matt was involved. I wouldn't have been surprised if he hated me for this, having to take in an animal he loathed so much. It would be like me having to babysit that spoiled brat Mrs. B.

I shut my eyes and tried to stuff all my panic and

frustration into some impenetrable part of me. The process was near impossible—like trying to close a huge, virtual suitcase crammed full of ugly clothes. Eventually my breathing steadied enough for me to approach Matt's door.

*Brace yourself. He's going to be mad,* I thought as I knocked.

Matt opened up, took one look at me and smiled. "You're back," he remarked. "Come in."

"Thanks," I said, disarmed by his good mood and (as always) his cuteness.

I headed into his condo, which had the exact same layout as ours only more guy-like. He had modular, comfy-looking furniture, all in different shades of brown—whereas our décor was more little-old-lady, circa mid-1980s, with a heavy wiener dog motif.

Seamus was lying on the rug, gnawing on something white and floppy. He saw me and immediately ran over, his tail a wagging blur.

"Hey, fella," I said, picking him up. It felt good to be greeted so warmly—although I wondered if he would still love me if his canine brain could fathom what a loser I was.

"Have a seat," Matt said. He scurried about, picking up books and stacks of dirty dishes. It was then I noticed how messy the place was.

"Oh no. Did Seamus . . . ?" I gestured helplessly at the papers and Starbucks cups strewn about the carpet.

Matt looked confused for a second, then started

laughing—a deep, musical laugh that reverberated through me. It was like Kinky's bass cranked up to eleven, only better. "You think Seamus did this?" he asked, chuckling. "No. This is all me. I'm a pathological slob. *Slob-a-noid maximus* I think is the clinical term."

"Good," I said, letting out my breath. "I mean, I'm glad he wasn't a big problem. Or was he?"

"No, he was no trouble," he said, tossing a pile of clothes and other debris into the linen closet. "He just got a little . . . chewy. That's all." He walked over and picked up the white thing Seamus had been munching on: a mangled athletic sock.

I sucked in my breath. "I'm so sorry!"

Again Matt laughed, and again my insides hummed. "Don't worry about it. *I* made half of these holes." He gestured to an empty spot he'd cleared on the couch. "Sit down for a sec."

"Okay." As soon as I settled onto the couch, Seamus struggled in my arms, trying to get at the sock dangling from Matt's right hand. "Uh-uh," I said to Seamus. "You've chomped on enough stuff today."

"It's okay," Matt said. "Let him go for it. I don't mind."

I released Seamus and Matt tossed the sock into the air. Seamus caught it and ran to the far corner, where he proceeded to whirl about, play-growling and flailing the sock as if it were a stray rattlesnake.

"Keep it. It's yours," Matt called out to him. He kept

his gaze on Seamus as he lowered himself into a fudge-colored recliner. Gradually his features slackened into the usual bummed-out expression he wore around us.

Guilt shot through me as I thought about how difficult these last two hours must have been for him—how he must have been battling his dog hatred the entire time. Mrs. Krantz was right. He was extremely nice. And it was thoughtful of him to hide it all from me.

"I really, really appreciate your taking him in," I said, leaning forward. "Especially with . . . you know . . . the way you feel and all."

His eyebrows disappeared beneath his hair. "What do you mean? How do I feel?"

It was cute how surprised and slightly worried he looked. He seemed almost embarrassed that I'd picked up on this aversion of his. "It's okay," I said. "I could tell the first time I saw you that you don't like dogs. No big deal."

"Don't like dogs?" he repeated. For a while he just looked at me as if I were speaking in code. Then suddenly, a bemused smile stole its way across his face. "Ohhh. No. You've got it all wrong. I love dogs."

"You do?" It was my turn to stare at him suspiciously.

"Yeah. It's just that . . ." He pressed his hands together and leaned forward, elbows on his knees. "You see, I had a dog. A golden retriever named Jessie. Had her for ten years. She, um, died two months ago." He said all this in a strained tone, as if hurling the words from deep within him.

"I'm sorry," I said softly. I sat there, completely riveted, battling an overwhelming urge to touch his face and try to smooth away the sad cracks on his brow.

"I found a lump on her belly," he went on, gazing down at the carpet. "It was cancer. The vet did everything, but . . . after a while it was clear nothing was helping. So we . . . so I . . . stopped her suffering." His voice petered out at the end.

I wanted to say *I'm sorry* again, but I couldn't. I felt almost too heavy for speech. The phrase wasn't good enough anyway—it was way too skimpy to truly impart how I felt. All I could do was stare at him and feel his heartbreak.

Ever so slowly, Matt seemed to particle-beam back to the present. His gaze lifted and he shifted awkwardly in his seat, rubbing his hands as if cold.

"Anyhow, that's probably why I seemed so out of it around Seamus," he explained. "It just, you know, reminded me."

"Yeah," I mumbled. "I imagine."

He turned and looked at Seamus, who was chomping merrily on the toe of the sock as he held it between his front paws. I studied Matt as he watched my dog, wondering how I could have misunderstood him all those times.

*It's his eyes,* I decided. Those sleepy, hooded eyes. They made him appear brooding when he was simply thinking—or remembering.

Seamus caught Matt looking at him and dropped the sock, his ears pricking like perfectly folded cloth napkins. Springing to his feet, he ran forward and leaped onto the coffee table, surfing on a piece of paper and knocking an assortment of pens, notebooks and Styrofoam cups to the floor.

"Down!" Matt shouted.

Seamus instantly hopped to the floor, his ears flattening against his head and his body bowed with guilt. He seemed totally taken aback by Matt's reaction. Even I had to fight the urge to hit the carpet.

"Sorry," Matt said, grinning awkwardly. "Force of habit."

"It's okay." I reached for Seamus, thinking I should comfort him. I really didn't want him to dislike Matt, especially now that I'd discovered Matt *didn't* dislike him. But to my surprise Seamus walked over to Matt and licked his hand. Matt's lips curved into a grin, and he bent down to scratch Seamus on the head. "You can crash here anytime you want, little guy," he said sort of wistfully.

A Christmas bulb pinged on inside my head. "Hey," I said. "What are you doing tomorrow morning?"

"I've got a class and then a couple of hours of rat holding. Why?"

"Damn!" I slumped back against the cushions. "It's nothing. I just need to figure out something to do with Seamus."

"What do you mean?"

I proceeded to fill him in on almost everything: my impulse decision to adopt Seamus, his wild behavior, my lack of sleep, my promise to Christine not to let him run loose, his skirmishes with Mrs. B, and my promise to Mrs. Krantz to keep him away from them. The entire time I babbled, Matt sat and listened patiently, stroking the long fluffy fur on Seamus's ears.

"So I can't keep him on the terrace. And now, apparently, I can't leave him in my room either," I concluded, having worked up to a full whine.

Matt sat back in his seat. "Maybe you could try what I used to do with Jessie."

"What's that?"

"Leave the radio on."

"Huh?" Matt struck me as a smart guy, but it seemed that adding music would only make Seamus howl louder.

"Seriously," he went on, chuckling at my reaction. "Set it on one of those morning talk programs. It always calmed my dog. I think the sound of voices made her feel less lonely."

"Really?" Maybe he was on to something. After all, Seamus hadn't howled when the party was going on, and our place had been full of yammering people. Of course, maybe he had and I just didn't hear it over all the noise.

"You know, it just might work." I nodded slowly. "Yeah. I'll give it a shot. Thanks."

"No prob."

We sat there grinning at each other for an immeasurable moment. Gradually, I could feel the skin on my face begin to sizzle. Just when my hair seemed ready to catch fire, I mustered my strength and turned away.

"Come on, Seamus," I called, standing. "Let's go."

Seamus rose up and glanced from me to Matt, stamping his paws and whimpering slightly.

"Go on," Matt said, giving him a gentle nudge.

Seamus gave him a wide-eyed, soulful look—the one I thought he only gave me—and scurried over to my feet. I scooped him into my arms and headed for the door.

"Thanks again," I said. "For everything."

Matt got to his feet and shoved his hands into the pockets of his baggy shorts. "Not a problem. I guess I'll see you around."

"Yeah. See ya."

As I opened the door and stepped out onto the landing, Seamus started to whine. Clearly he was reluctant to leave Matt.

He wasn't the only one.

"Do you hear something?" I asked, pressing the Lower Volume button on the TV remote.

"Will you stop?" Christine said irritably. "That was just the ice maker. Everything's fine."

We were sitting on the carpet with our backs against the couch watching a behind-the-scenes documentary of *Gilligan's Island*. Or at least I was trying to watch it. I had left Seamus in my room with the radio on in order to test Matt's method before tomorrow. So far it seemed to be working, but I still jumped at every teeny-tiny noise.

"Sorry," I said, increasing the volume again.

She repositioned the stuffed wiener dog she was using as a neck pillow and slouched farther down the front of the couch. "You're as bad as Robot when we're making out at my dad's house."

"Where is Robot anyway?" I asked tentatively. I was half afraid uttering his name might conjure him up—like a perfectly timed sitcom character entrance.

"He and the guys needed to practice," she explained. "They're going to enter the Battle of the Bands at the Danger Zone next week."

"Oh." I nodded as if I knew what she was talking about.

"Besides, we needed a break. You know how it is? When you're with your boyfriend so constantly he starts to get on your nerves?"

"Yeah." Actually I had no idea what that was like. I'd mainly spent the last two years plotting ways to spend *more* time with Chuck. But getting Mom to ease up on curfews was like requesting leave from a prisoner-of-war camp. Of course, looking back now, I saw that Chuck always needed plenty of space—the better to arrange secret meetings with Trina, no doubt.

I grabbed a handful of Cheetohs and glanced over

at Christine's sharp profile. Was she worried that Robot might be off getting to know a female fan better? Somehow I doubted it. It was weird. I always thought all boyfriend-girlfriend relationships were the same. But she and Robot were nothing like me and Chuck. She squabbled with him, bossed him occasionally, and even enjoyed time away from him—like now. My friends and I would never do that to our guys. In our circle, who you dated declared who you were—and how important you were. So you always had to treat your relationship as a sacred thing. Not so with Christine and Robot.

"So, I've got to ask." I rubbed off the orange cheese powder on my T-shirt and turned toward Christine. "This morning Robot didn't sound British at all. What's up with that?"

Christine just sat there, concentrating on a montage of all the visitors to Gilligan's Island: the rock band, the headhunters, Leonardo da Vinci, the Gilligan look-alike spy. . . . Finally she glanced over at me, her features set in a sour scowl.

"Okay. So he fakes it a little. So what? His mom was born in London and they fly to England every Christmas to visit relatives."

"All right. I'm sorry," I said, waving my hands in a surrender gesture. "I just don't understand why he does it."

She shrugged. "I think he started it to get girls. Now he does it because it gives the band some cool cred."

"But don't people know? Or won't they find out? I mean, he can't keep it up all the time, right?"

"But he does." Christine sat up straight and pivoted about to face me, hugging the patchwork dachshund to her chest. "His older brother once told me that Robot started using the accent when they moved to San Antonio. I think Robot was, like, twelve and realized how popular it made him. His parents just let him do it, figuring it was his right to creative expression or something. They're both therapists."

"Really?" I forced myself not to laugh. Not only was Robot not from England, but the fact that his parents were both professionals sort of debunked the whole greaser-punk persona.

"Anyway," Christine went on, "the only time he drops the accent is when he's really sick or tired. I guess it takes too much concentration or energy or whatever."

"But doesn't it ever bother you?" I asked, peering closely at her. She didn't strike me as someone who could put up with much bull.

She shook her head. "Nah. I did crap like that too when I was in fifth grade. I told all my friends my dad was a CIA agent and that was why he was never around." She started to laugh. "I even said if they ever told anyone they would go to jail or die mysteriously. You know, like deadly germs in their glitter lip gloss or something. Actually, I think a couple of those girls still believe it!"

I laughed. Knowing Christine, I wouldn't doubt that.

Just then, I heard a faint *clunk*. "Did you hear something?" I said, leaning in the direction of my room.

Christine whacked me on the head with her wiener dog pillow. "That was the air conditioner."

"Sorry," I mumbled.

"You know, you say that a lot. It's kind of annoying."

"Really? I'm sor—. I mean . . . Oh." I stared down at my orange-streaked lap. "Anyway, thanks for not ratting me out to my mom about Seamus."

"No biggie. You won't tell anyone Robot's little secret, will you?"

"No way."

"Good. Thanks." She grabbed some Cheetohs and turned back to the program. "God, I can't stand Gilligan. He screwed up their chances to get rescued so many times, you'd think they would have barbecued him."

I laughed. "I never liked him either. I always had a crush on the professor."

She cocked an eyebrow at me. "Seriously? That's sad."

"Come on. Out of all the men on that island, who would you pick?"

Christine thought for a moment. "Yeah. I guess you're right," she conceded. "But then, you love that ugly dog too."

It was my first day of the summer curriculum program, and except for my compounding lack of a good night's sleep (my eyes were starting to look as if they'd been pushed farther into my head), everything was going perfectly.

My classes had gone well. In both history and world literature, they'd utilized the standard meet-and-greet pattern. Vital schedules and syllabi had been handed out. Teaching assistants had been introduced. And instructors launched into overviews of what we should have already learned in high school.

Whenever I would glance around the giant lecture halls, the other hundred and fifty-odd students looked as if they felt the same way I did—slightly awestruck and eager to please. Everyone cranked out several pages of notes, and there was hardly any talking. We all felt as if the word *newbie* flashed in neon across our foreheads, so we were desperately trying to give off the laid-back vibe of *real* underclassmen.

As I headed toward the West Mall, where I was supposed to meet Christine, I glanced at my reflection in the glass walls of the Flawn Academy Center. I had tried hard that morning to dress the part of a bona fide college student, deciding eventually on the following: a pair of cropped, khaki carpenter pants, lightly dusted with black fur (from Seamus); a red tank with a fresh hole in the side seam (also from Seamus); and leather flip-flops that had been chewed to the moist, spongy consistency of Twinkies (ditto). My hair was swept up into a no-nonsense ponytail, and my backpack was slung casually over my right shoulder. I was kind of glad Seamus had chewed on that as well. Shiny new packs were a dead giveaway that you were a high schooler. Only a lunch box would be worse.

Christine was already waiting for me in front of the West Mall fountain. With her unique look and who-cares attitude, she had no problem passing as older. After our conversation the night before, I felt we had a closer bond now. Maybe even a real friendship.

I was in such a good mood, I felt charged up and bouncy. As I walked toward Christine, I marveled at the faint rainbows in the spray of the fountain and how the sun gleaming through the oak leaves made dotted patterns on the sidewalk.

"You look high," Christine said as I approached. "What's with the big smile?"

I didn't even realize I was smiling. "Nothing," I said, trying to play it cooler. "I just like it here."

We headed for the nearby intersection and blended into a crowd of about two dozen others also crossing Guadalupe Street. I glanced at everyone around me, feeling an overwhelming sense of camaraderie. These were my people. This was my world.

"Are you on crack or something?" Christine asked irritably. "Your cheesy grin is back."

"I was just . . . checking out the guys," I mumbled, keeping my eyes focused in front of me.

"Man, you're a lousy liar."

We turned the corner at Twenty-second Street and walked west, then turned on Pearl Street toward our building. As we headed for the front door, Matt walked out of it, looking amazing in a pair of blue running shorts.

"Hey," he said, tossing his head to sweep the hair out of his eyes.

A warm, squishy sensation swept through my chest. "Hey," I said back. Christine gave me a teeny nudge with her elbow. "Oh. Um . . . this is my roommate, Christine. Christine, this is our neighbor Matt."

"Hi," she said, nodding at him casually.

He nodded back. "Nice to meet you."

"So Katie . . . ," said Christine, heading toward the entrance, "I'm going to run upstairs and grab some lunch." As soon as she walked behind Matt, she shot me a wide, knowing smile.

"Okay. See you up there." I waited until she'd disappeared into the building before turning back toward Matt. "How are the rats? Still happy?"

"They're fine," he said, raking the hair off his forehead. "How did things go with Seamus? Did you try the radio trick?"

"I tested it last night and it worked great," I said. "So I set it up again this morning. Have you been here a while? Heard any howling?"

He shook his head, causing his forelock to fall back across his brow. "Haven't heard a thing."

"Great!" I bounced on the toes of my flip-flops, then realized how spazzy I probably looked and stopped. "Thanks for the advice," I added. "You really saved my butt."

"Sure thing."

Just like the day before, we smiled dopily at each other for a few beats. Then Matt clapped his hands together, breaking the spell. "Anyway," he said, his eyebrows lifting until they disappeared beneath his bangs. "I should probably start my run before it gets too hot."

"Yeah, I should go too," I said, walking toward the building as if suddenly in a hurry. "Bye."

"Later!"

From the safety of the foyer, I watched through the

glass door as Matt jogged down the sidewalk and out of sight. It was an amazing view.

I was just turning around when a high-pitched scream echoed down the stairwell. An icy tingle spread over me.

"Christine?" I called out.

Another scream. This time louder.

*Oh my God, oh my God, oh my God!* I charged up both flights of stairs, two steps at a time, desperately trying to remember the self-defense moves we'd learned in athletics class. Let's see. . . . Using your elbow was one. Using their weight against them was one. Running into danger was *not* one. . . .

As I bounded onto the third-floor landing, I saw that our door was ajar. Mustering all my courage, I flung it wide and raced into the condo, ready to crotch-kick however many masked intruders were lurking inside.

But there were no masked strangers. Not a one. Just Christine kneeling on the floor of the living room.

She whirled around and gave me the most lethal, Medusa-like death glare I'd ever seen. "Your . . . *dog*!" she spat, her cheeks the color of a Christmas stocking.

And that's when I noticed the mess. Scattered all over the carpet were pieces of colored felt, tufts of puffy white stuffing, and various severed limbs from Christine's wiener dog collection. It was a horrible, gruesome sight—like wandering onto the set of a Muppet slasher movie. Here lay a foot . . . there a pink tongue . . . a floppy ear . . . a big plastic googly eyeball . . . all ripped and mangled and damp with drool.

"Oh no, Christine. I—I'm so—"

"Don't even say it! Don't you dare!" she whispered angrily. Her face was all twisted, and lasers of pure hatred seemed to beam forth from her narrowed eyes—aiming right for me.

"I'm sorry," I rasped, choking on the final syllable. I had to say it. It was the only thing I could say. It was how I felt.

But it didn't do any good. Christine shot me one last heat-guided glare, marched off to her room and slammed the door behind her. And everything between us, all the friendship and trust I had felt last night, was left in smoking rubble.

I found Seamus underneath my bed, vomiting wiener dog parts. Christine's shrieks must have freaked him out pretty good, because it took a full fifteen minutes to wrestle him out of there. Whenever I reached in from one side, he would scooch in the opposite direction. Then, when I tried the opposite side, he would go the other way. And so on and so on. Meanwhile some guy on the radio kept babbling about the failures of the educational system, and I could hear Christine cursing and throwing things in her room.

"Why do you always have to do this? Why can't you just *be good*?" I cried out as I made another desperate swipe for him. "Don't you know what will happen if you don't?"

Seamus just eyed me cagily and wriggled away.

It felt like I was losing my mind. The virtual suitcase of horrors had burst open inside me—ejecting all its hideous contents. Just a half hour before, I was so happy, and now I was inches away from complete mental implosion. If one more thing went wrong, they'd find me racing down Pearl Street in my bathrobe, screaming and boinging my lower lip.

Finally I got hold of Seamus's left hind leg. He let out a yelp and tried to scramble away, but I slid him toward me, careful to steer him around the mucky vomit.

"Stupid dog," I muttered as I held him tight and clipped the leash to his collar. My shock at seeing the massacre was slowly wearing off, replaced by a helpless, shaky anger. "Come on!" I had no idea how Seamus had gotten out of my room, and I was in no mood to investigate. All I wanted was to get the hell out of there.

Since Seamus was in full-on passive resistance mode, I carried him down the two flights of stairs. The instant we stepped outside, his tail started wagging and he struggled to be let down. I complied, but seeing him scamper happily down the sidewalk only made me madder. He could dismember stuffed animals and destroy my friendship with Christine and then shrug the whole thing off with "walkies." Meanwhile I was left having to pick up the pieces—literally. It was so unfair.

Why couldn't I have been born a dog?

As per our routine, Seamus pulled me all the way to the park, stopping occasionally to sniff out a smell or pee on a tree or trip me for no discernable reason whatsoever.

"Will you *stop*?" I hollered as Seamus suddenly caught a scent and charged between my legs, sending me backward into a nearby bicycle rack. I fantasized about dropping the leash and letting him run in whatever direction he pleased—and me running the other way, free of all the worry and responsibility. . . .

Only I couldn't. I knew if I let him go he would end up hurt or killed, or back at death row in the shelter. As furious as I was, I just couldn't allow that to happen.

By the time we entered the park and found an empty picnic table (at a safe distance from the pool), my anger was pretty much spent. I plopped down on the bench and stared off into the distance, too weary even to think. Soon something warm and wet touched my chin. I glanced down and saw Seamus stretched out across the tabletop, staring at me. He licked me again, this time right on the nose, and made a half-grunting, half-whimpering noise in his throat.

"What am I going to do with you?" I whined as I scratched the top of his head. Seamus panted gleefully. "No. You don't understand! You've got to behave!" I pleaded. Hot tears filled my eyes, blurring Seamus's face into a wiggly blob. He whimpered again and inched forward a little, sniffing me with his damp nose.

"Please, Seamus. If you aren't good, Mrs. Krantz will—"

Suddenly it hit me. Mrs. Krantz was supposed to give me her answer this evening. This was D-Day. Decision Day. Even if she had originally decided to let him stay, by now Christine had probably transformed into Pollyanna and run tattling to her, convincing her to change her mind. Not only that, but she would surely blab to Mom too the next chance she got.

Seamus was doomed, and there was nothing I could do about it.

At that point, I was just too stressed and sleep-deprived to take it anymore. Whatever flimsy pillar of strength that had been holding me up completely dissolved, and I lurched forward with a giant sob, slumping over the tabletop.

I could hear Seamus whine and feel his tongue lap against my hand. Poor guy. How would he feel when I ended up taking him back to the shelter? Would he think I was giving up on him like the creep who'd had him before? Just thinking about it tore me up inside. In my mind I could see the sadness in his chocolate brown eyes as they carried him off to the gas chamber, or lethal injection gurney, or whatever ghastly device they used, and I started crying even harder.

"Katie?"

It took me a moment to realize someone else was there. Eventually I felt Seamus strain hard on his leash and glanced up. Matt was standing at the opposite side of the table, damp with sweat, his beautiful hooded eyes scrunched with worry.

"What's wrong?" he asked.

I was *not* glad to see him. Not like this, with me bawling like an infant. I knew my face was a wet, splotchy mess, and my lips and shoulders were twitching uncontrollably.

He circled the table and stood behind me. "Come on, tell me," he murmured.

I tried to tell him I was fine, but the concern in his voice only made me feel more pathetic. All that came out was a series of shrill throat rattles that disintegrated into more sobs. I surrendered my head to my arms again, wanting to hide and hoping Matt would just get a clue and go away.

Instead I felt the bench shimmy as he sat down next to me.

"Hey . . . ," he said softly in my ear. His arm draped across my back, and his hand began gently stroking my shoulder. "It's okay," he repeated over and over.

The weight of his arm and his gentle tone melted my feeble resistance, and I collapsed against his shirt, allowing myself to be comforted by him. Little by little, my blubbering lost force and volume until I was left limp and sniffling in his arms. As I came back to the present, I also became overly conscious of the fact that Matt was holding me close—and that I most likely resembled some B-movie swamp creature.

I pulled away from him rather shakily and sat upright, swiping my cheeks with my hands.

"You all right?" he asked, still lightly rubbing my back.

I kept on wiping my eyes, trying to avoid looking at him. "Yeah," I said croakily. "Sorry I got you all soaked."

"Are you kidding?" He chuckled and tugged on the front of his T-shirt. "I was already wet. I'm just sorry you had to smell my sweat."

I laughed weakly and snuck him a small smile, not quite so self-conscious anymore. All that crying had left me drained and headachy, and now that Matt's strong arm wasn't around me, I felt strangely exposed.

Seamus scooted forward and shoved his head in between us, letting us know he was still there.

"It's okay," I said, scratching his back. My throat constricted automatically, and I stopped myself from looking into his eyes in order to stave off another crying jag.

Matt sat back and drummed his palms against his knees. "You want to tell me what's going on?"

*No,* I thought. Only, I sort of felt like I had to after all that. Besides, Matt already knew more about my situation than practically anyone—except maybe Christine, and she *definitely* wasn't all that sympathetic at the moment.

Taking a deep, shuddery breath, I launched into the whole epic disaster: about Scamus eating Christine's collection and how it would surely blow his probation with Mrs. Krantz; about how Christine would probably ruin things with Mom and get me sent away to San Marcos; and about how my lame attempt to save Seamus had totally blown up in my face, and now he would be euthanized anyway.

My voice was shaky and squeaky, but I somehow managed to tell him everything without the tears restarting. Through it all Matt listened patiently, watching me with those mournful green eyes of his.

"I don't understand," he said when I'd finished. "How did he get out of your room?"

"I don't know," I whined. "I guess the latch didn't engage all the way."

"But you said the radio trick worked before, right?"

"Yeah."

"So if you fixed it so he couldn't get out again, it would probably still work, right?"

"Maybe. But that doesn't help the fact that I can't make him behave. Let's face it, he's a major handful."

Matt reached over and patted Seamus's head. "Aw, he isn't so bad. I heard about some other dog named William that's been terrorizing the park kids. Just be glad he isn't like that."

"Uh . . . yeah." I swallowed hard and glanced nervously around the park.

A breeze wafted over us, shaking the leaves of the nearby live oak. Behind me I could hear the shrieks and laughter of kids splashing in the pool. It didn't seem right that the day should be so beautiful. I wanted steely clouds and menacing thunder—something that would fit my misery.

"I had a hard time with Jessie in the beginning, too," Matt said, staring off toward the playscape, his brows knitted in deep thought. "She used to jump our fence and roam around the neighborhood. Then my parents made me take her to obedience class, and everything got easier." His gaze pivoted toward me. "You might think about signing Seamus up for something like that."

"I don't know," I said, shaking my head. "Even if it worked, what about Mrs. Krantz and Christine? I'm totally out of chances with them."

"What if you offered to pay Mrs. Krantz a pet deposit? I had to do that last year to keep Jessie in my old apartment."

I bit my thumbnail, thinking about all the money I'd already spent on Seamus. My savings was rapidly depleting. "How much exactly?"

"Maybe a couple hundred dollars or so. Enough to cover expenses if he should tear stuff up or break anything."

I remembered the broken cat figurine. A couple hundred bucks would take a huge bite out of my account, but I could absorb it. Besides, I probably owed Mrs. Krantz for her pain and suffering anyway. "I could do that," I said. "But what about Christine?"

He lifted his shoulders. "I don't know. But don't give up. Try to make it up to her some way."

"Yeah, right," I grumbled. The only way that would happen was if she were to come home and find little Seamus pieces all over the rug.

All those days I'd thought I'd been seeing hatred in Matt's face when he looked at Seamus, but I'd been wrong. Now, remembering Christine's scrunched, maroon expression, I realized *that* was hatred. Christine clearly despised Seamus. It would be impossible to change that. If only I could make her see him the way I did. Or the way Matt did.

Just then, a flare of brilliance blazed through my mind. Suddenly I knew exactly what to do. It made total sense. The answer to all my problems.

I pivoted around and looked directly into Matt's eyes. "You should take Seamus," I said, a fresh sob catching in my throat.

His face fell slack. "What?"

I squeezed my trembling lips together and nodded. "You should. You're so much better than I am. I totally suck at taking care of him, you know it yourself. And Seamus really likes you. And I could still visit him. And then he won't have to be put to sleep. And—"

"Whoa. Hold on." Matt held up his hands. "First off, I don't think you suck at this. Second . . . I can't take him. I just can't. I'm sorry, but I just don't want another dog after . . ." His voice trailed off into the breeze. Matt raked his fingers through his hair and blew out his breath. "Tell you what. Try the obedience class. If it doesn't work, I promise I'll help you find a good home for him. Someplace where he'll be safe. Deal?"

I looked over at Seamus, who lay flopped against the table, his eyes half closed. He looked so relaxed and carefree. Happy, even. I'd do anything to keep him feeling that way.

I couldn't give up. Not yet.

"Okay. Deal."

I stood in front of Mrs. Krantz's door, shuffling my feet and chewing on my first two fingernails. Closing my eyes, I carefully reviewed my prepared speech one last time before rapping on the wooden cat cutout. Then I stepped back and held my breath, my heart walloping against my ribs as if it, too, were knocking to be let in.

It seemed as if days passed. Finally, the door opened and Mrs. Krantz's owl-like eyes peered out at me. "Oh, Katie. It's you." She opened the door wide and gestured behind her. "Come in, please."

"Thanks." I cautiously strode into the floral-smelling living room, stopping at the coffee table. Mrs. B sat curled in her rocker. She gave me an indifferent glance and went back to her nap.

A trembly feeling came over me, as if I were an escaped felon returning to the scene of my crime. I inhaled deeply and focused on the frayed ends of my pants. I couldn't let anything throw me. I was on a mission and had to see it through.

Mrs. Krantz shut the door and trotted up behind me. "I've been expecting you. I suppose you're here to hear my decision concerning your dog?"

"Yes, ma'am."

"Well, then. Please have a seat."

I perched on the end of the parlor chair while she settled into the exact spot on the loveseat she'd taken the day before. I noticed the piece of gauze taped to her arm and felt the familiar dread creeping back inside me. *Stay cool,* I told myself. *Keep focused.*

"So where is . . . um . . ." She paused, pushing her glasses up to the bridge of her nose. "What is his name again?"

"Seamus," I replied. "He's at home in my room." *With the door shut tight,* I added silently.

Luckily Christine wasn't home. She was gone when we returned to the condo, giving me ample time to clean up the wiener dog slaughter and prepare my little plea for Mrs. Krantz. But I kept an ear out for any sounds on the landing in case she should return bearing some sort of weapon.

"Mrs. Krantz," I began, sitting up straight. "I realize it might be too late and that your mind may already be made up, but if I may, I would like to say a few things regarding Seamus."

She looked surprised. "Very well. Go right ahead."

My hands shook in my lap and a warm tingle spread down from my scalp. This was going to be harder than I thought. "I . . . I want to apologize again for the distress Seamus has already caused you," I began hoarsely.

She nodded primly.

I cleared my throat and resumed. "And I want you to know that I take this matter very seriously and plan to do everything I can to prevent any more problems." I paused to take a breath. When I'd rehearsed, I'd tried to come off as calm and proper as Christine when she's playing her priggish church-mouse role, but it just wasn't working. My words tumbled out on top of one another, leaving me gasping after every sentence. Still I kept at it. "I'm enrolling Seamus in an obedience class and will make sure he either stays safely in my room or under my control at all times. Plus, also, I would like to give you this." I leaned forward and held out the crumpled and slightly sweaty check I'd been keeping in my grasp.

Mrs. Krantz took it from me. Repositioning her glasses, she studied it carefully. When she glanced up again, her forehead was puckered in bewilderment. "I'm afraid I don't understand. Two hundred dollars? What is this exactly?"

"A deposit," I replied. "To insure against any damage Seamus might cause—um, or has already caused. For example, I already owe you for the broken kitten figurine."

"That old thing? Please, dear. It was an accident." She tried to hand the check back to me.

I held up my hand. "No. Keep it. It's to show my good faith. If Seamus does anything wrong, I want to take full responsibility and cover all the expenses."

"Well . . . all right." She sat back and placed the check on the table in front of her. "Of course, you're assuming I will allow him to stay."

Another wave of prickles swept over me. "I   I'm sorry. I meant *if* you let me keep him."

She sat silently for a moment, scanning me with her bulbous eyes. I tried to meet her gaze bravely, but my body slowly withered until I was hunkered against the back of the chair. *I blew it,* I cried inwardly. *She's going to say no. She's probably debating whether to let* me *stay.*

"Katie, dear," she began, finally. "I think you are a very sweet, responsible girl."

My stomach clenched. *Here it comes,* I thought. *The big "but."*

". . . and I think you will do a fine job with Seamus," she concluded. "He can stay."

*She—what?* "Really?" I asked skeptically. I was half scared she would shout "No!" and start cackling maniacally, then say, "Yow! Girl, you should have seen your face! I totally had you going!"

"Yes." She stood and smoothed her long denim skirt, signaling the end of our conversation. Her mouth was curled in a small, almost smug smile, making her look a lot like Mrs. B. It was almost as if she knew she was blowing my mind—and enjoying it.

"Oh my God! Thank you so much!" My chest

swelled with an intense, unrestrained joy. Before I realized what I was doing, I leaped from the chair and ran to her, gathering her petite frame in a hug.

"Oh!" she exclaimed, laughing lightly.

"I know I can do this," I said, to myself as well as to her. "I know I can make this work."

"Of course," she said, patting my arm. "You certainly showed a lot of courage coming over and presenting your case like that. But you know, I was going to let him stay anyway."

"You were?"

She chuckled again. "Yes."

"So you haven't spoken with Christine today?"

"Christine?" She looked confused. "No, I haven't. Why?"

My body trilled with a second, lesser shock. Christine hadn't told her! At least, not yet. "No reason," I said quickly. "Thank you again, Mrs. Krantz. I promise I'll do my best."

"I know, dear." She walked me to the door and opened it. "Good luck now. Let me know if I can do anything to help. I know how it is to love a pet no matter what they do."

I stepped out into the landing and turned to face her. *She really understands,* I thought, looking at her kind, sympathetic expression. "I can't tell you how much I appreciate this," I said softly. "I hope . . . I hope I don't let you down."

"You won't," she said, before disappearing behind

the door.

I stood there, smiling to myself. It felt good to have someone believe in me.

Now I just had to believe in myself.

"The main purpose behind Alpha Dog," Mr. Willard was saying in his nasal monotone, "is to strengthen and clarify the owner-dog relationship."

Seamus chose that very moment to heave against his leash, sending me topping into a large metal trash can. The resulting clang echoed throughout the unfurnished wood-paneled classroom and beyond.

Mr. Willard paused and looked right at us. So did the others in the class, including, it seemed, the dogs. Five minutes into our first session and we were already causing a scene.

"Sorry," I said, my cheeks broiling. I straightened up and tried to pull Seamus sideways a few feet, a safe distance away from the trash can. Unfortunately he was busy trying to sniff a scared-looking corgi beside us, and it ended up taking quite a bit of time. Eventually he gave up and began wandering in little circles, wrapping my legs with his leash.

Mr. Willard waited until we were relatively calm and quiet before resuming his speech. "Stop and think for a moment," he said, pacing back and forth across the front of the room with his hands clasped behind his back and his squat body stooped forward slightly. He reminded me of one of those sheet-metal ducks people shoot at in those carnival games. *P-ting!* I thought as he stopped and turned to go the other way. *P-ting!* "I want you to think," he added, pausing dramatically, "about why you are here."

I huffed in frustration as I slid two loops of Seamus's leash off my legs. It was a no-brainer why I was there. Seamus was so spastic, our walks were like extreme cardio workouts. Every item of clothing I'd brought to Austin now had chew holes. My dog's snoring was waking me up several times a night, so I was starting to fall asleep during my classes. And my roommate was probably plotting our murders this very minute. All just for starters.

But I did wonder why the others had come. Besides Seamus, there were four other dogs in the class: the corgi; a lazy-looking basset hound; and Natasha, the Great Pyrenees, with her beautiful long, white-blond fur and perpetual drool lines. Natasha had been the first dog we met when we walked into the classroom. She'd bounded right up to us, all one hundred pounds of her, and proceeded to slobber all over Seamus as if he were her very own lollipop. Roughly translated, their brief introduction went something like this:

NATASHA:   DAAAH-link! Geev to me large kiss! *(Pounces on Seamus, licking and salivating profusely)*

SEAMUS:   Aaaaaauuuugh!!!! *(Runs between Mom's legs, knocking her to her knees)*

And last, but not least, there was Ollie, Mr. Willard's border collie. Most of the time Ollie sat slightly behind and to the side of his master, looking bored and a little disgusted by the rest of the pack until Mr. Willard would call him for a demonstration. Then Ollie would eagerly trot forward and flawlessly perform the trick like some state-of-the-art cyberdog.

Because Alpha Dog was one of the university's community classes, the dog owners were as diverse as the dogs. Natasha's owner was Barry, a tall, bearded, painfully shy man in his mid-thirties. The basset hound belonged to a huffy-looking woman in an expensive suit who appeared to have a cell phone surgically attached to her right ear. The only other youngish person there besides me was the corgi's owner, a cute, athletically built guy who reminded me of a nineteen-year-old Will Smith. "Aw, come on, Floyd, chill," he would say whenever the corgi got spooked—which seemed to be any time another dog looked at him.

"Canines, as you know, are pack animals," Mr. Willard said, resuming his waddling. "They are social creatures who take their behavior cues from the other, stronger dogs around them. It may surprise you to realize that *you* are part of their pack. You have to take the lead. If *you* do not teach them proper behavior, they will never learn."

I thought about what he said as I reached down to pet Seamus and furtively unwind the leash from my leg again. What exactly did he mean about me being part of the pack? Was he implying that I should act like a dog? I envisioned myself tumbling about on the condo carpet, going, "Watch me roll over, Seamus. See? Like *this.*" Somehow, I really didn't think that would work.

"How many of you have had problems with your dog jumping on people?" Mr. Willard asked, halting his laps long enough to survey us.

Everyone but the corgi's owner raised a hand.

"How many of you have discovered your dog chewing on something he shouldn't?"

Everyone raised a hand.

"How many of you find that your dog ignores you when you give a command?"

Again, all of us raised our hands.

"Have any of you taught your dog a command?"

Everyone looked at one another. Finally the cell phone lady raised her professionally manicured right hand. "I have," she said.

"What is the command?"

"I taught him to sit," she said with a superior-sounding lilt in her voice.

We all looked down at the basset hound. It looked like he did nothing but sit.

"I see," Mr. Willard remarked. He also seemed a little skeptical. "Now then, the first thing you need to do if you want to train your dog," he went on, "is take control. When you are in this class or practicing lessons learned in this class, your dog should be wearing its special choke collar and leash."

He clasped his hands behind his back and slowly rotated on his heels, inspecting each dog-owner pair. When he got to me and Seamus, he paused and walked up to us. I ducked my head reflexively. I knew exactly what was coming.

"Where is his choke collar?" he asked.

"In my backpack," I replied, gesturing to where it lay against the wall.

He looked a little perturbed. "Why isn't your dog wearing it?"

"I just . . . I thought it seemed sort of . . . mean."

It was as if I'd hit a magic switch. Mr. Willard turned to the rest of the class and announced loudly, "Disciplining your dog is not being cruel. These methods you will learn, while they may seem harsh at first, are necessary to establish the fact that you are in control." He said all this with the repetitive cadence of a practiced speech. Apparently I hadn't been the only one to have such misgivings. Pivoting back toward me, he said more quietly, "Don't worry. You aren't hurting him when he wears the collar. Think of it as a wall. You can't hurt someone with a wall, although they can walk into it. But then they learn not to. Do you understand?"

"I guess so," I mumbled. Actually I had no idea what he was rambling on about, but I realized I had to do what he said if I was going to give this class a real chance.

"Good." He smiled encouragingly. "Go ahead and put the collar on him, and we'll get started on the first lesson."

I wrestled Seamus over to my pack and pulled out the choke collar. It looked innocent enough, but its name conjured up images of iron shackles and metal racks and other sadistic devices. *It's just a wall,* I told myself, still not quite grasping the metaphor.

"It's all right. Come here," I said, pulling Seamus closer. He seemed to pick up on my thinly veiled trepidation and went all stiff. His legs locked straight and his head jerked back. I pulled the leash hand over hand and he glided toward me, like the incredible unbending dog.

I should have known better than to unclip him from his buckle collar without somehow restraining him, but everyone was watching and I wasn't thinking straight. Maybe I just thought he'd remain statuelike long enough for me to switch collars. I don't know. In any case, the second I undid the clasp, he bolted away so fast, I could have sworn I saw one of those curlicue cartoon streaks. Round the classroom he ran, skirting the corgi, leaping over the bassett hound, and giving Natasha a wide berth.

"Seamus! Come here!" I yelled futilely. I ran after him.

By the time I finally trapped him and held him down long enough to attach the new collar and leash, the class had wasted a good ten minutes waiting on us.

I was beginning to wonder if this was worth the time and the tuition of one hundred thirty-five dollars. What if Seamus flunked? What would happen then? And why did I have to get professional help anyway? Why couldn't he just do what I asked?

Suddenly I was beginning to understand some of the frustration my mom must feel toward me.

After class we headed to the park to practice. With the choke collar on, Seamus did a better job of not bolting and throwing me off guard. Any time he tried, the collar would catch and he would automatically rear back.

I still felt guilty, though. It seemed like he'd been flashing me mournful looks ever since I first wrestled the thing onto him. However, I also realized this could be the first dog walk where I didn't come home limping, bruised, bleeding or mud-stained. I had to admit it was working.

I walked Seamus to the corner farthest away from the pool and playground—right beside the table where I'd cried all over Matt only a few days earlier. Just looking at it made my skin go tingly.

We came to a halt a couple of yards from the table. After scanning the area to make sure no one was watching, I turned toward Seamus. "Sit?" I tried, hoping I wouldn't have to use the choker.

Seamus cocked his head at me, but otherwise didn't move.

"Sit," I said again.

He stamped his feet excitedly and barked.

"Okay, okay. We'll do it the hard way."

I pressed down on his rear end while yanking up with the leash. "Sit," I said, drawing the word out.

Seamus sat.

"Yes! Good boy!" I stroked his back vigorously.

I made him sit over and over again, praising him each time and rewarding him with pats and cuddles. Then it was on to the homework: teaching Seamus to *stay* sitting.

I dug the folded photocopied sheet from my pack and read Mr. Willard's directions. They seemed easy enough. Get the dog to sit. Signal for him to stay. Move a short distance away, making sure the dog remains sitting. Count to five.

"We can do that, right boy?" I asked, returning the

paper to my book bag. Seamus smiled and wagged his back end.

"Okay, boy. Sit." I pushed and pulled him into the correct stance. "Good! Now st—"

Seamus jumped on me, panting and wriggling, eager for his reward.

"No! Not yet. You have to stay. *Stay*."

I decided to try again, only this time I wouldn't praise him until after he stayed put.

"Sit," I said, repositioning him. I turned and walked a few steps away. But when I spun back around, there he was right behind me, looking oh-so-proud of himself.

"No!" I groaned, grabbing a handful of my hair.

"Hey! What's going on?" a familiar voice sounded behind us.

I looked back and saw Matt jogging toward us in his running attire, his skin dewy with sweat.

As usual, my heart did its little happy dance at seeing him—not unlike Seamus's hyper, slobbery greetings whenever I returned from classes. But at the same time, I was a little annoyed by the interruption.

"Hi," I said. "We're just practicing."

"Obedience class?" He stooped over to pet Seamus, who was literally choking himself trying to get at Matt.

"Yeah. We had our first class today."

"How'd it go?"

"Uh . . . pretty good." I could feel my cheeks ignite. "Okay, I guess."

"So, what are you practicing?"

"The sit and stay."

"Cool. Want some help?"

"No. It's okay. You don't have to."

"I don't mind. I just finished my run and I don't need to be anywhere for a while." He gave Seamus a final pat and sat down on top of the picnic table. "Let's see what he can do."

"Okay," I said, biting back my annoyance. I really didn't want or need an audience right then. Or the distraction of a really cute guy.

I stood next to Seamus, leash in hand. "Sit," I said, moving him into place. Slowly, quietly, I backed away and held up my left hand. "Stay."

As soon as the word left my mouth, Seamus ran right up to me.

"No!" I groaned irritably. "Listen, Seamus. Sit." He sat. "Now *stay*." I held my palm right in front of his face. He licked it and leaped to his feet. "No, no, no!"

My face was roasting and I refused to glance over at Matt lest I spontaneously combust from embarrassment. This just couldn't be *that* hard. Maybe if I tried again, this time taking it real slow.

"Sit." At least that part was going well. I barely needed to touch Seamus now to get him to obey. "Now . . ." I stepped in front of him and hunkered down.

"You know what you should do?" Matt said.

I ignored him and held up my right palm. "St-a-a-y—

*oof!"*

Seamus bounded toward me so fast, it caught me off guard and knocked me flat. I heard a yelp as my left arm flailed backward, yanking the leash and choke collar. For a long moment, I just lay there, staring at the sky overhead and quietly fuming. Suddenly Matt's face loomed into view.

"Can I make a suggestion?" he asked, holding out a hand.

I grabbed hold and let him hoist me up. "What?" I grumbled, trying to avoid his eyes.

"Your voice is too soft. You don't sound firm enough."

"Fine. Whatever," I grumbled.

"Don't give up. Try again, and this time say it like you really mean it." He sat back down on the bench, resting his elbows on the tabletop behind him. All he needed was a box of Milk Duds and a bucket of popcorn.

Thankfully, Seamus was still in one piece and didn't seem to be harboring any ill will over the sudden choking. Dusting the dirt off my shorts, I went to stand beside him.

"Walk like you mean it," Matt called out. "Move like you're the boss."

I bit my lip and started pulling up on the leash while simultaneously pressing on Seamus's haunches. "Sit," I said.

"Hear the way your voice rises up at the end? You

sound like you're asking a question instead of giving a command."

I gritted my teeth as I raised my palm toward Seamus. "Stay."

Out of the corner of my eye, I could see Matt shake his head. "You did it again. You sound real unsure of yourself. If you listen to your instincts, you—"

*"Do you mind?"* I whirled around, shouting at him. "How can I even hear my instincts with you talking all the time?"

Even as I yelled, I knew I was freaking a little too much, but I couldn't help it. All my frustration had built to a critical mass and was now spouting out of its own accord. Matt was a sweet guy, not to mention really hot, but I was getting *real* tired of him wandering into the middle of my most embarrassing moments.

"I didn't ask to be coached!" I went on. "Believe it or not, I want to do this by myself!"

For a few seconds, my voice rang out over the treetops. Then it was like someone hit a giant Mute button. Mockingbirds quit singing, cicadas quit whirring, even the wind stopped rustling the leaves. There was only the faint throbbing of blood through my skull and Seamus's lonely whimper.

Matt's grin widened as he stood and walked past us, heading for the sidewalk. "See?" he said, breaking into a run. "I knew you had it in you."

A mixture of shame and anger fizzed through me as I watched him jog away. Why, why, *why* did I have to have some wiggy meltdown every time I saw the guy? Any day now his psych professors would be knocking on my door wanting to escort me away as their latest case study.

I felt a pull on the leash and looked down at Seamus. For some reason he was all worked up. He was wriggling about as much as his choke collar would allow and his mouth was hanging open in a wide, panting grin. If it were at all possible, I'd think he was laughing at me.

"Oh, what are you staring at?" I snapped. *"Sit!"*

Seamus sat.

I blinked in disbelief. It actually happened. He obeyed—without any help from me.

With sudden conviction, I held out my palm. "Stay!" I commanded. Taking a deep breath, I walked a couple feet away and turned around.

And wonder upon wonders . . . Seamus stayed.

I practically skipped all the way back to the condo. Seamus knew "sit"! He could even stay—not indefinitely, but at least to the count of five. He was also doing a pretty good job of heeling on the leash. From the park to our building, I only stumbled twice!

After witnessing these minor miracles in the park, I was buzzing with all the mad joy of a religious convert. In fact, my arms had been pumping so wide as I pranced rapturously down the sidewalk that I accidentally choked

Seamus a couple of times.

"Good doggie! Yes! Goo' boy!" I was still saying as we walked into the condo.

Christine was sitting on the couch. As soon as we entered, she rose up and turned to face me, propping her foot and folding her arms across her chest so that her elbows and knee were cocked toward me like bony artillery.

"I need to talk to you," she said, her eyes narrowed into thin slits.

My newfound elation spurted out of me so fast, I wouldn't have been surprised to hear a whoopee cushion noise.

Ever since the stuffed dachshund slaughter, I'd been avoiding Christine as best as I could. I got up extra early, ate in my room, and only ventured into the living room if I knew she was out with Robot. I'd been afraid of exactly this: a nose-to-nose confrontation. Because I knew I could never win. Not with Christine. I could only hope to avoid it indefinitely.

And yet, somehow, I was managing to meet her gaze head-on.

"Okay. Let's talk," I said rather calmly.

Christine lifted her chin as if pointing another weapon at me. She didn't seem to have expected this reaction.

"It's about your dog," she said, glancing down at Seamus long enough for the disgust to register on her face. "He's been a total pain in the butt since you brought him here and you know it."

Instinctively, I broke my gaze and stared down at the floor. She was right. Seamus had been a terror. Although I was hoping that would change now.

"He tore up three of my favorite wiener dogs," she continued, picking up strength and speed. "And one of them I'd had for eight years. Can you imagine what it was like for me to find it all shredded up like that?"

I shuddered slightly, remembering Christine's hysterical screams, the trail of plush body parts—every ghastly detail. "Sorry," I said, then immediately regretted it. How many times would I have to apologize? I was getting a little tired of it.

"You should be sorry!" she cried, her mouth twitching and her nostrils flaring wide enough to emit flames. She took a deep breath and moved her hands to her hips. I could tell she was tensing up for the final assault. "You can't keep him," she blurted. "You have to take him back to the shelter."

And there it was. She'd unleashed her ultimate threat. The bomb to end all battles.

For just a nanosecond or two, I felt truly licked—the exact same belly-up, pathetic defeat I'd felt when Chuck broke up with me. And then . . . it passed. I didn't have to do her bidding. I was not some cowed dachshund she could boss around. *I* could be the Alpha Dog here.

I picked up Seamus and looked her right in the eye. "No," I said. "I'm not going to." I didn't sound like me at all. It was strange, like I was a life-sized marionette for a loudmouthed puppeteer.

Christine's entire face seemed to lengthen. Her mouth dropped open and her eyebrows flew to the middle of her forehead. "What do you mean, you're not going to? You have to! If you don't, I'll . . . I'll tell Mrs. Krantz!"

"I've already talked to her," I said calmly. "I paid her a pet deposit and showed her that I'd registered him in an obedience class. She said he could stay."

I set Seamus on the floor and took the choke collar off him, replacing it with the buckle collar and leash I'd fished out of my backpack. I couldn't believe how cool-headed I was. Maybe I'd just been pushed and pushed so much, I had nowhere left to go and finally had to stand and fight. Or maybe I'd lost my mind and hadn't realized it yet.

Christine charged around the couch. "You can't do that!" she said, sounding almost whiny. "If you don't get rid of him, I'll tell your mom!"

My hands shook ever so slightly as I finished clipping on Seamus's old collar. I felt the familiar wringing sensation in my gut, and then, just like before, it vanished.

I walked Seamus over to the yellow armchair and sat down. "Go ahead," I said, scooping Seamus into my lap. "Tell her I said hi."

I knew what I was doing was dangerous. Mrs. Krantz I could handle. Christine I was somehow handling. But Mom?

And yet, what did it really matter? I lost either way. Backing down to Christine would mean giving up Seamus, and I wasn't prepared to do that without a fight. I could only hope she just didn't have it in her.

"You are being so unfair!" Christine shouted, marching over to us. "That is just so wrong! You can't make me live with him! It's selfish!"

"*Selfish?*" I set Seamus down and got to my feet, staring directly into Christine's wild-eyed, pink-tinged face. It suddenly felt as if that one word had stabbed right through me, tearing open a jagged hole, and all my pent-up fury came blasting out. "You mean selfish like inviting three guys to crash here whenever they feel like it? Letting them eat your roommate's food and use all the hot water? You mean that kind of selfish?"

I was really yelling now, even though I was smiling and over-enunciating like a scary schoolteacher. Christine's head slowly retracted and her shoulders seemed to be folding inward.

"Because if that's the kind of selfish you mean, go right ahead!" I continued ranting. "Tell my mom! Tell the world! And then . . . then it'll be *my* turn. I'll tell Mrs. Krantz and Mrs. B and anyone else who cares all about your selfish ways. It'll be a contest! A pageant! We'll let the people decide who's the most selfish one of all!" I took a step toward Christine, still wearing my loony Jack Nicholson grin, and made a big sweeping flourish with my arms. "Come on! What do you say?"

By now Christine looked small and concave. She eyed me warily for a few seconds before marching off to her room and slamming the door behind her.

I blew out my breath and closed my eyes. My head was pounding at the temples, but overall I felt kind of good.

"Well, buddy. If nothing else, maybe I bought you a little time." I looked over at Seamus. He was standing as far back as the leash would allow, whimpering mournfully. Poor guy. It couldn't have been fun for him to see me lose all control like that.

*Control . . .*

And right then, I got it. The whole Alpha Dog thing. I finally understood the "wall" and the collar and why it supposedly worked. Seamus *needed* me to be in charge. He needed to know that he was in good hands.

"Sit!" I commanded.

And he sat.

"Good boy."

I just hoped he got to stay.

That night when Mom called for a report, Christine was still stewing in her room. I lied and said she was at her Bible group.

"Again? She's been awfully busy with that group lately. Oh well, I'll just talk to her later. So how are you enjoying your classes?" she asked.

"They're fine."

"Have you given more thought to what you might want to major in?"

"I've been thinking about journalism."

"Oh no, you don't want to do that. They make so little money. Besides, you have to be a real go-getter, and I'm afraid that's just not you, honey."

"Way to support me, Mom," I said, then yawned loudly.

"What's wrong? You sound sleepy."

"I am."

"I knew it! You've been staying up late, haven't you?"

I shut my eyes and grabbed a tuft of hair on the top of my head. Stupid, stupid. Why'd I have to go admitting I was tired? But that was the thing. I was too tired to have my guard up. "No, Mom. I'm not staying up late. I just haven't been sleeping all that well. It's . . . um . . . it's just extra noisy around here. You know, traffic and all."

"You and your father. The McAllisters always were light sleepers," she muttered, as if suddenly angry at my dad for this glitch in my genetic makeup. "You know, I have just the remedy for that."

"You do?" I asked, feeling hopeful.

"Yes. You should come home this weekend. You could go to bed early in your own bedroom, without all that big-city noise. I'll pick you up Friday after my hair appointment."

"No! I can't leave," I blurted out, my voice shaky with panic.

"And why not?"

I paused. Should I just go ahead and confess about Seamus? I had to tell her sometime. "Because I have . . . I have . . ." My heart seemed to leap into my esophagus, making it hard to talk. " I have . . . some writing labs I have to go to," I finished somewhat lamely.

"Oh. Well, good for you. Classes are more important than any visiting. I remember. I didn't graduate with honors by skipping school, you know."

"I know," I mumbled. "Hey, Mom. I really need to get off the phone. I have a ton of studying to do and I want to get to bed early," I lied, knowing being the ultra-good Stepford daughter was the only way to beg out of a conversation with her.

"I think that's wise, dear. Hang on, your father has something to tell you."

I heard a rustling sound and then my dad's voice came on the line. "Hey, Kit-Kat. How are you?"

"Good."

"Who're you going to root for when Texas baseball plays Notre Dame next week?"

"The Fighting Irish, of course."

"Good girl. Bye, Sweetheart. Love you."

"Love you, too, Dad."

I could hear my mom scolding him. "Is that all you're going to say to her?" She sighed loudly and got back on the receiver. "Okay, then. We'll talk later. Get some sleep, sweetie."

"I will. Bye, Mom."

As I hung up the phone, my hands felt weighty with guilt. Why couldn't I just tell the truth about Seamus? I couldn't put it off forever.

I just needed a little more time, that's all. Just a few more days. Or couple of weeks. A month tops . . .

# 10

"Ready?" Mr. Willard looked somewhat fearfully at Seamus and me and scratched the side of his head. Along with pacing, I'd noticed he tended to do that when anxious. He was one of those men who tried to make up for being bald by letting the rest of his hair get long and bushy. Thanks to our little group of canine misfits, he usually abused his head so much throughout our lessons, he'd look like some washed-out Krusty the Klown by the end of them.

"We're ready," I answered, holding Seamus's leash firmly in my hand.

"All right," he said in a lackluster voice. "Begin."

I took off walking around the room with Seamus,

weaving around the others, who stood in a very loose circle. We were spending the hour doing heeling exercises, and Seamus was the worst of the bunch—except for maybe Natasha, and that wasn't totally her fault. She was just so huge, a simple turn of her Volkswagen-sized head would send poor Barry scrambling sideways.

"Heel," I said as we wended our way around Yoda, the bassett hound, and his mommy. "Heel. Heel."

Seamus tried to stop and sniff them, and I turned toward him, ready to correct his behavior with some sharp words.

"No!" called Mr. Willard, grabbing a tuft of hair on the back of his head. "Don't wait for him! Snap the leash!"

I nodded and gave a quick jerk on the choke collar. "Heel," I said a little more strongly.

"Good. Now faster. Faster," Mr. Willard cried out. "Take the lead. Make him catch up with you."

I quickened my pace. Sure enough, Seamus lagged, distracted by Floyd, the corgi, who was cowering against his master's legs.

"Snap the leash!" Mr. Willard shouted.

Again I jerked the line, somewhat reluctantly. I still felt like a big meanie every time I half choked my dog. It worked, though, and Seamus caught up to me.

"Good," Mr. Willard said. "All right, now. Slow down."

We were making a curve and approaching Natasha

and Barry. Natasha saw us coming and smacked her jowls eagerly, her drool making a small puddle on the floor in front of her. Seamus seemed to notice and sped up, veering away from the amorous Great Pyrenees.

"Snap it! Snap it!" Mr. Willard cried, tugging his hair with both hands. He was wearing the cramped, puckered expression of someone watching an impending train wreck.

I gave a good sideways yank and corrected Seamus's trajectory. As we rounded Barry and Natasha, Seamus appeared to cringe slightly. Sure enough, just as we were even with the two of them, Natasha bounded forward and licked the side of Seamus's face. Seamus ducked his head, tucked his tail between his legs and dove between mine. The next thing I knew, I was falling face-forward, with chaos erupting all around me. I could hear Barry yelling, "No, Natasha!" and Mr. Willard shouting, "Snap it! Snap it!" Then Seamus let out a yowl as I hit the hardwood floor, jerking him backward by the choke collar.

I rolled over and untangled myself from the leash. Barry ran up and offered me a hand, stuttering and apologizing profusely. Meanwhile Natasha chased Seamus all around us.

"It's okay," I said as he helped me back up. "Really it's Seamus's fault. He drives the ladies crazy."

He laughed and pulled Natasha back to their spot.

Mr. Willard, who now resembled an electroshock-therapy patient, made me and Seamus run the gauntlet again. This time, it went much better. I wasn't as shy about snapping the leash, and when we headed toward Natasha, Barry commanded her to stay in a booming voice that surprised everyone, including a very obedient Natasha.

Soon we had rounded Mr. Willard and Ollie and returned to our spot in the circle. I stopped and Seamus came to a halt beside me.

"Sit!" I ordered.

Seamus immediately sat down and looked up at me with his baby-deer eyes, waiting for his praise.

"Good boy," I said.

The entire class clapped.

When we left the lecture hall, instead of going to the park to practice, I decided to take Seamus for a long walk.

I shielded my eyes as we crossed Guadalupe at Twenty-first, the afternoon sunshine bouncing off cars, shop windows, and flaxen-haired sorority girls. It was one of those beautiful, sparkling days the Texas Tourism Board loves to advertise. The kind that makes people run like lemmings into lakes, streams and swimming pools and plasters a big, dippy smile on everyone's face. At the corner we stopped and stared northward, down the seven-block stretch of Guadalupe's west side—more commonly known as the Drag.

I absolutely loved the Drag. I loved the dense cluster of bookstores, cheap eateries and hip boutiques; the commingling of various drool-inducing smells wafting out of its many ethnic restaurants; and the harsh symphony of street musicians, boom boxes, and thou-shouldst-repent soapbox ranters, underscored by a steady hum of traffic.

But most of all, I loved watching the people. You name it, the Drag had it. From pampered coeds scoping the latest fashions to chain-smoking philosophy majors debating Kierkegaard in the coffeehouses, to mumbling, disheveled drifters squatting in doorways. There was even a guy who liked to rollerblade up and down the bicycle lane wearing skimpy gold lamé shorts.

I'd gone to the Drag a few times with Mom to shop and once with Ariel to meet her older sister, but I hadn't really been able to explore it much since I moved down here—mainly because I knew I couldn't navigate the foot traffic with Seamus.

But now it was time to test that out.

"You can do it, buddy," I said to Seamus.

He lifted his shaggy triangle ears and gazed back at me.

"Good boy," I said, heading down the sidewalk. "Heel . . . heel."

At first it was scary. Throngs of people seemed to come right at us, as if some Hollywood director were standing atop a cherry picker a few blocks down yelling into a bullhorn. "Group of chatty Tri-Delts . . . go! Woman with six shopping bags . . . go! Lovey-dovey couple, fuse hands and . . . go!"

But then, when I realized Seamus was staying even with my ankle, it was great—exhilarating, even. I steered him effortlessly through the crowd and around parking meters, just like we practiced in class. Only once did I have to snap his leash—when he stopped to sniff a discarded, half-eaten taco.

By the time we reached the little plaza at Twenty-fourth Street, I felt like I'd been pumped full of helium. My chest was swollen with pride and I was praising Seamus over and over in a squeaky, munchkin voice. "Good boy! Good, *good* boy!"

Seamus grinned up at me, his back end swishing like a fish tail.

People continued to rush past us, many of them heading to and from the plaza, where over a dozen carts and kiosks had been set up, displaying all sorts of handcrafted wares. Feeling bold, I let Seamus into the mini marketplace.

It was much slower going than on the street. The cramped aisles and crowds of onlookers made it difficult to maneuver around. Seamus stayed close to my legs, his bristly fur tickling my skin. He appeared to be extra alert and cautious.

"Good boy," I continued praising.

It had been a while since I'd had the time or freedom to browse. I scanned the different items displayed on the cloth-covered tables. There were stalls full of beautiful silver jewelry, rainbow-colored tie-dyed shirts, milagros, Santeria candles, woodcuttings, pottery and hookah pipes. Everything looked exquisite in the liquid gold sunshine.

"Great dog," came a voice from behind me.

I spun around and spied a man sitting at an easel. He had extremely long, graying dark hair and crinkly blue eyes that seemed to be smiling even when his mouth wasn't.

"Thanks," I said, beaming like a proud mommy.

Seamus appeared to realize he was being talked about, and he strained to approach the guy. I knew in theory that I should snap the leash, but since he'd been behaving so well, I allowed him to lead me over there.

"What's his name?" the man asked as he scribbled something on his canvas.

"Seamus," I replied.

"Ah. A good Irish name. It fits him. It sounds intelligent, and I can tell this is one sharp little guy."

"Yeah, well, he's smarter than me, that's for sure," I said, reaching down to rub the soft fur behind Seamus's ears.

The man laughed. "Where did you get him?"

"The pound."

"Good for you." He grinned at me, his eyes scrunching into tiny starbursts. "You saved his life. That's the most powerful Karma of all—the holiest of mitzvahs. Maybe someday he'll do the same for you." He turned back to his easel and began scribbling furiously.

"Uh . . . maybe. I hope so." The guy was super nice, but he was obviously a wee bit of a crackpot.

I tried to picture Seamus performing some Lassie-like deed, like dragging me from a burning building or running for help while I slowly sank in quicksand. But I just couldn't. I knew Seamus cared for me in his own simple canine way, but a superhero he was not. Not when any rescue attempt could be easily foiled by a half-eaten taco.

"Here you go." The hippie guy stood up and handed me the drawing he'd been working on.

I gasped, then laughed. It was a caricature of Seamus and me. He'd exaggerated us perfectly. Seamus's wedge-shaped ears were as large as garden spades and his eyes and nose were like perfectly round buttons. For me he'd drawn a heart-shaped mouth and Tweety Bird eyes, and he'd definitely embellished my body curves. I looked like a grown-up, PG-13 version of Cindy Lou Who.

"You like it?" he asked, his eyes all twinkly.

"Yeah!" I exclaimed. Then suddenly it occurred to me that he probably wanted to sell it to me. "Oh, I'm sorry. I don't have any money. I hadn't planned on coming here, it was just an impulse decision."

"No, no. Take it. It's a gift." He placed his calloused fingers in the center of his Guatemalan shirt and bowed slightly.

I shook my head. "No, I couldn't do that. It's too nice." I tried to give it back to him but he just waved his hands.

"Please. It's yours. If you don't feel you should have it, give it to your boyfriend."

"I don't have a boyfriend," I said, thinking of Chuck. The usual pang came and went, but the squeezing sensation was less fierce—as if it had switched from a choke collar to a buckle one. "Nope. Seamus is the only guy I can handle right now."

He nodded. "I totally get it. I have four dogs waiting for me at home myself." He reached down and stroked Seamus's back. "It's great, isn't it? There's nothing as pure and unconditional as the love of a dog. You know, you should keep the drawing for him."

I looked down at Seamus, who was panting happily under the man's touch. The man was right. Seamus might have chewed up my stuff and complicated relationships with my landlady and roomie, but he would never purposefully hurt me.

"I think I will keep it," I said, holding the drawing to my chest and bowing to him the way he did to me. "Thank you."

"My pleasure."

I waved goodbye and tugged Seamus's leash, guiding him back toward Guadalupe.

At the southeast corner of the market, the crowd grew thicker. While I stood off to the side waiting for an opening, something glittered, catching my eye. At first I thought it was some trick of my vision—a special effect my brain threw in to commemorate my good mood. Then I turned and saw a stall of cut crystals. The afternoon sun angled in behind them, creating an explosion of tiny multihued sparkles. I couldn't help gawking.

"See anything you like?"

I squinted through the pyrotechnics at the cute, pixie-looking girl on the other side of the table.

"Yeah. But I'm just looking," I explained.

I was about to move on when I spotted a familiar elongated shape in the display case: a tubular piece of cut glass with stubby legs and long, flappy ears. It was a wiener dog, about the same length as a deck of cards, completely clear except for its nose, ears, tail and feet, which had been tinted a faint red color.

"Actually," I called out as she was turning away. "How much is this one?" I pointed to the dachshund.

"Let me check." She glanced at the paper it was standing on. "You're in luck. It's on sale for only forty-five dollars."

*Forty-five bucks?* I imagine that would have been a good price for someone who hadn't already shelled out half her summer funds on a new dog, dog classes, dog supplies, and a dog deposit. I wasn't even sure if I had enough money for my own food for the rest of the session. And Mom had made it absolutely clear that I was only to use the credit card for emergencies. Fifty bucks for a hunk of glass was out of the question.

But Christine would love it. And she deserved to have it. I knew there was no way I could replace the stuff Seamus had destroyed, but I could at least try to make it up to her in a small way.

I decided to buy it for her—as a peace offering.

"Do you take checks?" I asked, digging through my backpack.

"As long as you show an ID."

Just then, Seamus started growling and straining against the leash. A squirrel had scampered over to a nearby trash can and was busy ferreting out food.

"Seamus, sit," I ordered.

He glanced up at me and lowered his hind end.

"Stay," I said firmly, holding up my hand.

He swallowed and made a faint whining noise, but otherwise stayed put.

Holding the leash tight, I handed the vendor my hastily scribbled check and driver's license.

"Wow!" she exclaimed. "Your dog is so well behaved."

I looked back at him and smiled. Seamus saw me and pricked his ears, his tail sweeping back and forth against the stone walkway.

"Yeah," I agreed. "He is, isn't he?"

As I stood outside our door, I could hear muffled voices from within. Christine was definitely home. I walked into the condo with Seamus and saw her sitting on the couch with Robot. Lyle and Kinky sat in the flanking armchairs.

Immediately the room grew quiet.

"Hi," I said.

"Hey," the guys said back. Christine didn't say anything.

I set my keys on the console table and started changing Seamus into his buckle collar. The silence was unbearably strained. And it didn't help that Lyle, Kinky and Robot kept staring from me to Christine wearing identical eager-yet-tense expressions.

"Your mom called," Christine said without turning around, making it seem as if her voice was emanating from the back of her head.

"She did?" I asked, barely able to hear myself over my heartbeat.

*Did she sell me out? Is Mom on her way right now with an application to an all-girls boarding school in Denmark?*

"Don't worry." Christine laid her head against the arm of the sofa and looked at me. "I didn't rat on you or anything."

"Thanks," I said, trying to look casual. "I didn't think you had."

"Yeah, right." Christine's face smoothed in a semismile before she turned back around.

I finished with Seamus and set him out onto the balcony. Still no one talked, but at least some of the chill had left the air.

"Your dog seems different," Robot remarked in his accent. "You been giving him pills?"

"Uh-uh," I said, smiling. "We're taking obedience classes. He's getting pretty good at sitting and heeling. He's really pretty smart."

"Man, my brother's dog should take some of those," Kinky said. "Every time I go near him, he barks and runs away."

Lyle frowned at him. "Dude, *you* should take some of those classes. The dog doesn't like you 'cause you tried to put a shirt on him that one time."

As I slipped off my backpack, I felt the lump of Christine's present in the side pocket. "Hey, Christine," I said, pulling out the box. "I have something for you."

Her forehead crinkled in surprise. "For me?"

"It's just something I saw and thought you should have."

I handed it to her. She peered at me quizzically before lifting the lid off the box and pulling back the tissue paper. The wiener dog lay nestled on a bed of cotton. "Ohhh!" she exclaimed, picking it up. It sparkled in the lamplight as she slowly twisted it in her grasp. The guys huddled around for a closer look.

"I know it isn't the same. I know I can't make up for what Seamus did," I babbled, "but I just wanted to try to make it up to you a little."

"Thanks," she said. Her eyes were still a little guarded-looking, but her voice sounded softer than I'd ever heard it.

"You're welcome."

"*Awwww,* isn't that sweet?" Lyle said, his eyes

blinking mawkishly behind his glasses.

Robot nodded. "Bloody heartwarming, that is."

Kinky sniffled and wiped an imaginary tear from his eye.

"Cut it out," Christine snapped, giving Robot a shove.

"Yeah," I jumped in. "Go watch *Zoom* or something."

"Actually, we've got to go soon, love," Robot said, stabbing out his cigarette on the top of an empty Dr Pepper can. "We've got a sound check in less than an hour."

"You guys have a gig?" I asked, trying to sound casual.

"It's the Battle of the Bands, man!" Lyle whooped.

"Yeah!" Kinky nodded, his Chia Pet hairdo boinging up and down. "We've been practicing really hard. I think we could actually w—"

"Stifle!" Robot shouted. "Better not say it, bloke!"

"Oh. Right." Kinky leaned toward me and lowered his voice to a whisper. "Robot's superstitious."

"Well, good luck," I said, trying to sound casual. I sat down in the armchair vacated by Kinky and pretended to stretch.

"Man, oh man," Lyle said, hopping around in his striped high-tops. "This is going to be so cool!"

*Yeah. Cool for you,* I groused silently. Once again I went all weak with self-pity. What made me think I could actually start up a whole new social scene here in Austin? Even my own roommate didn't want to be with me.

The guys loped toward the door, but Christine remained standing in front of the couch, still holding the box with the wiener dog in it. She was staring at me intently. "You know, you should come with us," she said.

"Really?"

She shrugged. "Why not?"

"Great!" I squealed, leaping to my feet. It was the exact opposite of cool, but I didn't care. Even if I ended up having a horrible time, the fact that Christine wanted me along meant a lot.

"Um . . ." Christine pressed her lips together and looked out onto the balcony. "What about him?"

"Seamus? I guess I'll just put in my room with the radio on. I promise I'll make triple sure the door is shut all the way. He's been really good lately when I go to classes. But it might be different at night." I stared at her uncertainly and bit the nails of my right hand.

Christine smiled reassuringly. "Hey, you've got to test it sometime. Why not tonight?"

It felt good to hear her vote of confidence in my dog. And she was right: I had to leave him alone some night eventually. Besides, I really wanted to go. "Okay," I said. "I just need a minute or two to get him settled."

"Yo!" Kinky's bushy head poked back through the doorway. Behind him, I could see the other guys standing impatiently on the landing. "What's taking so long? We want to grab some burritos on the way."

"Hold on. Katie's coming with us," Christine shouted back at him.

"Cool," he said, his head bobbing to an unheard song. "We'll meet you guys at the van."

We could hear them rumbling down the stairs, arguing about where to stop for food.

"You know what?" Christine grabbed my arm. "You should so ask that guy Matt to come with us."

"Um, yeah." The last time I'd seen Matt, I was screeching at him for trying to help me. I had a pretty good feeling he wouldn't want to go anywhere with me. "I don't think so."

He was someone else I needed to apologize to, but I wasn't sure how. At this point, the damage was pretty much done.

"Whatever," Christine said with a shrug. "You can always hang with me if you like."

I grinned at her. "Actually, I would like that. A lot."

The ride downtown was a unique thrill. Christine, Lyle and I sat squeezed in the backseat of the van, while Kinky and Robot sat up front. The van's interior had an odd, wet-carpet smell. The vinyl seats were ripped, bandaged here and there by long lengths of duct tape, and my feet were ankle-deep in fast-food wrappers. Whenever Kinky would put on the brakes, the equipment piled up behind us would slam into our seat.

Eventually Kinky pulled up in front of the warehouse-district club called the Danger Zone, where the Battle of the Bands was taking place, and let Christine and me out.

"See y'all inside!" Kinky called out the window as he turned the van down the nearby alley to unload the equipment.

A line to get into the club was already forming. Most the people in the crowd were the same pale, funeral-garb-wearing types I'd met at our party. But there were also quite a few jocks, each sporting ironed khaki shorts, a polo shirt and a bleach blonde on his arm.

I headed for the end of the line, but Christine grabbed my elbow. "Uh-uh," she said. "Follow me."

She led me to the entrance, where a truck-sized Hispanic guy sat perched on a stool collecting the cover charge.

"Hey, Ernie!" she called, pushing past a few people.

"Christine," he said, smiling. "Thought I'd see you. You on the guest list?"

"Yep. And this is Katie. She's helping us out tonight, so you've got to let her in too."

He tipped his Astros baseball cap at me. "Welcome," he said. "You ladies can go right in, but first I need to stamp you as minors."

Christine made a face. "Come on, Ernie. You know we'll be good."

"Sorry, *chula*. This is a big night. The newspapers are here and everything."

"Really?" She held out her hand for the stamp, peering past Ernie into the darkness and noise. "That's awesome."

Ernie grabbed my hand and stamped a glow-in-the-dark image of Marvin the Martian onto the back of it. "Have fun," he said, nodding toward the interior of the club.

"Don't worry," Christine said. "We will."

We walked down a short corridor into the main area of the club. A guitar-heavy rock group with a female lead singer was on stage.

"Oh God, I *hate* these guys," Christine shouted to me over the noise. She halted at the end of the corridor as if refusing to go any farther. "She wants to be Courtney Love so bad, and it is so not happening. She just likes to shake her boobs in front of a roomful of strangers."

"She's shaking more than that right now," I said, pointing to where the singer was now lying on the stage, bellowing into the microphone and writhing around into various contorted positions. "You know, if she wasn't so skinny, I'd think she was in labor."

Christine cracked up.

The song ended then and the crowd began clapping and cheering—especially the guys. Christine climbed onto an empty chair and began yelling, "Boo!" with her hands cupped around her mouth. A few other people nearby, girls mainly, joined in.

I shook my head, marveling at her. It amazed me

how Christine could feel so at ease in a pack of strangers when I didn't even feel at home . . . well . . . at *home*. Would I ever feel that carefree? Or would my mom's voice always sound in my brain, warning me to behave as properly as she did at my age and not smear our good McAllister name?

Well, frankly I was sick of acting like a good McAllister. 'Cause apparently all McAllisters were twee, namby-pamby little killjoys.

Tonight, I was going to have a great time. Even if it meant becoming someone else.

"Whoooh!" I shouted over the heads of the cheering audience. "All right, New Bile! Whoooh!"

Christine said something I couldn't hear and shoved my shoulder playfully, sending me flailing about for a second or two, trying to regain my balance.

We were standing atop a long, built-in counter that flanked one side of the club's seating area. Christine and I had climbed up there in order to dance—since the actual dance floor was crowded with lame poser types who just wanted to stand there and nod along to the beat.

I was having fun. Not just the "stand around with a polite smile and force yourself to laugh at people's lame jokes" type of fun—I mean *fun*.

New Bile was two songs into their three-song set and had the last slot in the competition. They were also, without a doubt, the best band there. They were freaking incredible—much better than I remembered them being at the party. But then, I hadn't been my best that night either.

"This next song is brand-new and goes out to me lovely girlfriend," Robot said, shielding his eyes from the overhead lights so he could stare out at Christine. "This one's for you, love."

"Ohhh. How sweet!" I exclaimed, clasping my hands together over my chest.

Robot had never really struck me as the sentimental type. I'd figured he was like Chuck in that department: the no-nonsense-type boyfriend who bought flowers only when the occasion required it—if then. But there he was, about to serenade Christine with her very own love song.

He strummed a couple of chords and turned toward the rest of the band. "One . . . two . . ." Lyle tapped his drumsticks together a few times, and then . . .

*Wang! Boom! Bow, b-b-bow, bow!*

Instead of a slow ballad, the band launched into an up-tempo number with a thrashing beat and jangly power-guitar melody.

Robot half screamed the lyrics into the microphone.

> *I got my ears pierced with needle and thread,*
> *Got my nose pierced by a bloke named Fred,*
> *But you pierced my heart with the things that you*
> *said,*

*But I never bled.*
*Instead,*
*I knew . . .*
*That I fancied you . . . ooh . . . ooh.*

"Yeah!" Christine shouted, pumping her arm in the air.

Everyone on the dance floor was hopping up and down. It seemed like the entire building was shaking to the beat. Christine and I danced on the ledge and hooted at the breaks. It felt as if all the stress I'd been storing up the past few weeks were rising up out of me.

Near the very end of the song, Kinky quit playing and Lyle's drumming slowed to half tempo.

Robot gently plucked out the melody and began crooning hoarsely:

*Fancy you, Fancy you,*
*Fancy that it would end up you . . . oooh . . .*
*I'll always be true.*

And then it was over. The crowd roared with applause and whistles, cameras flashed, and a few girls screeched loudly. I looked over at Christine, who was hunkered over slightly, wiping the corner of her left eye.

"You okay?" I shouted over the still-cheering audience.

"Yeah," she said, straightening up. "It's just smoky in here."

I nodded back, not believing it for a second. His song had moved her, I could tell. And although his lyrics weren't exactly Shakespeare or Keats, they seemed heartfelt. Even I was a little touched.

"You know, they were the best band by far!" I hollered. "I really think they're going to w—"

"Don't say it!" Christine held her hand out in front of me. "You know how Robot feels."

I looked over at the stage and watched the guys take their bows, Robot keeping his gaze on Christine. *Yeah,* I thought. *I guess I do.*

They did win that night. New Bile was treated like conquering heroes. After the official announcement, the guys pulled Christine and me onstage and we danced alongside Robot as they did a raw, semi-acoustic version of "Twist and Shout" for their encore. It was the most amazing time I'd ever had.

To top it all off, Seamus was sleeping peacefully at the foot of my bed when I got back. And I fell into the first blissful, uninterrupted slumber since I'd adopted him.

In a way, I felt like I had won, too.

# 11

"*Fancy you, fancy you, fancy that it would end up yo-o-ou* . . ." I sang out as I opened a can of Alpo Hearty Classics with Beef.

Seamus stood beside me, smacking his jowls.

I turned the can upside down and shook it. The contents slid out with a loud squelch and plopped on the plate, retaining their cylindrical shape.

As soon as I picked up the dish and turned toward him, Seamus stood on his hind legs and began dancing about, his nostrils quivering at top speed.

"Seamus, sit!" I commanded.

He sat down, licking his chops and keeping a close eye on the plate.

"Stay," I said. I waited for a count of five and set the food in front of him. "All right. Go ahead."

I'd splurged and bought him the special treat after doing so well in doggie class that day. We'd practiced lying down on command, and he'd been practically perfect. In fact, all the students were doing much better. Floyd the corgi was much less skittish. And Barry had been so proud of Natasha, he'd promised her a treat too—although I couldn't imagine what that would be. A thirteen-ounce can of chopped meat would be like a Tic Tac to a dog that size. Maybe a rack of lamb? A couple dozen sausages?

Unfortunately Yoda the bassett hound and his wireless mommy had quit the class. Barry joked that she was so busy, she'd probably decided to send Yoda off to boarding school instead.

Come to think of it, Barry was also becoming less skittish.

Seamus scarfed down the glob in about three gulps, then proceeded to lick the plate so hard, he pushed it all around the kitchen with his tongue. After a while he stopped and looked over at me. His button eyes twinkled and his cotton-candy pink tongue hung out of his mouth slightly. He was the picture of bliss.

I sat down next to him and began stroking his wiry, unruly fur. "You're my good boy, aren't you?" I crooned. "That's right. Who's the bestest boy? You are!"

It was probably a good thing Christine and Robot

had gone to the movies or I would have irrevocably squandered any cool points I might have earned with them.

Seamus snorted happily and flopped onto his back.

"Yes. That's right," I went on as I scratched his swollen belly. "You're my superstar doggie! My super duper pooper! My—"

My fingers brushed over something hard, making me stop. I retraced my path and found it—something round and solid just above his stomach. At first I thought it might be a burr or blob of mud stuck in his fur, but as I examined it more closely, I saw it was a raised lump of skin.

Cold prickles raced down my spine. I remembered what Matt had said about the lump he found on Jessie. How the vet had tried everything, but she was just too sick. And the heart-wrenching decision he'd had to make . . .

In a burst of speed, I scooped up Seamus, cradled him against me, and ran across the hall to Matt's door.

"Please be home. Please be home," I chanted as I pounded on the door over and over.

A few seconds later Matt opened up. "What?" he said irritably. As soon as he saw me, his face fell slack with surprise. "Katie?"

"I was feeding Seamus and then I was petting him and he rolled over and then I found this thing on his stomach and now I'm scared he might be sick!" I babbled. Tears were seeping out of my eyes and my voice was all squealy like a scared puppy.

"Whoa. Slow down," he said gently. "Why don't you come inside?"

I stepped into the condo and Matt shut the door behind me. His place was even messier than the last time. Papers and books were strewn all over the coffee table and floor, and I noticed he had a ballpoint pen tucked over his right ear.

"Okay," he said, laying a steadying hand on my shoulder. "Tell me what's wrong."

I took a shaky breath and launched into the whole story again. I started out relatively calm, but by the time I said "lump," my throat constricted and the rest of my words took on a shrill, nails-on-blackboard pitch.

When I had finished, Matt's big, sleepy eyes were gazing at me with so much sympathy, I could barely look at him. I suddenly realized what I was doing to him by coming here. I was making him relive his worst memory ever.

"Show me the lump," he said.

I set Seamus on the couch and held him down on his back. His legs were stiff and his eyes were wide and suspicious-looking.

"It's okay, bud," I said, keeping my left hand firmly on his chest. With my right hand I slowly stroked his belly until my fingers found the bump. I pushed the fur aside and pointed to the raised nodule. "Right there," I said, my voice wobbly.

Matt poked it with his index finger a few times and then looked back at me. "Uh . . . I think he's going to be okay," he said. His mouth was quivering slightly, and a pale pink tinge was spreading across his cheeks. He seemed to be choking back some strong emotion.

"But how do you know?" I wailed.

"Because . . . because that's his nipple." Matt pursed his lips together. A small snort escaped through his nose, and then his whole body just seemed to cave in. His mouth burst open and peals of loud laughter came ringing out, rocking him backward and forward.

"Really?" I plopped onto the couch, half stunned. *His nipple?* I had no idea boy dogs even had nipples.

I felt both immensely relieved and utterly, squeamishly embarrassed. I closed my eyes and ducked my head, wishing I could just retract it, turtlelike, into my blue tunic top.

Matt flopped down beside me, still convulsing with laughter. "I'm sorry. Really," he would say each time he came up for air, then he would break up all over again. Finally he stopped and let out a long, audible sigh. "Aw, man," he said, wiping the wetness from his eyes. "That was great."

"Glad I could help," I muttered.

At this point Seamus had taken off away from the couch and was peering at us from the far side of the recliner. I couldn't blame him. First I freak out over his nipple, and then Matt explodes like some crazed clown. If he'd known how, he probably would have dialed 9-1-1.

Matt grabbed my shoulder and shook it in a good-buddy sort of way. "I'm sorry," he said. "I shouldn't have laughed so much. It was just . . . just . . ."

"Funny as hell?" I finished for him, smiling in spite of my humiliation.

"Yeah. That."

I shook my head. God, I was such a dork. In fact, I was probably beyond simple dorkdom. I was a *Dorkus maximus*. A *Dorkus rex*. I couldn't imagine what Matt must think of me.

I thought of our last meeting in the park and a wave of guilt washed over me.

"Um, hey," I said. "Sorry I was such a monumental bitch the other day. I don't know why I went off on you like that."

"*I* do. 'Cause I was being a total ass."

"But you were just trying to help."

"Without being asked." He shook his head. "I was awful. I'm sorry."

"Okay, fine. We're both sorry."

"Yeah, we're sorry, all right." He smiled wryly.

*God, he's cute*, I thought. I stared at him until my cheeks felt warm and liquid, then turned away.

Something on the coffee table caught my eye—something familiar. It took me a moment to realize it was my own face grinning up at me. I slid the picture out from underneath some papers and held it up. It was a clipping from the *Austin Chronicle*—their story on the Battle of the Bands and a photo of me and Christine onstage with New Bile. Robot was "oohing" into the microphone, with sweat dripping down his face, and Kinky was bent furiously over his bass. Behind them you could just make out the top of Lyle's bald head gleaming under the stage lights. And Christine and I were frozen in mid-dance, both of us sporting wide, openmouthed smiles.

"You saw this?" I asked.

"Yeah," he said, shifting uncomfortably. "I thought it was a good shot."

Actually, I liked it too. If I didn't know it was me, I'd think the girl in the photo led a charmed, carefree life. It made me feel . . . hopeful. In fact, I had it up on my wall next to the caricature of Seamus and me.

"You look happy," Matt said, peering over my shoulder at the photo.

"I was," I said. "I mean, I am."

"Good."

Maybe it was the carefree me in the photo, or maybe I was just a little intoxicated from the heady mix of emotions that had shot through me that day, but for some reason I was feeling incredibly bold—incredibly *alpha*. I could almost hear Mr. Willard's flugelhorn voice urging me to take the lead.

"What are you doing this weekend?" I blurted out.

Matt looked surprised. "Uh . . . nothing. Why?"

"We're all going to the lake for the Hill Country Music Fest. You want to come with us?"

"Yeah. That sounds cool."

"Great."

We grinned at each other and my heart skipped merrily about in my rib cage. *He's coming!* I thought. *We have a date!*

Was it a date? I wasn't exactly sure. But the fact was *he was coming!*

Just then, Seamus started whining. He was standing at the door looking back at me dolefully.

"Uh-oh," I said, rising to my feet. "Time for walkies again."

I hurried over to Seamus and picked him up. Matt followed and opened the door.

"So," he said as I walked out. "You want to maybe grab some coffee before we leave for the music fest?"

"Sure!" I replied, a tad too quickly and loudly.

"Cool. I'll knock on your door around nine, then?"

"Okay. Sounds good. See you!"

"Bye."

As soon as he shut the door, I hugged Seamus to me and danced like Snoopy all the way down the stairs. It was unbelievable. I was going out with Matt! He asked me to coffee and I asked him to the festival!

And at least one of those *had* to be a date.

You have **14** new messages.

"Huh?"

I hadn't checked e-mail in forever. I'd been too busy. Besides, seeing how little mail I was getting these days always made me depressed. Now suddenly my in-box was full of postings from friends back home, all sent within the last two days. I clicked on the first one from Ariel.

> OMG! Everyone is passing around the *Chronicle* down here! How cool that you know New Bile! What's the sitch with that? Can I meet them?

She went on to relay some relatively lame gossip about Debby Ellis and Todd Haskins and then closed with another pitch to meet the band. I noticed she didn't say a word about Chuck or Trina, which meant things must still be hot and heavy between them.

The next message was from Tracy, saying pretty much the same thing, followed by one from Bethany. She was at least subtler. She apologized for not having written sooner and wanted to know what I was doing for fun in Austin.

*Oh, so* that's *it,* I thought, hitting the Delete button. After almost three weeks of nonexistence, I'm suddenly back in the game because of a newspaper photo? I had no idea New Bile wielded such power.

I scanned the others relatively quickly. There were a few more from Ariel (just some forwarded jokes and a reminder that she'd be out of town the first weekend in August), a couple of invitations to parties this weekend (one even asking if I could get New Bile to play), another "sorry I haven't written in a while" from Tonya Snodgrass, San Marcos High School's biggest party girl (who, coincidentally, had never written to me before), and one from Mom giving me Aaron's cell number and asking for the seven-thousandth time why we hadn't met up yet.

Weird. I couldn't figure out why I wasn't flipping all over the room in sheer relief. It was over, mostly. I had my status back. People deemed me worthy of contact once again. And yet, as I fumbled through my feelings, I realized I didn't care all that much.

Ever since I got Seamus, I'd been too caught up in him to deal with the situation back home. And I had to admit, it hadn't even crossed my mind the past couple of days. Maybe all the pressures of owning and training a dog had boiled my brain. Or did I not care about all this because I didn't care about those people anymore?

While I sat there lost in thought, someone started pounding on the front door. I leaped up from my chair. As I headed into the living room, the knocking grew louder and faster, and I could hear muffled cries from the other side. I quickly opened the door to find Mrs. Krantz, all tearstained and disheveled.

"Katie, thank goodness you're home," she said, dabbing her eyes with a dainty embroidered handkerchief.

"What's wrong?" I asked, ushering her inside and closing the door.

"It's Mrs. B. I can't find her anywhere! I put her on the balcony for her afternoon nap and she disappeared. She's never been gone this long!"

It felt as if I'd been punched in the gut. "Oh God," I said, more breath than voice. "I put Seamus outside too."

I ran to the patio door and flung aside the blinds, memories of mutilated stuffed animals whirling through my mind. Mrs. Krantz trotted up behind me, gasping and sobbing.

And then I froze. I was just about to open the door when I saw them.

"Look," I said, pointing.

Mrs. Krantz gave me a bewildered, glassy-eyed glare and then followed my finger, wincing slightly. "Oh my," she whispered. "I didn't . . . I never thought . . ."

"Me either," I said.

I beheld the sight again. Seamus and Mrs. B were lying in the shade, curled up together in a nap.

# 12

I stood ankle-deep in discarded clothing, studying my latest ensemble in the mirror.

*Cinched cargo capris with gauzy tank?* I turned to the left, then the right, then climbed onto my bed to view my bottom half.

Verdict: a good maybe.

Matt would be here in five minutes and I had yet to decide on an outfit. The dresses were too dressy and the shorts seemed too, well, short. I didn't want to wear obvious date clothes if this weren't an actual date, but I didn't want to slob out either.

I heard a distant pounding and Seamus charged out of the room barking.

*He's here!* I thought, leaping off the bed. Guess this look would have to do.

I smoothed my hair and straightened my top as I walked into the living room. For some reason, I wasn't as nervous as I thought I'd be. My pulse had definitely quickened, but there was no palm sweat, no trembling, no gelatin joints. I was just . . . happy.

"Okay, okay," I said, shooing Seamus away from the door. "Sit! Stay! Good boy."

I stood there for a second with my hand on the knob. I considered making Matt wait a moment or two, just so I wouldn't seem overly eager. But then I reminded myself that he was early. I took that as a good sign.

I unlatched the door and flung it open. "Hi th—"

My voice died away in mid-greeting and my smile broke, reassembling itself into a gaping grimace. There on the landing stood not Matt, but *Chuck*.

It felt as if I'd passed through some weird time distortion. Right place, wrong guy. Or was it former right guy, wrong place? He looked great, I noted irritably. Obviously he'd been spending a lot of time in the sun. His skin glowed a beautiful caramel color and his spiky hair was almost Q-tip white.

"Hey," he said coolly, as if I'd been expecting him.

"What are you doing here?" There was no anger in my tone. My voice had kicked in to its Chuck default setting: passive and meek.

"Can I come in?" he asked.

"Um . . . okay."

He loped into the living room and I shut the door behind him. Seamus started growling. His snout twitched, revealing his toothpick-thin fangs, and his whole body vibrated.

"Aw, man," Chuck said, laughing. "They're making you live with some spaz dog?"

"He's my dog," I corrected.

I picked up Seamus and carried him, still snarling, onto the balcony. My limbs felt heavy and floppy, as if I were moving under water. And I still couldn't shake the feeling that I'd slipped into some alternate reality.

"So, what are you doing here?" I asked again as I walked back toward Chuck.

"I came to see you," he said with a grin. "You look great, by the way."

My face flushed automatically. *Dammit!* I thought. *What the hell is he doing to me?*

His smile widened as he noticed my reaction. "How've you been?" he asked, taking a step closer.

*How have I been?* It was such an odd question. So much had happened in the past few weeks, I didn't know what to say. I still couldn't even believe Chuck was right there in front of me.

I was about to give a standard nonanswer, like "fine," when another knock sounded. In a daze, I walked over to the front door and pulled it open.

"Hi!" Matt stood on the landing, grinning at me. "You look great. Ready to go?"

"Uhhhhh . . ." I couldn't speak. I couldn't move. I couldn't do anything but stand there gripping the doorknob like a lifeline.

Matt looked past me and saw Chuck. His back stiffened and his smile washed away. "Oh . . . hey."

"Hey," Chuck said, lifting his chin at him.

Their eyes locked for a moment. I fought the urge to tiptoe down the staircase and race out of the condo, back to some place that made sense.

"Um, Matt?" I said, rediscovering my voice. "This is Chuck. Chuck, Matt."

They smiled stiffly at each other. Chuck took a swaggering step toward me and folded his arms across his chest.

"Hey, uh . . . why don't I meet you at the park later?" Matt said. I could read confusion and disappointment in his eyes.

"O-okay," I stammered, feeling a big swooping sensation behind my ribs. I really didn't want him to leave, but I had no idea what to say. How could I explain things to him when I didn't understand them myself?

He pursed his lips and gave me one last nod before ambling back to his condo.

"Who was that?" Chuck asked when I shut the door. His tone was slightly sharp, almost accusatory, and I felt guilty in spite of myself.

"He's . . ." I paused. Was there a one-word classification for Matt? If so, I couldn't think of it. And even if I could, I probably wouldn't want to tell Chuck. "He lives next door."

My numbness was starting to wear off and crude emotions came bubbling to the surface. I stared into Chuck's Ken-doll face and felt the old hurt and longing and anger. "Why are you really here?" I asked testily.

His sapphire eyes grew big and round. "I just wanted to talk to you about stuff. About us."

Various feelings jostled inside me, all trying to assert themselves. "I don't know . . ."

Just then, the door flew open and Christine entered the condo, followed closely by Robot. Each one carried a McDonald's bag.

"Hey," Christine said, looking surprised. "How goes it?"

"Hi, guys," I said wearily. "This is Chuck."

"Aw, man. I know you." Chuck walked over to Robot and held out his hand. "You're in New Bile, right?"

Robot puffed up slightly and grabbed Chuck's palm with his free hand, pumping it up and down. "That's right, mate. You a fan?"

"Yeah! I caught you guys last fall at the Hot Spot. You were awesome!"

"Thanks." Robot beamed at me. "Katie, your friend here is bloody brilliant. Where've you been hiding him?"

He and Christine walked over to the coffee table and set their food down. Chuck followed at their heels, practically genuflecting.

"Man, I've been telling everyone about you," Chuck went on. "Told them you'd be huge. Didn't I, Katie? Didn't I say that?"

"You said that," I muttered.

"Then we owe this bloke," Robot said, plopping on the couch and digging a bagel sandwich out of his bag. "We should get him into our next gig."

"Aw, man. That'd be awesome!" Chuck cheered.

"You could come with Katie," Robot added through a mouthful of food. "She's our good-luck charm."

Chuck smiled at me. "Yeah, she's great."

"Hey, I know!" Christine exclaimed. "What are you doing today? You want to come out with us to the music fest?"

I flashed her a bug-eyes warning look, but Christine didn't see it.

"What do you think?" she asked Robot. "We've got room in the van."

"Sure thing, love," Robot said. "Whatever you say."

"Dudes! That is so cool!" Chuck cried. "Isn't that cool, Katie?" He looked over at me, smiling broadly.

"Yeah. Great."

🐕

"Jesus, Katie. I'm sorry. I had no idea he was the jerk who dumped you."

"It's okay."

"No, it isn't!"

275

"Really, Christine. I can deal."

We were already at the campgrounds, sitting on an itchy blue blanket Kinky had brought and listening to an amazing bluegrass band. While the guys played Hacky Sack nearby, I filled Christine in on what happened that morning before she came home. Seamus lay between us, keeping a close eye on Chuck, an occasional rumbling rising up inside him.

"So . . . you think Matt will show up?" she asked cautiously. "Or did he just say that to get the hell out of there?"

I shook my head, tracing my finger along the satin edge of the blanket. "I don't know," I said glumly.

"You should have told me you'd invited him. Then I wouldn't have been so accommodating to Johnny Bravo over there."

"I didn't get a chance. You guys were out last night and he showed up first thing this morning." I watched Chuck bounce the Hacky Sack on the inner part of his Nikes and frowned. "It's weird, you know. He probably had to get up pretty early to make it here before nine. He would have never done that for me while we were dating."

"What's up with that, you think?"

"Beats me. Guess I'll find out." I'd reached the acceptance phase. We were here. Things were already in play. Now I just wanted to ride it out as quickly and smoothly as possible.

I still had no answer from Chuck on why he was

there. He'd spent most of the morning hanging with Robot, talking about New Bile and scarfing down the rest of his hash browns. Then later when we all piled into the van, it became clear that four of us couldn't fit in the backseat and Robot suggested I ride on Chuck's lap.

So for the entire drive, Christine held on to Seamus while I sat snuggled up against my ex-boyfriend. It was a bizarre experience. Horrifyingly awkward, but not entirely unpleasant either. I could smell the familiar scent of his cologne and feel the weight of his long arms around me. Snatches of memories replayed in my mind—many of them good. And I remembered how it used to be.

Of course, the ache of him dumping me was there too, looming like a giant monolith in the middle of my nostalgia. I spent the ride in a detached state. It seemed to last forever—made even longer by the many stops at fireworks stands, where the boys wanted to load up.

"He's cute, you know," Christine remarked as we watched the guys. "Not my type, but definitely hot. Like a soap opera star or something."

"You think he's *my* type?"

She peered closely at me, as if X-raying me with her eyes. "Yeah. . . . No. . . . Maybe. When I first met you, this is exactly the kind of guy I would have pictured you with. But now . . . I don't know."

I heard Chuck's familiar chuckle and saw him walking backward away from the guys. "Y'all go ahead," he was saying. "I'm going to take a break." He loped toward us and Seamus immediately jumped to his feet, growling like a revved hot rod.

"Down!" I ordered. "Stay!"

Chuck stopped at the edge of the blanket and bent forward, his hands on his knees. "Katie? Can I talk to you a sec?" he asked, eyeing Seamus cautiously.

"Uh . . . sure." As I rose to my feet, I glanced over at Christine, who gave me a bolstering look.

"Be careful," she mumbled.

Chuck, Seamus and I strolled alongside the lake, away from the noise of the festival. Since we'd arrived, the campground had filled up pretty fast. People, kids and dogs were milling around the different booths or sitting on colored blankets that were spread out in front of the stage like a gigantic, loose patchwork quilt. After walking several yards, we stopped beneath a lush pecan tree and plopped down on the grass.

For a while, we just sat there. Chuck threw rocks in the water and I nervously plucked blades of grass. Seamus stayed hunkered up against my side, like a little trembling, snarling outboard motor.

Eventually Chuck turned and stared at me.

"I know you've been mad," he began.

My brow furrowed. *Mad?* No. Mad is how you feel when someone cuts you off in traffic, or breaks your favorite bracelet, or makes you wait an hour while they do their hair. It doesn't even begin to describe the emotions churned up when your boyfriend messes around with one of your friends and then breaks up with you on your birthday. *Shattered,* maybe. *Depressed,* definitely. But not just mad.

I bit my lip and let him continue.

"I was a real loser to do that to you. I guess I was just mad that you were coming here for the summer. I thought it made me look bad. Like you'd rather study than hang out with me."

"Really?" I'd never heard Chuck talk this way before. He sounded kind of whiny.

"Yeah. I guess the thing with Trina was just me trying to get back at you."

At the sound of Trina's name, my back arched and my fingernails dug into my cargo pants.

"Anyway, I know it was a bad thing to do and I'm sorry," he went on. "I've really missed you, you know. Me and you, we're totally right for each other." He hunched his shoulders and looked at me with a doleful expression. "You think maybe . . . we could get back together?"

I stared at him blankly. Again time seemed to tilt. For days I had dreamed he would say those exact words. But now that it was actually happening, it felt a little off—as if I weren't me, and Chuck weren't Chuck, and we'd accidentally slipped into some strangers' skins and started reciting lines.

"I don't know," I said slowly.

"Aw, come on," he said. "Is it Trina? Because she is totally yesterday. We aren't even friends. And I promise, I *swear,* I won't ever mess around again."

I felt a slight charge. Once again, it was just what I wanted and needed to hear. I had my rep back. And now I could have my boyfriend back. This could be all over with.

But still I couldn't quite get into the moment.

"Please, Katie?" Chuck dipped toward me, his mouth curled in his trademark, sultry grin.

It was his secret weapon. That look and his husky voice. They had never, ever failed to work on me.

Until now. Looking at him, I felt stiff and embarrassed and even a little disgusted with myself—like when you hear a song on the radio that you used to be crazy about and realize it's kind of cheesy and lame.

Chuck had lost all his luster. He had no power over me anymore. I no longer loved or hated him.

"Chuck," I said, scooting closer. I wanted to let him down easy. After all, in a completely warped way, I was sort of grateful to him for breaking up with me. If he hadn't let me go, I might not have realized that I didn't really want him. Or I would have realized it too late.

But Chuck misinterpreted my forward movement. He reached out with his arms and started pulling me toward him, his face dipping toward mine in pre-make-out formation.

I was just about to pull away when Seamus came out of nowhere. He dove between us, barking at Chuck while pushing back against me, trying to wedge us apart with his little body.

"Stupid dog!" Chuck shouted, pushing Seamus with his right hand and slamming him onto his side.

Something popped inside me—like a grenade being unpinned—and everything went hot and loud.

"Don't you dare hurt him!" I screamed, picking up Seamus and holding him against my chest.

"I—I'm sorry." Chuck's eyes were as wide as compact discs, and it occurred to me that he'd never seen me really mad before. "I thought he was going to bite me."

"If you touch my dog again I'll bite you myself!" I raged.

"Okay, okay. I'm really sorry," he said again. He ducked his head and smiled sheepishly, trying to turn on the charm again.

But I was *waaaaay* past letting that work. "I can't believe you," I said angrily. "I can't believe you would come down here and act like everything's all better, just because you say so! After what you did!"

I must have been making a pretty sizable racket because people all around us were craning their heads and staring. Soon Christine, Robot, Lyle and Kinky ran over.

"What's going on?" Christine asked, breathless from running.

"He—he pushed—" My anger was finally starting to subside, leaving me shaky and stammering.

"Did you hurt her?" Robot asked, getting right up in his face.

"Aw, dude. That's uncool," Lyle said in a menacing voice, stepping up beside Robot.

Kinky made fists and lined up beside his bandmates.

"No way!" Chuck shouted, staring at each of them. "I'd never hurt her. I just sort of pushed her dog!"

"Aw, dude. That's uncool," Lyle said again.

"You lousy liar!" Christine said, pushing her way through the line. "What do you mean you'd never hurt her? What do you call that asshole stunt you pulled on her birthday?"

Chuck opened his mouth as if to protest, then quickly shut it and stared down at his Nikes.

"Know what, lad?" Robot laid a heavy hand on Chuck's shoulder. "I think you need to find a new ride home."

Chuck stared into each of their set faces before slumping in defeat. He then turned and fixed me with an expression both hurt and wrathful. I met his eyes full on, still clutching Seamus against me and stroking his shaggy backside. Eventually Chuck broke off his gaze and walked away.

I watched as he slowly ambled off toward the parking lot. Most of his swagger was gone, and he looked kind of reedy and slight. Once again I was struck by the nothing I felt for him. Just a little pity, some residual, stinging anger, and a tiny pocket of warmth.

Chuck was leaving the park, but I knew he was also leaving my life. And that was okay.

Everything was going to be okay.

# 13

"He's not coming, is he?"

"You never know," Christine said as she tied back her raven tresses with a red scarf.

We were stretched out on the blanket with Seamus, listening to a pretty blonde play guitar and sing densely poetic songs in a birdlike voice. The guys were standing nearby, trying to get a better view.

After we chased off Chuck, I was in a whole new mental state. I felt lighter somehow. Unshackled. And with it came a new clarity of thought.

Unfortunately, the main thing I was able to deduce was that Matt was still not there and probably wouldn't show at all.

"It's not that late yet," Christine went on.

"Yeah, right," I mumbled. It was almost dusk. The sun was dipping behind the trees, and the sky had taken on a faint lilac hue.

Yep. He wasn't coming. Finding me tongue-tied with Chuck probably reeked something awful. And it was too much to ask that he would give me another chance. The guy had already forgiven countless temper tantrums and freak-outs; I couldn't expect him to let anything else slide.

And then, just as the blond girl finished her set and was bowing to the crowd, I noticed someone pushing through the audience. Sleepy eyes . . . a wide, curvy mouth . . . wavy forelock tumbling across the brow—It was him!

I jumped to my feet. "Oh my God, Christine! He's right over there!" I cried, keeping my eyes on him. Now that blondie was leaving the stage, people were scurrying everywhere, and I was afraid I might lose him in the crowd.

"Don't just stand there! Go!" she said, giving me a little push on my leg.

"But Seamus—"

"I'll watch him. Just go!"

"Thanks!" I bent over Seamus and gave him a little pat on the head. "Stay!" I ordered. "Be good!" Then I took off into the throng.

I veered through the tide of strolling, chatting people, keeping my eye on the top of Matt's head. Eventually the masses parted enough to provide a full view.

"Matt! Over here!" I shouted, waving my arms.

He halted and turned slowly in place, glancing at the faces passing by. Finally he saw me. "Hey!" he said, his lips parting in a wide, moon-slice grin.

We walked toward each other, meeting in the middle.

"I'm so glad you came," I said. I grabbed his arm and gave it a tiny squeeze.

His smile cocked sideways and he shook his head. "Man, the traffic was *horrible*. And when I got here, I couldn't find a place to park." He put his hand on my shoulder and slid it down my bare arm. "Sorry I'm late."

"That's okay," I murmured, suddenly feeling short of breath.

"So, where're the others?" he asked. His eyes darted around, scanning the field behind me.

"Over here. I'll show you." I grabbed his elbow and pulled him toward our blanket, trying not to skip with glee.

Suddenly a series of loud pops sounded nearby, startling me. I looked past Christine and saw Robot and the guys standing a few feet away, setting off firecrackers. A few more loud bangs went off, and the next thing I knew, Christine was yelling and waving her arms. Following her gaze, I could see Seamus racing away, with the leash trailing behind him.

"Seamus!" I hollered.

I tried to run after him, but a big group of people passed in front of me. I skirted sideways and finally got around them, heading for the spot where I'd seen him last, but he wasn't there.

"Seamus?" I mumbled, my heart battering against my ribs. I looked left and right and then turned in a slow circle. I couldn't see him anywhere.

Seamus was gone.

Everyone was talking at once—everyone except me.

"Oh my God, Katie. I'm so sorry. The stupid guys set off those firecrackers and he just . . . freaked!"

"Which way did he go?"

"You morons! What the hell were you doing setting those off?"

"It's a bleeding festival! A celebration! You were supposed to be watching the little bugger!"

"I didn't even see what happened. Did you?"

"Uh-uh."

"Katie, are you okay?" Matt was peering at me closely, but his voice sounded far away. All I could think was *He's gone.* Seamus had disappeared. Somehow, it didn't feel real.

But it was. And there we were, standing around our blanket while Seamus was out in the crowd, lost and freaked. We had to do something, and fast.

"Guys, this isn't helping," I said.

Only Matt heard me. The others were still shouting

and pointing in several different directions.

"Listen," I tried again.

Still no response.

*"Stop!"* I yelled.

Everyone finally stopped talking and looked at me. *"Sit!"*

Lyle plunked down on the blanket. The rest of them looked confused.

"This place is huge and crowded, and it's starting to get dark. We've got to split up and look for Seamus now!"

Everyone agreed. Robot and Christine took off to search the field where the portable toilets were lined up. Lyle and Kinky left to search the area between the stage and concession stands. And Matt and I headed right down the middle, trying to follow the path I'd seen Seamus take into the crowd.

"It's going to be okay," Matt said. "He's wearing his leash, so he can't go very fast."

*Ha!* I thought, remembering those early days in the park. Seamus could be anywhere at this point.

We moved through the crowd, scanning the ground in front of us for anything dark and furry. "Seamus!" I kept calling. "Seaaaaaamus!"

People were looking at us strangely, and I found myself getting frustrated and angry with the whole crowd. There were just so many of them. And they were all sauntering lazily past us, chatting and smiling as if everything was so great. I wanted to take a giant broom and sweep them all into a big gummy pile of flesh and sunblock. Then I could search the grounds for my dog without anyone in my way.

I was on the verge of losing it. As I stooped and scanned and called Seamus's name, I felt as if I were skating the frozen surface of a raging river. Each moment that passed with no Seamus created a new crack in the protective surface.

We reached the edge of the grassy field and stopped. Directly in front of us was a wide gravel trail, and the parking lot lay just beyond that. To the right was the back of the concession stands, and to the left lay thick oak woodlands and a carpet of high wild grass.

"What do you think?" Matt asked, looking back the way we had come. "Should we head back to the blanket in case he returned? Maybe check with the others?"

"I don't know." I said croakily. Panic was rising inside me now. I could feel myself slipping into the icy rapids. "What if we don't find him? What if he headed into the woods? We'd never find him in there. Or what if someone took him?"

"Hey." Matt wrapped an arm around me. "It's all right. We'll find him. Hell, Seamus is so smart, he might find us."

"I hope so."

Just then we heard shouting out by the parking lot. A car horn sounded and someone yelled, "Stupid dog!"

Matt and I exchanged urgent looks and took off running toward the area. The parking lot was covered with limestone gravel that sent up flumes of chalky white dust any time a car drove over it. We followed the trail of powdery vapor down an aisle to the far edge of the lot. And there, pacing up and down the grassy edge of the lot, was Seamus, looking lost and confused and very, very small.

"Seamus!" I cried out, relief spilling through me.

He saw me and smiled a doggie smile, his pink tongue poking out between his open jaws.

"No, wait!" Matt shouted.

But it was too late. One second I could see Seamus scampering our way; the next second, a blue Volkswagen backed out of its space, blocking my view. I heard a horrible *thunk,* followed by a plaintive yelp and the squeak of brakes. Then everything went quiet. There was just a faint *whooshing* sound as the cloud of dust settled back down to earth.

I screamed and ran down the row of cars, Matt following close behind me. As soon as I reached the back end of the Volkswagen, I skidded to a stop and dropped to my knees.

Seamus—my buddy, my dog, my best friend ever— was lying motionless on the ground.

It's a little hard to remember what happened right after Seamus was hit. The memories have all the vague, soft-focus qualities of a bad dream. I can only conjure up a jumble of sensations—my wails, the stares of curious onlookers, the frantic apologies from the guy driving the Volkswagen. The one thing I can picture clearly is Seamus lying limp and twisted on his side, his fur ashen gray from the layer of dust.

After that, I faintly recall Matt helping me pick up Seamus and leading us to his car. On the way he spied Kinky's frizzy head over the crowd and shouted something to him. I was crying so hard that I didn't hear. Soon after, we were on the road. It seemed to last forever. I held Seamus gently the whole way, making sure he was still breathing. He was still alive when we arrived at the twenty-four-hour animal hospital. Once there, a tall, pretty vet whose name tag read Dr. Skyler rushed over and carefully took Seamus out of my arms.

When I tried to follow them in to the examining room, she looked me straight in the eye and said, "You need to wait out here. I'll come speak to you as soon as we know anything." Then she disappeared behind the doors with Seamus and her assistant.

"How long have they been in there?" I asked Matt.

"Just over an hour," he said, glancing at his watch.

It seemed as though time had stopped. As I paced up and down the empty lobby, the only sounds were my shoes squeaking against the vinyl floor and the faint buzzing of the overhead lights. Outside there was an eerie twilight. Night had fallen, but the glow of the city brightened the darkness to a somber gray. It felt as if we were the only two inhabitants of a strange night-mare void.

"You should sit down," Matt said.

"I can't."

"Why?"

"Because he's in there."

There was a pause. I could tell Matt was patiently trying to decipher my reply. He was going to make a damn good psychologist.

"But . . . he's going to be in there no matter what you do," he said slowly and carefully. "You might as well relax."

"No! I can't!" I shouted. For some reason I was really irritated with him, even though he'd done nothing but help me.

My anger didn't seem to faze him at all. "Why not?"

"Because! Because I don't deserve to!" My voice seemed to catch on something. Before I realized it, a new round of tears began streaming down my cheeks. I stood there wavering while my sight went blurry and my legs grew weak.

Matt came up, put his arm around me and led me to the chairs.

"I don't deserve to sit down!" I cried, even as I sank into the seat. "It's my fault he got hurt!"

There. I'd said it. I'd voiced the horrible thought that had been lurking inside me. Now that it was out and I was forced to face it, an agonizing pain was shooting through my body at soul-level. My breath came in short ragged gasps, and tears dripped all over my dusty clothes.

"It's not your fault," Matt said, still holding me steady. "It was an accident."

"But if I hadn't called to him, he wouldn't have gotten hit!" I choked out. It actually hurt me physically to admit it aloud. My shoulders shuddered and something sharp was hacking at my heart. Instinctively, I crossed my arms over my chest and doubled over, sobbing.

For who knows how long, I sat there, folded over like a pill bug and crying. Images of Seamus whirled past my closed eyes. Seamus in his cage at the pound; Seamus wet and muddy at the park; Seamus gazing at me fondly with his round, root beer–colored eyes. It just wasn't fair. Seamus and I had come so far. He was truly the best thing that ever happened to me; and now he was being taken away.

"It's not your fault," Matt kept murmuring as he bent down next to me.

I didn't believe him, but his soft tone and supportive hold did manage to calm me down—or maybe I just ran out of power. Eventually my sobs dwindled into sniffles and I sat there like a deflated ball.

After a while I heard Matt say, "Here comes the vet."

I sat up quickly, my head pounding from the sudden change in elevation. Through the glass partition, I could see Dr. Skyler walking down the corridor toward the lobby. I tried to read her expression, but she just looked really tired.

We stood up to meet her as she pushed through the glass door.

"Well, he's out of surgery," she said, looking right at me.

"Is he awake?" I asked.

"Not yet."

"Will he—" I stopped myself. I just couldn't say it. *Will he ever wake up?*

Dr. Skyler tilted her head sympathetically. "We don't know what will happen. We managed to stop the internal bleeding, but he's pretty banged up. At this point we just have to wait and see."

"Can I see him?"

She sighed heavily. I could tell she was about to say no.

"Please," I added quickly. "He's my dog. I just want to see him, that's all."

"Okay," she replied, giving me a sad smile. "But prepare yourself. He's still under the anesthesia, and he looks pretty bad."

She led us back down the corridor and into a white room with a big stainless steel table in the center. Seamus lay in the middle of it, crumpled and lifeless. His legs flopped aimlessly at his sides, his fur was matted and his eyes were shut and puffy. Heavy gauze bandages covered his stomach, and a clear plastic tube ran from an IV pole into his left foreleg. I couldn't fully believe it was Seamus. Instead, the little figure seemed more like a Seamus-looking stuffed animal someone had pulled out of a Dumpster.

A strange choking sound gurgled up out of me and I instinctively reached toward him.

"I'm sorry, but you can't touch him," Dr. Skyler said.

I nodded weakly, my throat too constricted for speech.

"It's almost two. Why don't you two go home and rest?" she said, motioning toward the door behind us. "We probably have a long wait ahead of us."

"No," I croaked, shaking my head. "I want to stay."

Matt grasped my shoulders and gently turned me to face him. "Katie, you're exhausted. You can't help him by wearing yourself out like this."

"But what if he needs me? What if he wakes up and gets scared? Or what if he . . . what if . . ."

"I promise I'll call you if there's any change," Dr. Skyler cut in, her voice low and compassionate.

I broke my stare off Seamus and looked at her. "Promise you'll call no matter what? Even if it's ten minutes after we leave?"

She gave me a small smile. "I promise."

"Thanks, Dr. Skyler," Matt said, shaking her hand. "Thanks for everything."

"You're welcome." She turned to me. "Please come back after you've gotten some rest. Okay?"

"Okay. Thanks."

As we headed out the door, I looked back over my shoulder at Seamus. It felt wrong to leave him there. It was like taking him back to the shelter. His life was on the line, but this time there was nothing I could do to help him.

*Don't leave me, buddy,* I urged silently. *Hang in there. Please!*

# 14

I barely remember Matt walking me up the staircase to our landing. Only it didn't feel like our landing. The eggshell-colored paneling and Berber carpeting looked only vaguely familiar. It was as if, instead of coming home, I'd entered a strange building and was experiencing a really strong sense of déjà vu.

"You all right?" Matt asked, still gripping me tightly as if he were afraid I might float up to the fluorescents if he let go.

"Yeah," I replied croakily. And I was. *I* was just fine. It was my poor dog who was a mess. While I stood in front of my door pondering a scuff mark on the tips of my sandals, Seamus was lying unconscious and bandaged, with tubes threaded into his veins. I didn't deserve any concern at all compared to him.

"Get some sleep, okay?" Matt said as he let go of me. I hadn't thought I was leaning on him all that much, but as soon as his hands left, I felt weak and floppy. I quickly grabbed the doorknob and unlocked it.

Matt was peering into my eyes as if he could somehow see past them. It occurred to me that he wasn't saying "Don't worry" or "It will be all right" anymore, and for that, I was grateful. He'd been so amazing to me and Seamus, but right now I just needed to be alone. To slip off into my limbo and ignore everything in the world for a while.

"Good night," I mumbled.

"Good night."

His image slowly disappeared as I shut the door and locked it.

The condo was dim and silent. I still felt eerily detached from myself—a walking ghost. There was a note from Christine and Robot on the console table. I didn't read it, but I did notice the word *sorry* had been written in all caps and underlined four or five times. Seamus's training collar lay beside it.

I picked it up and twisted it around in my hands, studying it as if it were some valuable ancient relic. So many memories associated with that thing, both good and bad. A squeezing pain shot through me, but I didn't cry. I couldn't anymore. Except for the dense pressure in my chest, I was completely numb.

Setting the collar carefully on the table, I tiptoed to my room. The first thing I saw when I switched on the light was Seamus's cartoon face staring down at me from the drawing on the wall. I felt another wrenching sensation in my gut and immediately turned out the light and crawled into bed, fully dressed. Only I couldn't sleep. I was so thoroughly depleted, my body felt as if it had been trampled, but every time I shut my eyes I would hear the sound of screeching brakes and see Seamus sprawled against the crushed gravel. I missed him, too. It seemed too quiet without his snoring or the familiar tinkle of his tags as he shifted in his sleep.

I took a deep breath and rolled onto my side. In the faint light of the streetlamp outside my window, I could make out a face in front of me—one with big brown eyes and a black button nose.

*Seamus?*

No. It was my Scooby-Doo alarm clock. Its frozen, goofball expression seemed to be taunting me. Suddenly it was like coming out of heavy anesthesia. It began with a prickle of irritation, and then a surge of anger broke through my deadened emotional state, charging me up again. I jumped out of bed, lifted my window, and pushed open the screen. Grabbing the Scooby clock in my right hand, I reached back and hurled it as far as I could. I didn't see where he landed, but I heard a muffled crash and few pinging sounds.

For a moment, I just stood there, listening to the

crickets and the hum of faraway traffic. Then I lay back down and closed my eyes.

The next thing I knew, the apricot light of morning was streaming through the window. I struggled to my elbows and my head immediately began to throb. My insides felt shriveled, and there was a crick in the left side of my neck. Instinctively, I glanced over at the Scooby clock . . . but it wasn't there.

"Oh, no," I mumbled. Although it was wonderful not having to wake up to the blaring alarm, I had no idea how late I slept. What if I'd missed a call from Dr. Skyler?

Ignoring the pulsating pain in my temples, I leaped out of bed and rushed into the living room.

"Oh my God! Katie! I didn't even know you were here!"

Christine was standing in the living room talking to Mrs. Krantz. She stared me up and down, her features creased in an expression of half horror and half pity. I imagined I did look like a disaster survivor. My clothes from the day before were hanging off me all lopsided and rumpled, and I could tell by my constricted vision that my face was bloated up like a jellyfish.

"Where's Seamus?" she asked tentatively.

"He's in the animal hospital, recovering from surgery," I heard myself say in a dull, flat voice.

"Is he . . . going to be okay?"

"We don't know yet."

"Katie, dear! You poor, poor thing!" Mrs. Krantz trotted over and pulled me into a frantic embrace. The pungent smell of hairspray and floral perfume threatened to make my already aching head shut down completely. "Oh, poor Mrs. B will be so upset!"

She pulled back but kept a firm grip on my arms, her many rings pressing into my flesh. I was touched to see a tear roll down her heavily powdered face. "Please let me know if I can do anything to help you," she went on. "You do know how much Seamus means to me and Mrs. B, don't you?"

"Yeah," I mumbled. Actually I *hadn't* known. She was sweet to be so concerned, but she was freaking me out a little bit too. I expected her to let go, but for some reason she just kept holding on to my arms and gazing at me sympathetically. Her fingers were digging into my skin like jeweled barnacles, and her magnified eyes were like giant watery bull's eyes. In my posttraumatic, newly awakened veg state, I was finding it hard to deal.

Thank God for Christine. Somehow sensing my trouble, she stepped forward and draped an arm around Mrs. Krantz, giving her consoling little pats while simultaneously steering her toward the door. "Thanks for stopping by, Mrs. Krantz," she said, opening the door. "We'll let you know as soon as we have any answers."

"Please do," Mrs. Krantz said. She produced a lacy handkerchief from the pocket of her skirt and dabbed her nose with it. "I just know Mrs. B won't sleep a wink today!"

We waited until she'd toddled off to her apartment before shutting the door.

"God, Katie," Christine said, shooting me a less close-up version of Mrs. Krantz's mournful look. "Are you okay? Don't take this the wrong way or anything, but you look like death."

I winced slightly, and Christine's eyes widened.

"Oh, I'm sorry. I didn't mean to say—"

"It's okay." I trudged over to the answering machine. "Did anyone call?"

"There's a couple of messages for you. From last night."

"Really?" My heart started thumping frantically, echoing inside my ears. I pushed the Play button and held my breath.

"Katie, this is Mother. Call me when you get in. BEEP! . . . Katie, it's Mom again. Where are you? I hope you don't make a habit of staying out late. How can you concentrate on your studies if you're sleep-deprived? Call me. BEEP! . . . Katie? Are you still out? This is ridiculous. I'm going to bed. Call me first thing in the morning. BEEP!"

I hit the shut-off switch and gripped my pounding temples.

"You going to call her?" Christine asked.

I shook my head feebly. "No." I was barely holding it together as it was. A lecture from Mom could make me lose all structural integrity.

So Dr. Skyler hadn't called. What did that mean? Was Seamus still unconscious? Was she still working on him? Or . . . did the worst happen, but she hadn't had time to let me know?

Christine was still watching me cautiously. "Um . . . do you want something to eat?"

"No."

"Coffee?"

"No, thanks."

"Damn, this sucks! I'm *so* sorry, Katie! This whole thing is all my fault!" She trudged over to the couch and flopped down on the cushions, hugging one of her surviving stuffed wiener dogs to her chest. "I should have held on to him. I should have grabbed him before he got away."

Her voice was weak and tinny with emotion. I'd never seen Christine look so vulnerable before. Suddenly everything and everyone around me seemed surreal, and I wondered if I could still be asleep.

"It's not your fault," I said. I walked over to the couch and patted her shoulder awkwardly. "You did everything you could. He was just too freaked."

Christine snorted derisively. "Yeah, because of my boyfriend. It's Robot's fault too. He's such a little kid sometimes. I got so mad at him last night, I sent him back to San Antonio."

"Really? You didn't break up with him, did you?"

She stared down into her lap. "I don't know."

I plopped down beside her. "But it's not Robot's fault either. If anyone's to blame, it's me." My throat tightened and my face started twitching. "I called to him. I was just so happy to see him that I wasn't paying attention. I didn't see the car backing up." My voice broke and the familiar kick-in-the-chest pain came back. I'd thought I couldn't cry anymore, but my ducts were once again manufacturing big, hot tears.

Christine gasped. "Oh, no. Katie, don't even think like that. It was just an accident."

I shook my head, loosening the tears, which began streaming down my puffy cheeks. Matt had said the same thing the night before. But those guys just didn't understand. "I let him down," I explained hoarsely. "He was my responsibility—*is* my responsibility. I should have protected him." I slumped back against the cushions, hugging my knees to my chest.

She bumped me with her shoulder. "Stop that. Listen to me. You saved that dog's life! If it hadn't been for you, he would have never had a chance! And you not only took him in, you turned him into a whole new dog. A great dog!"

I stared at her blurry image. She was right about that; he really had turned out great. He'd come so far in such a short time. That was another reason this whole situation seemed incredibly unfair.

"And there's something I should confess to you," Christine went on, tugging the bottom of her black tank top. "You really made me see what it means to own a dog. All that hard work and perseverance. I'd wanted a wiener dog for so long, but watching you, I realized I wasn't ready. I've gotten two e-mails about dachshunds up for adoption, but I haven't replied. I know I could never be as good as you."

"Of course you could do it!" I countered. "You'd be great."

"Maybe someday. But not now," she said with a shrug. "So . . . do you want a ride to the animal hospital?"

"Yeah. Thanks," I said. As she started to stand up, I put my hand on her arm. "You know, you're a really good friend, Christine." It was a cornball thing to say, but I meant it. I'd been through so much with her these past few weeks that I truly trusted her. Probably even more than my friends back home.

I expected her to make some flip comment about how snorting Mrs. Krantz's perfume must have gotten me stoned. Instead her eyes got all murky-looking and she ducked her head sort of shyly. "Thanks," she said in a barely audible voice. "So are you."

"Thanks." I smiled weakly.

"Um, Katie?" she added as she studied her chipped purple fingernails. "I just want to say, I know I threatened it, but I want you to know I would have never ratted you out to your mom."

"I know. It's okay."

"No, it's not. I can be a real bitch sometimes and, I don't know, maybe I was jealous that your mom is actually interested in how you are—unlike my mom. I just . . . miss her sometimes." Her eyes widened. "Wow. I've never said that aloud before. Not even to Robot."

I grinned at her and bumped her with my shoulder. "Maybe you should. He really seems to care a lot about you."

A knock at the door made us both jump slightly. My hand flew up to my aching head.

"I'll get it," Christine said, leaping up from the couch. I heard her fumble with the latch and the pop of the door leaving its frame. Then her voice cried, "Hi, Matt!"

I jumped to my feet—a movement that seemed to dislocate my frontal lobes. "Hey," I said, gripping my forehead. I rounded the couch as he stepped inside. His sleepy eyes looked even sleepier than usual, and his wavy hair lay flat against his skull. I felt a spasm of guilt at having put him through such a rough night.

"Did you hear anything from Dr. Skyler?" he asked.

I shook my head gently. "No."

"Well . . . no news is better than bad news." His mouth curled into a half smile. "You want a ride to the vet's?"

"I . . . um . . . ," I glanced over his shoulder at Christine. She made a shooing motion with her hand. "Sure. I mean . . . are you sure? You really don't have to."

He lifted his shoulders slightly. "I want to."

"Okay. Just give me some time to clean myself up

and I'll come over."

"See you in a bit."

As soon as he'd shut the door behind him, Christine flashed me a knowing grin. "You know what? That guy seems to care about you too."

When we arrived at the hospital, a way-too-cheerful assistant informed us that there had been no change in Seamus's condition, but that Dr. Skyler would be available to talk to us in a little while if we wanted to wait. She then presented me with a bill for services rendered thus far, totaling $1,162.54.

As I handed her Mom's emergencies-only credit card, I realized I was setting off a self-destruct sequence. Mom would have a supernova freak-out when she saw the bill—especially considering I hadn't actually told her about Seamus yet. But I couldn't worry about that. My mind was too busy agonizing about my present situation to care about any future catastrophes. All I wanted was for Seamus to get better, no matter what it took.

The office looked different by day. It was brighter and busier. Jazz music was playing on an unseen sound system, and the perky assistant kept flitting about, opening drawers and answering the phone in a singsongy voice. A large birdcage sat on the counter. Inside, perched atop an orange rod, was a brightly colored parrot with a bandaged left wing. *"Here, kitty, kitty,*

*kitty,"* he kept saying in his shrill, nasal bird tone. *"Come here, kitty, kitty."* Again, I felt as if I'd fallen down the proverbial rabbit hole into a bizarre parallel universe.

"Here you go!" the assistant crooned merrily, handing me my receipt. "Please have a seat. Dr. Skyler will be out as soon as she can!"

I nodded mutely, focusing on the walls in back of her as if I could melt them away and see Seamus. Failing that, I trudged off to the waiting area, pinching the receipt in both hands.

"How're you holding up?" Matt asked once I'd settled into the seat beside him.

"Okay," I replied as I folded the paper into fourths and slipped it into the front pocket of my jeans. My voice sounded far away, even to myself.

Matt looked like he didn't buy it. "You sure?"

"Yeah. It's just weird being back here. It's hard not doing anything."

"I know," he said. "When they were working on Jessie, I felt . . . I don't know . . . useless. I knew I couldn't exactly operate, but I still wanted to help in some way—just hold a scalpel or something."

I nodded. That was exactly how I felt.

"Sorry," he said as if suddenly embarrassed. "I guess I shouldn't have brought up Jessie."

"No, it's okay. I'm glad . . ." I paused, unsure how to phrase it without sounding stupid. *Glad for your loss? Glad your dog died and you can help me in case my dog does?* "I'm glad you understand," I said finally. "You've been really great to me. Thanks for . . . well . . . every-thing." I smiled as wide as my puffy features would allow.

He smiled back, and a coziness oozed over me like warm syrup. I couldn't believe how amazingly nice Matt had been to me. The guy had seen me at my absolute worst. Holding a bag of poop, yelling at him, crying until I was a snotty mess. Even now, I should be embarrassed as hell to have him see me like this: half-swollen with grief, hair in a greasy ponytail, wearing a T-shirt and jeans I'd dug out of a pile of dirty clothes (I hadn't had a chance to do laundry). And yet for some strange reason, I wasn't embarrassed. And for another, even stranger reason, he was still there.

"Um, hey. There's something I should tell you," he said, shifting uncomfortably in his chair. "I didn't exactly tell you the entire truth before. About Jessie."

"What do you mean?"

"It's true that I was sort of avoiding Seamus for a while because I was still getting over her death. But . . . I was also avoiding you."

"*Me?*" I suddenly felt uneasy. "Why?"

Matt scowled into the distance. "About the time I lost Jessie, I also went through a bad breakup. She and I had been together for over a year, and even though I knew it was totally over, I was still sort of freaked. The last thing I wanted to see was a beautiful girl—especially one with a dog."

I sat completely frozen, holding my breath. *Beauti-*

*ful? Did he just call me beautiful?*

"At first I thought I could just ignore you guys all summer—not in a mean way, just not as friendly as I wanted to be. But you were right next door and I sort of got pulled in a little . . . then a lot. Once I got to know you guys, I didn't want to keep my distance anymore. I wanted to get to know you better. In fact, I still want to know you better—*a lot* better." He let out a sigh and raked his fingers through his floppy bangs. "You don't have to say anything. I realize you're with that guy Chuck, but I just . . . I wanted you to know how I felt."

If I was stunned before, I was near comatose at that point. Matt wanted to be with me? For real? In my broken mental state, it was near impossible to process it all.

"You . . . ?" I began, my voice tapering off weakly. I wanted him to keep talking, to explain in no uncertain terms what he meant, but my systems seemed to be shutting down into some sort of primitive protective mode. I just couldn't think about this right now. I couldn't handle another big shock.

A shadow fell over us as someone entered the waiting area. I glanced up and saw Dr. Skyler standing in front of the sunny window, looking slightly haggard.

I rose to my feet. "Seamus?" I cried. "Is he— Is there any change?"

Matt stood up and placed his hand on my back, lending me his strength.

"We've been monitoring him closely all night," Dr. Skyler said, "and it looks like he's going to be all right."

I let her statement slowly penetrate. Seamus . . . was . . . going . . . to . . . be . . . all right. He was going to live! "Oh my God! Oh, thank you!" I ran forward and threw my arms around her, tears of relief rolling down my cheeks. "Thank you so much!"

It was if I'd burst out of a gloomy cocoon. Suddenly everything around me looked shiny and beautiful. The worn plastic chairs. The flecked vinyl floor. Dr. Skyler with her tired blue eyes and blond Peter Pan haircut. I was in a sparse and rather antiseptic paradise.

Dr. Skyler laughed and patted me on the back. "He's awake now," she said. "Would you like to see him?"

"Yes!"

We followed her down the corridor into a sort of pint-sized ICU. There were shelves of medical supplies and all sorts of fancy machinery. Kennels had been built into the far wall, with large stalls for the big animals and a row of smaller cages on top. Dr. Skyler lowered the door of one cubicle and gestured for us to approach. Seamus was lying on his side, still heavily bandaged. Only this time, his eyes were halfway open.

*He's alive!* I thought as I raced to his side. *Thank God, he's going to be okay!*

"Don't pick him up," Dr. Skyler said. "And remember he's still medicated. He can't interact with you much."

I stepped forward and began stroking the wiry, unruly fur on his ears and the top of his head. "Hey, fella," I said softly. Seamus let out a low, happy-sounding moan and licked my wrist. He looked weak and kind of hungover, but it was Seamus. He was back.

"I'll give you guys some time to visit." Dr. Skyler gave me another warm smile and headed out the door.

I saw Matt start to follow. "Wait," I called. "Please stay."

"You sure?" he said, looking sort of hunched and uncomfortable. I thought about his earlier confession and how awkward he must have felt.

"Yes," I replied. "I really want you to be here."

He walked up beside me and grinned down at Seamus. "Hey, dude," he said, rubbing him behind the ears. "Glad you're going to be all right. You sure are a tough guy."

Seamus beamed back at him, his tail thumping sluggishly.

"I'll bring you home soon, buddy," I said. "I promise." I picked up his left leg and kissed the soft pad on the underside of his foot over and over. Then, without thinking, I slid my hand over on top of Matt's, lifted it off of Seamus, and raised it to my lips.

He smiled faintly, his forehead puckered in confusion. Reaching up with both hands, I cupped his face and pulled him toward me. As he came closer, I could see streaks of green in his wide gray eyes and a soft line dividing his pillowy lower lip. I saw those same lips lift slightly, and then . . . they were on mine.

It was not like kissing Chuck at all. With Chuck I'd always felt awkward and hyperconscious. Worried about my breath and hair. Confused about where to put my hands. But with Matt everything was more . . . well, *more*. More exciting. More right. There was no hesitation and I instinctively seemed to know what to do. Our bodies shifted, effortlessly settling into each other's contours. And our mouths just seemed to find each other, zooming together like magnets.

And there was something else. As we kissed I realized that I was happy. Not just ho-hum, can't complain, everything's-hunky dory-type happy, but really, truly *happy*. The kind of happiness that makes the sunlight sparkle brighter and the air smell sweeter and your chest flutter as if your heart is sprouting rainbows and roses inside your chest. Seamus was going to be okay and Matt was kissing me. Things hadn't felt this right in a long time. Maybe never.

Gradually we broke off. Matt leaned back and gazed into my eyes, his mouth curled into a sheepish and very adorable grin.

"What about your boyfriend?" he murmured.

"I don't have a boyfriend," I said, pushing his bangs off his forehead.

"Really?" His grin widened. "Would you like one?"

I smiled and we kissed for an unfathomable amount of time. It would have been longer, but a strange thwacking sound made us pull apart. We turned toward the noise and saw Seamus, grinning a broad doggie grin, his tail whapping against the cage as fast as my own heart was beating.

# 15

"Dudes! Check this out!"

Christine and I came out of the kitchen where we'd been making quesadillas for dinner. Robot, Lyle, Kinky and Matt were sitting in the living room, all of them huddled around something.

"Yo. Come watch this," Kinky said, gesturing Christine and me closer with a bob of his bushy head.

We exchanged tiny shrugs and ventured toward the guys. As we came up behind them, I noticed MTV had been muted. Seamus was sitting in front of the coffee table, his little chest puffed up with pride.

"Okay. What's the big thing?" Christine asked, resting her hands on the belt loops of her ripped, low-riding jeans.

"Kinky taught Seamus a new trick," Matt said, sounding slightly incredulous.

"No way!" I exclaimed. "We've only been out of the room fifteen minutes."

"Believe it," Robot said, nodding. "The little bugger is right smart."

"And Kinky's sort of like an animal," Lyle added.

Christine took another step forward and crossed her arms over her chest. "All right. Let's see it."

Kinky smiled proudly and hunkered down in front of Seamus. "Yo! Seamus, dude! Give me five!" He held his big palm out toward Seamus.

Seamus wobbled a little, lifted his right leg, and swiped his paw against Kinky's outstretched hand.

Everyone whooped and clapped. "Good boy!" I shouted. Seamus panted happily.

"Man, I want to teach him how to drum!" Lyle exclaimed.

I headed over to the gold armchair where Matt was sitting and perched on the armrest. "Did you witness this little miracle?" I asked. "Did he really teach him that?"

"He really did," he said, slipping his arm around my waist. In a quick movement he pulled me onto his lap and started kissing me. I laughed and put up some perfunctory resistance before blissfully giving in.

"Aw, man! There they go again!" Lyle whined.

Kinky shielded his eyes dramatically. "Dudes, get a

corner or something."

"Right," Robot said, rising to his feet. "I'm off to get a pack of smokes and some brew. Any of you blokes want to come?"

"I'm there," said Lyle, bouncing off the couch.

"Me too," Kinky chimed in, loping after Robot.

"Hey, could you guys get Seamus some doggie snacks?" I asked, struggling to stand so I could grab my purse.

Matt pulled me back down. "I'll do it," he murmured in my ear, sending little shivers down my back.

"You sure?"

"Yeah. Besides, I'll know what to get," he added in a whisper. "Those guys would probably get Seamus a can of beer and some Twinkies."

"You're right," I said, laughing.

Matt slid out from under me and headed toward the door, Seamus limping after him. "Hey, guys, hold up," he called. "I need to grab some stuff too."

"You mean something besides Katie?" I heard Lyle ask before the door shut.

Seamus looked back at me sadly, as if he had wanted to tag along too.

"Come on, buddy." I picked him up, mindful of his bandages, and carried him over to the patio. "Go see your pal." Sure enough, as I pushed back the blinds, there was Mrs. B waiting on the balcony. Seamus's tail started wagging rapidly.

I carefully set him outside and watched through the

glass as the two of them started sniffing each other all over. After a while, I headed back into the kitchen, where Christine had returned to her cheese grating.

"Stop it," she said when I rounded the corner.

"What?"

"Wipe that silly-ass smile off your face before I slap it off."

"Really? I'm smiling?" I said, patting my cheeks and mouth. I hadn't even realized it.

Christine groaned and rolled her eyes. "You've had one all week long—ever since you and Matt got together. You guys are so cute you make me want to puke."

"Come on!" I cried. "What about you and Robot?" I launched into a horrible, off-key rendition of "Fancy You."

I'd just reached the chorus when the phone started ringing.

"Thank God!" Christine exclaimed. She set down the grater, scurried into the living room and snatched up the phone. "Hello?" she said, turning her back on me and my singing. Suddenly she spun back around, staring at me with wide eyes. "Oh, hello there, Mrs. McAllister!"

I trotted up beside her, chewing four fingernails at once. This could be bad. I hadn't spoken to Mom in over a week—since before Seamus got hurt. It wasn't as if I'd been purposefully avoiding her; I'd just been so busy with school and nursing Seamus back to health.

In the meantime she'd left one message after another, still yelling at me about staying out late and never calling Aaron.

"Uh-huh," Christine kept saying into the receiver while shooting me round-eyed looks of sympathy. "Yes, well . . . actually, Mrs. McAllister, I really don't feel comfortable with this arrangement anymore. I think you should probably get information from Katie directly. In fact, she's right here." She held the phone out toward me.

I shook my head no. While I appreciated her gesture of resigning as official go-between and informant, I was also a little miffed that Christine was putting me on the spot. Talking to Mom was like storming an enemy beach. You had to be mentally prepared and equipped with several carefully rehearsed responses.

Christine mouthed the word *yes* and pressed the phone against me, stabbing my sternum with the antenna. Then she set it on the table and walked off toward the kitchen. *No!* I thought, glaring down at the receiver. Its antenna pointed toward me, wagging back and forth as if scolding me.

*Oh, what the hell. I have to face her sometime.* I picked up the phone and raised it to my ear. "Hi, Mom."

"Katie, what on earth is going on? Why have you been avoiding me? Do you realize if I hadn't gotten hold of you today I would have contacted the authorities?" Mom's voice rose with each rapid-fire question.

"I've been ready to call the police for three days now but your father made me wait. What's gotten into you, young lady? Why haven't you been returning my calls?"

"I'm sorry, Mom. I've just been really swamped."

"That was very thoughtless of you! Do you realize I've barely slept for days?"

"Sorry," I said again.

"Are you hiding something? Why have you been ignoring me?"

"I haven't. Really. It's just that school's been getting tougher and I keep forgetting to juice up the cell phone and I've had tons of errands to run this week."

"I see." Mom's voice was strangely subdued. "Would any of these errands include spending twelve hundred dollars at the North Austin Animal Hospital?"

My face instantly grew hot, smarting all over as if severely sunburned. "Uh . . . yeah, that," I said lamely. I'd thought I had more time. I had no idea she would get the bill so quickly. "That was for Seamus."

"Seamus? Who is Seamus?" she cried.

I took a deep breath. It was time rat myself out. "He's my dog," I said, pushing the words out of me. "I have a dog." And there it was—just a simple declarative sentence. I'd expected to go all meek and trembly, but I didn't. If anything, I felt relieved.

"You have a . . . *what?*"

"A dog, Mom. I adopted him the first week I got here."

There came a long pause, and I could almost hear a bomb ticking in the background. Finally Mom let out a long, staticky sigh. "Oh, no. You do *not* need a dog, Katherine Anne!"

I heard a slight rustling noise and her voice grew muffled. "Shane, I told you I should have driven up there! Do you know what she's done? She's gotten herself a dog!"

"Really?" Dad sounded somewhat interested. "What kind of dog?"

Mom let out an irritated grunt and came back on the line. "Really, Katie. Why would you even do such a thing?"

"Because the shelter was going to kill him," I explained. "I wanted to save him."

"It's the same as always. You are just too selfish and irresponsible to be left on your own!"

"What?" I yelled. "How can you call me selfish for wanting to save him? You're the one who's always going on about how I should take a stand and be a good citizen. So I did. I took in a dog that needed a home."

"Without consulting me first!" she snapped. "And you know perfectly well that that credit card was for emergencies only."

"It *was* an emergency! He got hit by a car! If I hadn't tried to help him, I would have never forgiven myself." I closed my eyes and recovered my breath. "I'm sorry I had to use the credit card. I just had no choice."

"I see. So you adopt a dog and then let him run in

the street? Katie, that is about the most irresponsible thing I've ever heard of! I should have never trusted you to be out on your own. I'm considering bringing you right home this instant!"

"*No!*" I shouted so loud that Christine peeked around the corner from the kitchen. "I *wasn't* being irresponsible and you *can* trust me! The accident was just an accident. I'm doing a great job with Seamus. I'm training him and taking good care of him and still keeping up with classes. I'm doing good, Mom. You should be proud of me."

"I will *not* be made the bad guy in this matter!" she cried, raising her volume to my decibel level. "I've tried to be nice. I've tried to set you on the right path, but of course you won't listen. As usual you had to do things your own way, no matter what. Do you think your father made it as far as he has by doing his own thing? Do you think *I* got to do whatever I felt like growing up?"

Mom's tone took on a reedy quality. She sounded almost resentful or jealous. Like maybe she would have liked to step out of her perfect facade once in a while and mingle among us mortals.

"Why do you always have to make things so hard?" she went on. "Is it so difficult just to do what I ask? To do the right thing?"

I braced myself for the usual torrent of guilt, the standard amount of whining and groveling on my part and the eventual shaky truce. But as I listened to

322

Mom's tirade, I realized . . . I was done. The guilt just wasn't there. I couldn't feel useless and irresponsible, because now I knew I wasn't those things.

"Sorry you don't trust me, Mom," I said. "But I don't think that's my problem. I've been doing my best for years and you're never satisfied."

"How dare you talk to me that way!" Mom was shrieking like a hawk. I'd never heard her so upset before. "When I was your age I would have never talked back to my mother that way!"

*When I was your age* . . . There it was, her usual catchphrase. I'd heard it thousands of times before, but this time it was different. As soon as she said it, a smoldering anger came spouting to the surface. "Maybe I don't want to be you at my age!" I yelled. "Maybe I want to be *me*!"

That did it. For a moment all I could hear was the white noise of her huffy breathing and a few disjointed vowel sounds as she started to reply and then stopped herself. It was unbelievable. For the second time in my life, my mom was speechless. Only this time, instead of letting a hunky Irish stranger do it, I was sticking up for myself.

Listening to the silence emanating from the other end, I felt like I was somehow growing, doubling in strength and size.

"I can handle it, Mom," I said loud and clear, as if issuing a proclamation. "You don't need to look out for me anymore."

"Shane, you won't believe what our daughter is saying to me!" Mom's voice grew distant again. "She suddenly thinks because she's lived away for a while she can make her own decisions about everything."

"Well, land's sake, Laura," I heard my dad say. "She is seventeen."

I could hear Mom sputter and gulp for a moment, and then her voice came back on the line. "Forget it. I can see the both of you are determined to act impossible," she said shakily. Then she hung up.

I replaced the receiver on its base and stood there, staring at it.

"Katie? Are you okay?" Christine said, rounding the corner of the kitchen nook. "That was awesome. I can't believe you stood up to her like that."

"Neither can I," I said truthfully.

She slowly shook her head. "Girl, you are my hero. I mean, I'm always totally ragging on my dad and sneaking stuff behind his back, but I've never just told it like it was. How'd you do that?"

"I don't know," I said, breaking into a smile.

Strange. When I first met Christine, I assumed she was so together. I thought if I studied her hard enough, I could figure out how to get a grip on my own life. Now she was calling me *her* hero?

But maybe that was it. Somehow I'd stopped worrying so much about what other people thought about me. Instead of looking to others for strength, I found it inside me, where it had been all along, puny and neglected like a stray pup.

Somehow I'd become my own Alpha Dog.

Later that evening, I took Seamus to the park. I was careful to slow my pace so that he could heel without straining himself. I could tell it was getting easier for him. Dr. Skyler had said he should be completely better by September, but I was beginning to think it would be sooner than that. He was a tough one.

We crossed the pea-gravel pit, circled the swimming pool and came to "our" picnic table beneath the live oak trees.

"Here you go, buddy," I said, lifting him to the tabletop. I sat down beside him and began stroking the dark wiry waves along his back.

To our left the sun was setting, bleeding orange-red streaks into the sky. The wind was picking up, and our grassy surroundings were taking on the heavy bronze hue of evening.

Seamus flopped down next me, resting his shoulder against my waist, and heaved a contented sigh.

"Yeah, I know," I said, petting the soft fur behind his ears. "I know exactly what you mean."